SELLING A GOOD TIME

SELLING A GOOD TIME

A Novel

Ken Scelfo

iUniverse, Inc.
New York Lincoln Shanghai

Selling a Good Time

iUniverse books may be ordered through booksellers or by contacting:

iUniverse
2021 Pine Lake Road, Suite 100
Lincoln, NE 68512
www.iuniverse.com
1-800-Authors (1-800-288-4677)

Because of the dynamic nature of the Internet, any Web addresses or links contained in this book may have changed since publication and may no longer be valid.

This is a work of fiction. All of the characters, names, incidents, organizations, and dialogue in this novel are either the products of the author's imagination or are used fictitiously.

Cover Illustration by Mikey G.

ISBN: 978-0-595-44118-1 (pbk)
ISBN: 978-0-595-88442-1 (ebk)

Printed in the United States of America

For Anna

Part One

1. No Future without the Present

*I*t was eleven in the morning, and I was standing with a group of salesmen in front of the distribution office in Buffalo, frigidly smoking a cigarette and listening to them trash a former employee. With hands tucked deep into their coat pockets and cigarettes dangling from their lips, they were moving seamlessly through a string of unruly comments, their visible breath barely distinguishable from the smoke. I just stared ahead, shivering through a fake smile.

"Why it took them so long to get rid of Anderson, I'll never know," said a hefty gentleman wearing one of those big fur hats with ear flaps. "The first time he showed up to the meetings with that polka dot bow tie, someone should have ripped it off and shoved it down his throat."

"The man was a walking curse," said another, before coughing violently and spitting into a muddied snow bank. "He couldn't give away a bottle of whiskey to a bum if his life depended on it."

"I heard he got caught stealing liters of daiquiri mixers from the warehouse. That's why he got fired."

"*Daiquiri mixers?* Ha! I always knew he was a fruit!"

Outside of this, and the constant sight of another regionally inadequate sports car sliding across the frozen parking lot, the morning was uneventful and boring. Due to an unforgiving concoction of heavy snow and swirling winds, the start of the sales meeting had been pushed back on the hour for three consecutive hours, waiting for winery representatives and other important industry people to arrive. This left the local sales force in a sour mood to begin with and had forced their managers to feverishly scramble about in an attempt to calm everyone down and keep morale high. It was of little help. These salesmen weren't being bought with small talk, pats on the back, and endless rounds of coffee and donuts. They wanted to get out of this meeting as soon as possible, and as feared, this delay had allowed them to begin showing signs of boiling over, most evident from the complaining that had been slowly spreading throughout the grounds of the office. There was simply no antidote for stopping them when this reached a certain point. Once the friendly introductions and handshakes had worn thin, the typical conversations would soon follow. Then the tension really becomes visible. You could only talk so long about "how things have been" and "what's new." It was like the Black Plague: no hope.

Regardless of the outcome, the two-day event was a complete waste of time. Management viewed it as a meeting to kick off the new year and hopefully boost sales in an otherwise slow month. But the salesmen and winery reps knew better. Coming on the tail end of the November-December holiday drinking season, January was typically a month to get away with as much vacation as possible *without* getting caught. As far as work was concerned, no liquor store owners wanted to see you—never mind buy anything—and no restaurant managers were even thinking of changing their wine lists this early in the year. So whether you called an account for an order from the base lodge of Killington in between runs *or* from the office, it produced the same results entirely. Naturally, in an effort to keep the sales force from completely dropping off the face of the earth, the heads of the distribution company decided to hold a meeting to help tighten the slack and prevent "runaway sales calls." While their plan to keep everyone in check may have worked, the general vibe continued to descend into uncharted territory with each passing minute. Over the next half-hour, a few isolated shouting matches had sprung up, the Italian winery reps had twice set off the fire alarm trying to smoke inside, and a strong rumor was circulating that the French reps were collectively ready to bail. This type of behavior shouldn't be taken as hostility—especially toward one another—but instead as a preference to wasting this day on our *own* time.

I was about to call it quits myself, when suddenly the front door creaked open. At the precise moment when it appeared there would be no possible chance for a civilized gathering to take place, our prayers had been answered.

"Hey! Get your asses in here," said a fat, bald head poking out. "The meeting has started."

The announcement came like a gunshot, setting off a flurry of activity in every direction. Birds scattered, car doors slammed, cigarettes were flicked left and right, and an assembly line of salesmen quickly slunk past me, amid several grunts, spits, and belches.

Rounding out the initial herd, I closed the door behind us and squinted out through the heavily scratched Plexiglas window. In the distance, several more figures were cutting through the fog and limping awkwardly across the dreary parking lot. It reminded me of a graveyard scene from an old black and white horror flick. Except these zombies were dressed in fine Italian suits and tugging on rolling bags stuffed with an assortment of promotional merchandise and loose wine bottles.

It had been a long and unproductive winter so far, and to say that my mental state at this particular meeting was like all the others would be a lie. The reason being that two weeks earlier I got *the call*: produce better results or start looking for new work. The business world's equivalent to a mob threat. Subtle, yet devastatingly real.

I hadn't exactly been a rookie phenom in my brief, six-month role as a winery representative for Bunglewood Vineyards, so this came as no surprise to anyone, including myself. With no background whatsoever in sales, I was practically hired on the spot last summer following a chance meeting with their owner. At the time I was working as a minimum-wage cashier in a small Manhattan wine shop when I happened to fall into a long conversion with this guy about what people were buying. Before he left, he gave me a quizzical look and said something like, "We could use a young guy like you out in the field." I didn't even know what that meant, but when he called later that afternoon and mentioned the words "salary" and "expense account," I quit the shop the next morning.

His name was Randolph Bungle, but everyone just called him "the boss." Although our conversations were mainly limited to work, he seemed to be an okay guy I guess; an old hippie/cowboy type with like five ex-wives and a ranch somewhere in the Sonoma Valley. The vineyard he purchased in the late '70s could be described as modest at best, with a knack for producing wines that no one seemed to enjoy, but somehow people continued to buy. Originally an apple farmer by trade, he also doubled, or rather quadrupled, as the CEO, national sales manager, director of marketing, and vineyard operator. The rest of the team was made up of about fifteen area reps placed around the country; our winemaker Paul, who no doubt dabbled in the production of "mind-enhancing" crops as well; and an aging office secretary named Betty.

I fully expected to go through some sort of sales training or interview process before they hired me, but there wasn't any of that. Outside of a basic outline of what the job entailed and a few discussions on sales technique, the boss more or less just said, "All right. Go get 'em." Talking to several other people about him, I'd begun to piece together the idea that the man either had an unorthodox view on life or was simply a poor businessman with a weakness for betting on instinct.

Which brings me to my own failures. In many ways, these occupational handicaps work on several varying levels—the most obvious being statistical. Based on the numbers that got sent every month from the vineyard office in California, I was downright terrible on paper. As some sort of competition, we received a list on how the entire national sales team was doing in terms of both total sales and our annual goals. I consistently resided at the very bottom of the standings. Not good. The necessary social skills weren't quite where I would've liked them to be either, especially since I hardly knew anything about tasting wine. I'm a beer drinker by nature: porters in the winter, lagers in the summer, and pale ales in the spring and fall. In turn, most of my days were spent giving run-of-the-mill explanations of the Bunglewood wines to various liquor store clerks and restaurant managers throughout the state of New York. These sales pitches were so rudimentary that it'd be like meeting with Vidal Sassoon and saying, "Wow. Red hair is cool. I think wavy curls are something everyone should have." And let's be honest here, the fact that I didn't have tits was also a downside as far as my sales promotion goes. No grumpy old store owners were jumping out of their seats to see my skinny ass first thing in the morning. Throw in a pair of cheap suits, a fairly weak work ethic, and you get the picture.

So they knew what they were getting. But what I'd come to realize later on was that when you were a small winery with little money to throw at some hardened veteran of the business world, you had to take what you can get. And I was about the only thing they could afford.

The situation had forced me to look deeper into my job. Not by concentrating any harder or through reading some lame textbook on how to generate sales, but by merely observing. I already knew why I was a terrible salesman; maybe I just had to inspect the game a bit more. See how others succeeded. Learn the rules. If anything, I thought, it could be a chance to redeem myself, or at the very least, an opportunity to look around at the business world and discover what lay buried within. My fate resting somewhere in between, my mind trying to make sense of it all.

A smell of stale coffee and rotten corks hit me as I entered the main hallway. Excluding the timeless brick exterior, the decaying, one-story office building had no aesthetic charm to speak of. The inside walls were, in most areas, a dull off-white color and thoroughly marked with an array of scratches, fingerprints, and dents. The carpet was in even worse shape: worn in the middle and with the dull trace of red wine stains in nearly every direction. Only a few poorly framed, warped vineyard posters and a fake palm tree here and there stood as any sort of decoration.

Making it through the initial hallway led you to a small waiting area, where a middle-aged secretary sat with a forced smile, double fisting phones and motioning for everyone to sign in. A set of doors were positioned on both sides of her desk, the one to the right leading to the office suites and the one on the left leading to the main lobby and meeting rooms.

Entering the doors on the left was like walking into a crowded bus station. Noisy and full of impatient travelers. It was hard to tell what the original use of this area was, but for some reason it had the look of an old cafeteria. Decoration was again minimal, with only a few small tables and a handful of folding chairs throughout, forcing the majority of us to either stand or sit on the ground against the wall. While the doors of the meeting room toward the back remained tightly shut during each presentation, the cavernous lobby was full of arguing Italians, Germans, Frenchmen, and Brooklynites, all of whom seemed to think that they were next in line to present their products to the upstate sales force. These uptight individuals were winery reps like myself, and they were here to represent their respective brand by speaking to those who will sell it. Though the importance of timing can be debated, no one—especially not in this sub-zero hamlet of outskirts Buffalo—wanted to wait around until nightfall to get in front of the already-scowling crowd.

"The longer you wait, the less interested and more hostile they get," said a sheepish little man leaning up against the back wall next to me. "You'd think it was high school all over again."

I'd been up in front of them before, so I knew what he was saying was indeed correct. A working relationship between a winery rep and the salesmen from the distributor was absolutely critical to the success of a brand. These salesmen were, without question, the unsung heroes of the entire wine industry. While the winemakers, vineyard owners, and restaurateurs got all the glorious headlines and awards, these were the people who actually got the product out there. They were the only direct link between the distributor (the company who represented and supplied your wine in a certain state or region) and the buyer (the restaurant or liquor store manager who actually sold it to the public). Each of these salesmen had a list of accounts which they were responsible for throughout these areas, and it was their job to help persuade these buyers to take in as much of the products that their particular distribution company represented.

Some of these big time distributors had thousands upon thousands of different wines and liquors, so for a small winery such as the one I worked for, it was important to stay on top of things and not get lost in the mix. Because these salesmen handled so many other brands, it was the winery reps' job to help inform and remind them about everything they needed to know regarding their particular brand, right down to the bare floor. This may or may not include, on a daily basis, the following: price changes, new products, new labels, available merchandise, vintage updates, special requests, stock checks, incentives, the position of the moon, and the weather. Because we had the ability to assist them in selling something that was part of their quota list, we were, in effect, a big help to them as well. In many ways, the winery rep position was very much a *sales* position, the only difference being we worked directly for the vineyard and not the distributor. I could go into any store or restaurant on my own and sell my wines—and I did—but working with a salesman from the distributor, who had daily contact with the head buyer of these places, was completely invaluable and ultimately much more successful.

As the ongoing scheduling debate continued, most of the reps were hunched over laptop computers and barking out long lists of code numbers and orders into their cell phones, with the occasional side arguments thrown in on whether or not there would be a lunch break, how the warehouse lost their samples again, and *olde-tyme* shit like why these meetings weren't like they used to be. As for myself, I had no money to buy a computer; my cell phone was lost over New Year's break; and at twenty-eight, I was easily the youngest of the winery rep crowd. This left me slumped in the corner of the lobby, next to an abandoned filing cabinet, sleeping. It was all I could think of to do, and I had more than enough time to do it. My original time slot to present was listed at quarter to eleven, but had since been crossed out twice and now stood at a time of five thirty, a good six hours away.

I was awakened a few hours later, at this point completely stretched out on the carpet, with a swift kick to my right thigh.

"You were scheduled to go on in ten minutes, but it's too late to continue," said Gene, one of the upstate managers. "You'll have to do your presentation tomorrow."

I thanked him for the update and asked if he could kick me again, on the other leg, just to even out the pain. "Walking with a pronounced limp could be taken as a sign of weakness," I said, "and I'm not looking for any favors."

He frowned and casually walked away.

Dusting off my pants and sitting up against the wall, the lobby had once again been transformed into a swirling mass of bodies. Cranky salesmen were yanking off their ties and hastily clutching piles of sale sheets, winery reps were hauling away boxes of wine and talking loudly on their cell phones, and members of upper management were either pacing around with their hands on their hips or rushing for the exits. In the far corner, leaning up against a doorway that led to the main offices, I even spotted a secretary with her head down, crying. The stress produced through hours of

fist-pounding demands, a relentless barrage of technical information, and an unmerciful schedule had proven to be too much for
some.

Besides myself, the only other stable human being in sight was a
man seated on the floor a few feet down from me. He had the back
of his head propped up against the wall and a slew of paperwork
across his lap. "You all right?" I said, clearing my throat and gathering up my own materials. He slowly turned his blank stare toward
me and nodded.

"Why the hell are we up here?" he mumbled, before putting his
head back against the wall. I didn't have an answer for him and
shook my head in a confused manner.

As I was about to leave, he said, "See you at the bar ..." When I
asked him what bar he was referring to, he told me that the hotel
bar at the Holiday Inn (where we were all staying) was having a
happy hour "just for us." At the exact moment he said this, some
stocky, bald fellow dropped an entire case of Zinfandel in the lobby,
making a gurgling mess of a stain creep across the carpet. No one
offered to help him out, and by the time I could even care, I was
already halfway across the parking lot, shivering in the dark looking
for my car.

The chaotic scene at the hotel was no different from the one I'd
just left. The loud, echoing noise emanating from the bar down the
hall was being matched by several men in suits who were arguing in
thick Italian accents to a surely frightened, seventeen-year-old front
desk girl.

"Do you *realize* that we have come all the way from Calabria? *Do
you understand that much?*" shouted one.

"Naturally, she does not. Or else we would have a room,
Ricardo," said another, flailing his arms around in a dramatic, yet
somehow strangely effective manner. "This is how they work in this
country."

The girl was on the verge of tears, trying to stall them until the manager returned from his smoke break.

"Listen, Mister, uh, Alignini … Alignani … I'm so sorry. We are completely booked. But like I was saying, there may be a chance of a cancellation due to the weather. When my manager—"

"I do not want to talk to him! Are you listening to me? *Just give me a fucking room!*"

The volume of his voice did nothing to interrupt the ongoing circles of conversation throughout the lobby. But the slamming of his briefcase on the ground, as well as the accompanying boot to the desk, did, as the crowd paused momentarily to see what the fuss was all about, before reverting back, unimpressed, into their own world of business talk.

I decided to skip checking in until later, feeling somewhat sorry for the girl and somewhat impatient for my own need of a drink. It had been a long day and I owed myself that much, so I left my bag with one of the bellhops up front and headed for the bar.

The place was a business nightmare. Strictly an old boys club. Toward the back corner of the bar sat the lone saleswoman. She had long, flowing blonde hair and a plunging neckline that revealed just enough to draw the attention of several optimistic drunks who crowded around her like she was some kind of art exhibit. The actual seating area wasn't that big, but there were tables full of what seemed to be dozens of salesmen and winery reps going over notes and drinking two-dollar Bud Lights—except, that is, for the Europeans, who stuck exclusively to red wine. Hanging clumsily behind the back bar and underneath a row of TV's showing the Knicks-Bulls game, a huge banner read "WELCOME GOAL STAR SALESMEN AND VISITING WINERY REPS." Which was kind of funny, because the company name was actually *Gold* Star.

I stood in the doorway for a few minutes, looking around. Taking in a scene such as this was like witnessing a pack of lions in the depths of the Serengeti. A rare, up-close glimpse at a unique breed interacting in its natural setting. I watched them closely—being careful to not create a visual disturbance—as they spoke the universal language of Sales, face-to-face, through a high-class delivery and an all-too-fake, overconfident grin.

There was definitely something to be said about these weary, hotel-dwelling businessmen who moved from town to town, state to state, to help sell and promote their products. They were, in essence, a dying tribe of road warriors—foot soldiers—in a world rapidly becoming more and more antisocial and less and less active. Like the toll booth operator and the milkman before them, it seemed inevitable that in some not-too-distant future their physical presence will be unnecessary. Meetings will all take place via satellite, deals will be brokered through conference calls, and inventory will be purchased from an Internet database. Even the handshake will be gone, most likely replaced by a smiley face icon at the end of an e-mail. Christ, it was happening already. Everywhere you turned, some technological breakthrough was being introduced as the industry standard. Just look at how the actual sale was completed. It had gone from submitting order sheets, to calling in from a cell phone, to transmitting straight through wireless handheld computers in the span of only a few years.

But many argue that changes like this have been going on for decades. There were those who predicted television would be the end for newspapers and radio at one point, too, remember. And although blues may have given life to rock and roll and then heavy metal, as jazz did to funk and rap, it wasn't like the original medium just shriveled up and died. Evolution did not *always* mean extinction. So let's not count these salesmen out just yet. They were still around—and strong in numbers, mind you—moving steadily across the land in search of the next sale. And the one after that. And the one after that.

Their cunning and persistent manner alone will most likely get them through the next century.

As I continued to watch them, I began to pick up on a few things—most notably their differences. Although they conversed and drank as one on this night, the division among them was clearly visible. They consisted of two core groups separated by ideals, purpose, and wrinkles: the Old School and the New School. Besides being predominantly younger, the few members of the New School were easy to pick out. With their business degrees and upper-crust internships under their belt, they hung together near the bar dressed in spiffy, pressed suits and that "just out of the salon" hairstyle. It was here where they compared watches and fought for bragging rights among various things like old girlfriends, new cars, and college football programs.

The Old School, on the other hand, occupied most of the seating areas and came from a variety of different backgrounds. Take for instance, the big guy who sat in the corner putting someone in a headlock. That was Max Duncan, the former middleweight champ. Or the skinny, balding fellow double fisting beers at a back table: none other than Sylvio Benetti, former guitarist for '70s punk rockers Cut Monkey. Others were simply lifelong salesmen who grew tired of selling things like shoes or copy machines. It should be stressed that what we were selling here *was* alcohol—"a good time" as someone once told me—not computers or insurance or medical equipment. For many of the old-timers, the good times were an integral part of the work week. The stories I'd overheard from some of these guys seemed to come straight out of a book on Led Zeppelin or Ozzy Osbourne. Hotel demolitions, strip club mayhem, all-night binge drinking, you name it.

But as the age of technology and health awareness came upon us, so went the fun. The increase of competition among countries, wineries, importers, and distributors had caused the wine and liquor business to become another endless numbers game—and the threats of cirrhosis (drinking too much), cancer (smoking too much), and a collection of STDs (screwing too much) had frightened the joy right out of it.

As you might expect, these nights of drinking in communal situations had become an increasingly rare occurrence. I could only recall a handful of times when I'd even *heard* of one happening since I'd been on the job. The actual moment where work ended and the rest of life began showed no boundary anymore. There were signs of this creeping all throughout the room. These salesmen may have appeared to be putting back a few drinks and enjoying the game, but if you looked closely, you could see the mind still at work. The eyes gave it away. Each person who entered the bar was immediately being stared up and down to see if they were someone important and worth talking to. It could be a chance to get an inside track on the market, or a chance to get a deal out of someone. This could also explain why everyone in here was turned facing the entranceway. One mistimed kneel down to tie your shoe could mean the difference between you getting in good with the boss or your fellow coworker.

As for myself, I attracted no such attention when I finally entered, and had to squeeze my way past several lurking packs of industry people—some with headsets still in their ears and small notebooks in their hands—just to get within shouting range of the bartender. Over the next few hours I would drink about a half dozen beers watching the game, talking only to excuse myself from bumping into people on my way to and from the bathroom. I was approached once throughout the night, though, by a creepy-looking man with slick black hair and a voice like a gangster. He caught my eye from across the room and immediately made his way over. "Do you guys make a Merlot under ten dollars?" he asked, for some reason rather discreetly. When I told him that *all* of our products were basically under ten dollars, he nodded his head, squinted his eyes for a moment, and vanished back into the pack.

As the last remaining seconds ticked off the scoreboard, I was one of the last remaining patrons in the bar. The floor was literally covered with business cards strewn all over the place, coasters with notes on them, and discarded gas station receipts. When I went back to the front desk, the girl from earlier in the night wasn't there. Instead there was a middle-aged lady with a poofy haircut and a hefty slathering of cheap makeup that made her face look like it would crumble upon any immediate movement. Staring straight at me, she wore a crooked smile, with her hands placed perfectly on top of the counter and her back kept stiff as a board. I wondered for a second if the young girl had snapped and even thought to ask, but this lady had such an annoying appearance and tone that I couldn't take it for any longer than what I needed: room number, key, vending machine location.

Walking around the corner of the lobby and toward the elevator, I happened to see the blonde saleswoman from the bar. She was giggling on a small sofa with another salesman. I faintly heard her say something like "No. I think I should just head up to my room," but I couldn't be sure. As I walked by, the guy looked up and gave me a standard "What's up, man." I flashed a half-smile and nodded in return, then made my way into the elevator, into my room, and into my queen-sized bed, falling asleep to a repeating edition of *Sports-Center.*

By the time I got to the warehouse the next morning, a crowd of about a dozen suits had already formed outside of Bay Nine, a vile, grimy spot where all sample pickups and exchanges took place. In the summer, this area was a haven for bees, and the smell of rotten liquor from the hundreds of bottles that had busted throughout the season would offend even the most ardent garbage man. Luckily, in the winter this was all nonexistent, the only drawback being the bad footing due to any spilled alcohol that had frozen overnight.

"Name?"

"Chet Fisher. Bunglewood Vineyards. There should be two cases of Cabernet."

"Yeah, yeah … two cases, right?" the warehouse manager grunted, taking a leisurely gaze across the endless case stacks. "I got it. One second."

The samples were a major part of the job. Like any other product—whether it be cars, cabinets, can openers, dogs, dope—everyone needed to see how it performed. Buying anything blind was simply a gamble. As for me, these samples were also my life force. When you worked for a winery that had no big press to gloat about, no commercials, no major history, and no fancy advertising merchandise, you had no choice. This left nothing besides what was in the bottle to help me sell it—which, in the end, should be the deciding factor anyway. Unfortunately people wanted to be pampered with ratings and celebrity endorsements as well. Does Bobby De Niro drink your wine? How about Leo? What score did *The Wine News* give it? For the most part, the wine I was selling was actually all right—especially for the price—but it paled in comparison to most of the big boys. The Merlot was weak, the Cabernet was tart, and the Chardonnay tasted like it was dunked in a vat of butter. Nevertheless, it was my job to push it, so I had no right to say differently.

It reminds me of the time I once saw a salesman at a big in-store wine tasting tell a customer that one of his wines was "crap." Little did he know that the customer was actually the store owner's elderly father. The old man literally grabbed the salesman by the tie, threw him out the door, and heaved his briefcase full of papers all over the parking lot while shouting at him in Russian. The moral of the story: if you told someone a product was crap, they'd believe you. If anything else, just lie.

Slumping back down the aisle and slamming the cases carelessly on the ledge, the warehouse guy slapped a clipboard down, huffed out, "Bunglewood. Two cases" and asked me to sign the invoice, which I did.

"Thanks man," I said, ripping the top of the case off and pulling out a bottle. "Happy New Year."

With a puzzled look, the man leaned over and grabbed it.

"You're gonna get in trouble, ain't ya?"

"I already am. Guess it's time to try something else."

"Cheers to that," he said with a smile.

Back inside, the office was visibly less hectic than the day before. With half the winery reps on an airplane home, the room had a much more passive feeling.

I checked the bulletin board and saw that I was scheduled to go on in less than a half-hour. Although I'd never sat in on anyone else's presentation, I'd heard of people getting their message across in any way from top-volume threats to shameless pleas. My normal procedure was to simply get up there and blabber for a few minutes about whatever new products were available. Whether they were half-asleep or under the table jerking off couldn't have bothered me the slightest. I was simply doing what I was told. Besides, I just couldn't get myself to believe the idea that berating these people was somehow going to motivate them to support my product.

A spattering of lazy applause went up as I approached the podium. The fifty or so members of the sales force looked unimpressed, most slouching back in their seats or propping themselves up with an arm to the head. As the wine was being poured down the rows by several office interns, I did my basic spiel about the vineyards location, the soil, the vintage, etc. In past renditions, none of this had ever been a problem, but for some reason my comfort level began to get the best of me on this day. It felt like a recording of myself. Really boring shit. As my lips moved, I struggled to come up with anything besides the same exact sales pitch that had been delivered to every sales team, restaurant manager, and liquor store owner in the greater New York area during my short reign as a winery rep. It was terrible. I could almost see the finish line in sight as I neared the end. One look to the clock on the side wall hinted that I had barely even talked for a minute. Before I could think of anything else to say, I slowly began to fade. "So ... uh ... anyway, that's about it ... and ... uh ... well ... *just sell the shit. It's not that fucking hard.*"

A couple of heads popped up wondering if I indeed said what I had said. As I walked off, only two or three people clapped, the sound of my shoes echoing throughout the board room. The vice president stared at me with his arms crossed at the door, unsure of whether to give me the complimentary "Let's give Chet a big hand" or simply ask if I was on crack. I didn't care. I just wanted to get out of there.

I would be more prepared next time ... I had to be.

The first thing I noticed back at my hotel room was the red "message-waiting" button flashing in the dark.

"Chet, this is Randolph Bungle. Why haven't you been picking up your phone today? I hope to god you made it up to the meeting. Please call us back at the vineyard at once. We have some new leads for you to look into. Also, there is some new merchandise that I think you'll really like. It's waiting for you up at the Buffalo warehouse. I hope you get this message before you head home. Bye."

Hanging up the phone, I considered going back down to the bar and grabbing a few pints, but chose instead to drink one of the sample bottles I had picked up. One turned into two rather quickly and before I knew it I was wearing nothing but my boxers and heading down to the pool with my third.

The place was empty and the water was warm. As I rested my arms on the wet concrete, slugging wine out of a plastic coffee cup, salesmen continued to walk by the open door every few minutes, talking loudly on their cell phones about dates and numbers, and hurriedly scribbling things down on whatever was available. At nearly ten o'clock, the work day was still going strong for many.

"Robots," I thought to myself, "fucking robots."

But who was I kidding. I knew damn well that's what it took to make it in this business—*any* business, for that matter. And more importantly, I knew I had no one to blame but myself for the situation I was in.

Whether it was all worth it was the real question. There was a time not too long ago when I would have cringed at the thought of being a slave to my job. Even the idea that I might someday have a sales job with a suit and tie and business meetings and all that was something that had never even crossed my mind. I wasn't going to be like everyone else. I was going to be *creative*, maybe a heralded underground writer or an "elegantly wasted" yet profoundly meaningful musician. Someone who set his own time line while the rest of the world anxiously awaited the release of each momentous project.

In a way, I guess I never accepted having a "normal job" as a viable option for a career. To some, this blatant dismissal of reality may seem completely irresponsible—unfathomable even—but I mean, honestly, what was supposed to be so enticing about doing the same thing every day, nine to five, only to come home on Friday feeling like the entire week was hardly any different from the one that preceded it? Guys like Bukowski and Harvey Pekar made a living writing about that shit. The doldrums of an ordinary life. One day it's a great opportunity, then a few years pass and it's like a sad, inescapable death march to the car every morning. To me that seemed to be the exact opposite of the so-called American dream. Yet, besides the times when we had to take a job just to *have* a job, so many of us have continued to choose them for reasons other than because it was what we wanted to do in life. Money, security, social acceptance, tradition. None of that ever appealed to me as a worthy substitute. I wanted more. I wanted a life that I could call my own. Something original.

But I never got around to taking actual guitar lessons or journalism courses. Instead I sat in my apartment, got drunk, smoked pot, and merely envisioned how cool it would be—a victim of my own lazy infatuation with the end result. Days turned into weeks and eventually years as I worked dead-end job after dead-end job, never once thinking that I would become, in the eyes of most of my friends, a sad, last link to a life of bar crawls and midweek hangovers. It all happened so quickly.

At some point, the fantasy of living someone else's life had ended … and mine had begun.

2. The Island of Discontent

I lived in a suburban area in North Jersey, about an hour outside the city. My apartment was cheap, near a small park, and, for the most part, located in a hassle-free environment. Acceptable given my single/borderline-poor status, but nothing to be terribly proud of. Passing by it in the early morning hours would have led anyone to believe it was nothing more than an abandoned motel. Two stories of concrete walls and a pool out front that was perennially drained and littered with shattered beer bottles.

I grew up not too far away, roughly thirty miles west, and had been here almost seven years at this point. The majority of my neighbors were either Mexican laborers, young couples saving up for their first home, or people just stopping through. We kept to ourselves—excluding a brief smile or hello—more out of convenience than dislike for one another. There was one fellow, though, that I eventually did become friendly with. His name was Gus, and he moved into the apartment to my left, D2, with his wife about a year earlier. He was a quiet man, in his early to mid sixties, who worked in a local construction site. With long, stringy grey hair falling underneath a trucker's cap and a boney frame that seemed all too brittle for his trade, I'd often come home to see him sitting on our shared front stoop, covered in dirt from a day's work, and with a can of beer in his hand. Our meetings at first were a bit awkward and politely forced, but congenial nonetheless.

"Evening, Gus."

"Chet."

"Long day at work?"

"Yep. Yourself?"
"Friday can't come soon enough."
Looking off in the distance, he'd just raise his beer and nod.
That was pretty much the extent of our conversations over the first few months. I was too deep into my job routine to attempt, care for, or even comprehend anything beyond it.
Yet somewhere along the way, our conversations grew. And although I thought little of these brief encounters at the time, I would go on to learn more from this man than anyone before or since. He was one of those people you didn't really think much of in the moment, but somehow, down the line, you never forgot.

Tuesday night, nine thirty, the following week. The downpour of freezing rain on the Long Island Expressway had made it nearly impossible to move more than ten feet per minute. The drive from my apartment to the hotel out on the South Fork could normally be accomplished in a reasonable four hours, but I was going on six, and at this rate it was a toss up of whether or not I could even get there by sunrise.

The floorboards in my Jeep were somehow flooded with two to three inches of water, and my windshield wipers had been on the short end of a losing battle. This left me hunched over the steering wheel, squinting through the one-inch gap of brown slush and caked ice that the wipers had been able to scrape off. Although the heat in my car was on and working, my feet were soaking wet and on the verge of becoming completely numb. Every few minutes I had to take my foot off the gas and slap it against the center console to avoid total loss of feel. To make matters worse, my antenna was ripped off in the city over the weekend and I forgot to bring any music, except for the one lone tape I found buried in my glove compartment: AC/DC's *Back in Black*.

Not that it was a bad tape to have—arguably one of the best hard-rock albums of all time—but at some point, the lure and fist-pumping tone of Brian Johnson's gruff vocals can do damaging things to a man's brain after several hours of constant repetition. I eventually started judging distances in between the ringing of "Hells Bells." Between that, the constant threat of careening off the road into a telephone pole, and some energy drink that tasted like a liquid gummy bear, I managed to keep my eyes on the road.

Even though it was the dead of winter and the area was a popular summer destination, I was informed by the vineyard heads that "this is a time to get ahead of the competition ... succeed when no one else is watching." I could understand the logic behind this, and I didn't doubt the fact that I needed to switch my game plan up. The only question that continued to be a problem for me was the possibility that no one was, in fact, actually *living* out here in the middle of January. In the past hour I had only seen two cars, and one of them was a snowplow.

By the time I got to the hotel it was close to midnight. The parking lot in front was surprisingly full, so I had to slowly inch my way toward the back side area for a spot. Within seconds of stepping out of the car, the wind was blowing snow into my ear and making it difficult to even keep my eyes open. I quickly realized that the entire parking lot was one big sheet of ice. Each step made a cracking noise like I was walking on a thin pond, so I shuffled my way over to my car tracks, which had made a trail of sorts over the frozen ground.

Walking inside the hotel, the first thing I noticed was a huge curtain in front of the back end of the lobby. There were also mounds of what looked to be cement shavings everywhere and plywood planked across several areas that ran along paths bordered by yellow tape. A sign read: PLEASE EXCUSE THE MESS WHILE WE UNDERGO RENOVATIONS. THANK YOU. There was no one at the front desk. I saw one of those old bells and hammered down on it. This was immediately followed by a loud squeak of a chair from the back room.

"One second," said a voice. "I'm just checking my lotto numbers on the news."

The ice that had covered my body had rapidly formed a pool around the front desk area. I was losing patience by the second.

"Sir, I'd really like to just get to bed if you don't mind. I've—"

"*I'm checking my numbers!*" the voice screamed back.

A few moments later, I heard another loud squeak, followed by the sight of a short, squat figure waddling out of the darkness. *Jesus,* I thought to myself; the man was almost perfectly round. I couldn't believe my eyes and quickly tried to regain my composure.

"Did you win?" I smiled nervously.

"Excuse me?"

"Did you win? The lottery ..."

The man's face twitched in a bizarre expression. His roundness was absolutely mind-boggling.

"*What do you think?*" he barked.

I said nothing else and threw my credit card on the counter. Deep down, though, I imagined rolling him into a large set of bowling pins positioned, to scale, at the opposite end of the hallway.

The hotel looked just like the many that I had stayed in before— so much so that it could become easy to forget, from time to time, exactly where I was. While the grounds of the hotel may have been slightly different, the second I closed the door to my room, they were all the same. In the bathroom to the right, a collection of various-sized towels hung above the toilet, with an empty garbage bin adorned with a fresh plastic bag placed next to it. On the sink counter, several bars of paper-wrapped soap were stashed inside a wicker basket along with tiny bottles of generic shampoo, conditioner, and moisturizing lotion. The shower curtain was usually left open upon arrival with a floor mat draped over the tub wall. Drinking cups and/or cotton swabs may or may not be available. Moving into the main room, a modest TV set rested atop a dresser along with a remote, a channel listing, and a weekly pay-per-view event schedule. On the other end of the dresser, single serving packs of coffee, powdered milk, and sugar accompanied a humble plastic coffee machine with two mugs. Taking up the majority of the living area was a standard queen-sized bed, tightly tucked in to the point of absurdity, with a night stand and a lamp on each side. A bible, which had forever been a hotel room institution (traditionally placed inside one of the night stand drawers), has been phased out in favor of Internet connections. The closet space, opposite one side of the bed, was fairly adequate for most business travelers, with half a dozen or so locked-in clothes hangers and an ironing set for good measure. On the other side, positioned in the far corner, typically sat a writing desk, with a pad of note paper and a cheap plastic pen (both embossed with the hotel logo) lying on top. There were also several flyers of local attractions no one ever went to, some take-out menus, a phone, and a local directory. Any framed wall paintings were either of ducks in flight or sailboats easing along a quiet shore town.

The room I was given on this night was the first one outside the lobby. Throwing my bag on the floor, I stripped off my wet socks and crashed on the bed. I was halfway asleep when I realized I had left my samples in the car. Shit. I had to go back outside and do the whole ice-skating thing all over again, because the damn things would have frozen.

The wake up call that I had requested the next morning never happened. I knew I hadn't slept through it because I was actually up before it would have gone off due to the sound of a half-dozen hammers outside my door. When I stumbled out of bed to see what all the racket was, my first sight of the day was some fat slob construction worker scratching his balls with one hand and using a straw to pick his teeth with the other.

I was scheduled to work this day with a young salesman from the distributor named Derek Brooks. Although I was surrounded by industry people every day; they were always different faces. I might work this one day with Derek, then not again for months, *years* even. It made no sense to keep covering the same ground with the same salesman, so each day was spent with someone else. And because there were literally hundreds of salesmen that I could work with in the state of New York, it was nearly impossible to keep track of all their names. This wasn't like working in the same town every day, in a cozy office building where everybody knew your name and who your favorite baseball team was. It was quite the opposite actually, and in some ways, it could be a very lonely job. There were no real everyday coworkers alongside me, and with all the hours spent on the road—traveling to the next city, or whatever—it left no time after work to spend with friends and family.

My local hangout was only still designated so because of the close proximity to my home, not because I was a regular anymore.

But I learned to deal with it. And while it could often be difficult to pin a name to a face, it took nothing away from how important these days spent working with a salesman from the distributor were. As I'd mentioned before, the chance to go into some of these stores and restaurants with someone who had a relationship already built with the head buyer of these places was an absolute invaluable experience. They understood their tendencies and purchasing history, and could prep you on what to say and what *not* to say. The last thing you wanted to do was walk into a place and randomly start bashing a movie you saw over the weekend, only to find out the owner's sister wrote the screenplay. Plus, with all the other brands these distributors handled, it guaranteed that for at least this one day, I'd have the salesmen concentrating on nothing else except *my* brand.

When I spoke to Derek on the phone last week, he mentioned that we'd met once before at a wine tasting, but I couldn't remember what his whole story was or what he even looked like. Sometimes my memory failed for other reasons. To be frank, I had a tendency to get rather bombed at tastings. Free alcohol was a damn tempting thing and a definite perk in this line of work. Especially to someone who, for the past ten years, had to scrounge up change just to get a six-pack of watered-down beer that tasted like tinfoil.

As strange as it may seem, drinking on the job was actually not that uncommon. I mean, it was right there in front of us. And with that solicitor's license in our wallets, those open bottles would be with us all day, as we spent the majority of the time outside our cars in wine shops, liquor marts, taverns, pubs, sports bars, cafes, and restaurants. I'm not trying to justify irresponsible consumption here, but it's important to understand that when you're dealing with selling alcohol for a living, it sure makes it tough not to sample the goods. I've had a lot of people laugh and tell me that if they had this job, they'd drink all day, and, well, there you go.

Anyway, the plan was to meet Derek out in front of the hotel at a quarter to ten, but I unfortunately got sucked into watching highlights of the NFL playoff games that I had missed due to the drive out here. By the time I made it into the construction site of a lobby, this error in clock management had caused me to be ten minutes late. A fine example of how my laid-back approach and disregard for priorities had continually caused problems between my on and off-the-job personalities. It wasn't that I didn't care about the job; it was just that I usually cared *more* about something else. Like football ... or music ... or looking at some chick's boobs on the subway.

Immediately, someone was yelling my name from across the roped off entrance hall.

"Hey, what's the deal? You were supposed to be here ten minutes ago! We have an appointment set for ten fifteen!" he screamed.

I assumed this was Derek.

"Sorry man. I thought we were gonna get some coffee or something first. I got caught up back in my ..."

Before I could even finish, he was already walking away from me and talking loudly on his cell phone. He turned around quickly before the door, gave me a frustrated look, and waved me over in a hurried manner. Fantastic.

Derek was driving a brand new silver Mercedes Compressor convertible with a beige leather interior. Although it barely had enough storage space to fit my wine bag in the trunk, he claimed that it gave him respect from all the store owners, saying, "They can tell how successful a salesman is before you even enter the store. You don't get that driving a fucking beat up Honda Civic." Right.

We were driving east on the Southern State Parkway, doing close to ninety and testing every inch of the road's condition. It was still bitterly cold, but the ice storm had stopped, and the sun was on the verge of peeking its head out among a few straggling clouds. Derek appeared to be in a monumental kind of rush, constantly riding on the tail of other cars in front of us. "Goddamn it," he would say, "look at this asshole." With every pass he would crane his neck forward and stare at them through my passenger side window, tacking on a fill-in-the-blank comment depending on their race/gender/sexual preference: fucking slut, fucking A-rab, fucking homo, fucking whore, fucking spic. All the while he was answering phone calls, typing into some handheld device on the dashboard, and flipping through the sales book, crossing out some things and circling others.

"Why don't you just call the guy at the store and tell him you're running a little late?" I said.

"*I'm* not running a little late. *You're* running little late," he snapped, looking over at me. "Let's get that straight. I am *never* late."

For a few moments I actually considered opening up the door and doing a commando-style roll out of the car, like John Goodman in *The Big Lebowski*. Instead, I turned and continued to look quietly out my ammonia-scented, spotless window. It was too early to do anything but that.

When we pulled up to the store, he told me to just "do my thing," and he'd handle the pricing. "I've got this guy eating out of my hand. He carries nearly all my products," he said, straightening his tie and looking at his watch. "Except yours," he added.

The store looked like many of the accounts I had visited before. Rows of bottles separated by country and variety, shelves along the walls covered with liquor, and a freezer in the back. A few old posters of vineyards desperately clung to the walls alongside a Jack Daniels mirror or two, with a radio quietly playing in the background. From what I could detect—due to the overdone harmonies, corny lyrics, and unnecessary guitar solos—it must have been some mid-'70s soft-rock station.

Derek spotted the owner in the Spain section and motioned for me to follow him over there. He made some dumb joke about the Giants game over the weekend and slapped the guy on the back.

"Tony, I want you to meet a friend of mine," he said, smiling at me. "This is Chet Fisher from Bunglewood Vineyards." Tony grimaced as he slowly stood up and shook my hand. "Chet has some of those wines I was telling you about. Great prices, Tony, *great* prices."

The man looked like he hadn't slept in a week, but had no trouble finding time to eat. His face was unshaven, he had some serious bags under his eyes, and was wearing a grey Giants sweatshirt that was most likely older than I was.

"Okay, let's go over here," he said, walking with a slow limp.

"Back still hurting, Tony?"

No response. Only a slight sigh and a shake of the head.

"Tony used to work in construction and, ah, is still bothered by a few injuries stemming from that," Derek explained to me. "How long have you had the store now, Tony? Five years?"

Tony made his way around the front counter and shoved a newspaper opened to the sports section and a half-eaten bagel smothered with cream cheese out of the way. Reaching into my bag, I pulled out the five wines I had with me and was about to start opening the first one when Tony asked, "What's the price?"

"Ah, yes, Tony. We're just about to get to that," Derek said. "Would you like to taste the wine first or—"

"I just want to know the price. I don't have time to taste this morning."

The place was completely empty minus the three of us.

"Well then, we've got some great discounts. This particular Chardonnay has a discount on three cases which bring it down to six dollars a bottle and ..."

I hadn't even opened my mouth yet. Derek continued to run down all the prices and add in his little quips about "how well this wine would sell here" and "how the store could really use another Merlot in this price range." Tony just nodded his head and said nothing. After Derek had finished, he looked briefly outside and stared at a lady in a fur coat walking by.

"You should see how she dresses in the summer," he said. "Some ass on that woman."

"Hahaha. Yes. I'm sure," Derek said. "So about the wines, Tony. What do you think?"

He mumbled and scratched his chin for a second.

"All right, gimme three of the Chardonnay and five on thee, ah ... Merlot. Just bill it for February."

"Certainly, Tony, certainly," Derek smiled, grabbing his pad and writing down the order. "And thank you very much for the business."

We shook hands and walked outside. Before getting into the car, Derek looked at me and said, "You see. This is why I deserve to be making twice as much."

The rest of the day was more of the same. Derek kissed ass, sold wine, and complained about the business not giving him his due. This was a common theme in the minds of most of the salesmen I'd been in contact with. Whether or not they could actually do this job well enough to warrant a bigger paycheck or promotion didn't matter. It was apparent that the majority had their eyes set on something higher up the totem pole anyway. Fine wine director, management, ownership ... that type of thing. The salesman position was merely a phase to them. In the same way you don't see many lifetime bartenders around anymore, there were very few "lifers" left among the traveling salesman profession. Get in, get out, move on.

That's not to say this day with Derek was totally uneventful. At twelve thirty, he nearly killed us driving straight through a four-way stop while trying to put an order in on his cell phone. At two, he gave the finger to a truck full of Mexicans for only going fifty in a thirty-five, leaving us scooting around some back roads to finally lose them. And at quarter to four, his in-car navigation system took us the wrong way down a one-way street, sending a plumbing van over the curb and nearly plowing into a group of high school Goth kids.

The entire afternoon we barely spoke, minus the complaining part of course. He spent most of the time in the car attending to his various computerized contraptions and countless phone calls. By the end of the day, we hadn't taken a lunch break (Derek said it was a waste of time) and I don't think he even knew one single fact about me (except that I drove a Jeep, which Derek said was a nice car "when you're in college").

We left on civil terms. As I was getting out of the car, I turned to say a simple thank you, but his phone rang again and that was that. I spent the rest of the night in a diner across the street from my hotel, drinking happy hour beers and stuffing myself with twenty-five-cent wings.

In the newspaper I was reading, there was a picture of Keith Richards hanging out at some backstage party in the city. I must have stared at that picture for an hour, wondering what it was like—for even one day—to have lived that kind of life.

I had little time to deliberate between my current situation and those of elderly rock stars. The next day I was working with a guy named Ed, a nice, clean cut, balding gentleman in his late thirties or early forties. We were in this store on the south shore trying—at least I was—to sell my crummy wine. I say this because Ed offered no help whatsoever and seemed to care even less. Not in any rude way, just very straight-faced. Somewhat resembling a Swiss Guard I guess.

To further dampen my spirits, the manager of the place was act-ing like a total douche bag, catching me on every minute detail, spitting out my wine, and obnoxiously screaming "Next!" after each one. Ed seemed to brush this off with ease, but I was beginning to think I may burn this place down later on.

"So you see, we get this wine from the Alexander Valley in Sonoma County, a very good place to—"

"Shut up and listen to me for a second, kid. I know all about the Alexander Valley, just give me the prices again. For Christ's sake, Ed, why do you waste my time with this shit?"

"Eighty-eight bucks on three cases for the Cab and Merlot, eighty on two for the Pinot, and seventy-two on three for the Chard," Ed mumbled, flipping boorishly through the latest issue of *The Wine Explorer*.

"Well, I have one more wine for you to try and then maybe—"

"I don't want to try it. *Look*, I don't like your wine! The only rea-son I'm even remotely interested is because of the price. Ed, just call me tomorrow. I have too much shit to do around here right now … I can't think straight!"

Ed tossed the magazine back on the counter and gave the man a gentle smile.

"Okey dokey. Let's go," he calmly said to me, raising his eye-brows.

Putting the corks back in my wines and placing them in my bag, I stood up and looked at the manager. His back was to me, setting some nips of vodka on the shelf behind the counter.

"Do you enjoy what you do, sir?" I asked.

He slowly turned around.

"What did you say?"

"I said, do you enjoy what you do?"

"What the hell does that mean?"

"It's only a question."

"Get the fuck outta here," he muttered. "Jesus … you got a lot to learn about life, kid."

It was the only thing we agreed on.

In most cases, the salesmen I worked with were very easy to read. They either loved the job or hated the job. They were happy with the way their life was going or they were a complete time bomb. This way of putting your emotions and personality in the forefront was as commonplace as getting dressed in the morning. Which made this particular day all the more a mystery. Where Ed fit in was entirely unclear, and for this reason, I guess, it intrigued me.

The foundation of his unique persona rested on his aforementioned nonchalant attitude. This laid-back demeanor was complimented by a certain serene quality that devoured any sign of stress or possible trouble that came his way. It was beautiful. Nothing forced or contrived, just very natural. At a stop later that morning, it was put on full display when a store manager accused him of placing the wrong order, called him worthless, and told him to get his head out of his ass and do his fucking job. While I sheepishly ducked behind a stack of wine boxes, Ed didn't even blink, and just smiled as he assured the manager that he would take care of the problem right away.

Now, this type of immediate restraint wasn't so surprising—it came with the territory—but what did surprise me was that there wasn't any sign of animosity or an obscenity-laced tirade once we left. I began to think that this manner of his was some sort of defense mechanism against the routine bullshit that a salesman must deal with on a daily basis. I couldn't be sure, but I also suspected he might be working on a higher level of consciousness, quite possibly through some Zen mind trick. Then again, maybe he was just stoned.

Mental strength aside, what confused me even more was his physical nature, mainly because he seemed to work in polar opposites. He drove a grey Dodge Caravan that was heavily littered with piles of merchandise, empty coffee cups, and rotting fast food wrappers—but he was impeccably dressed, with a stylish, well-cut light brown suit and matching leather coat and gloves. At lunch he ordered a garden salad and a sparkling water with lemon to start, then tacked on a T-bone steak with mashed potatoes and gravy. And while he was rather meticulous about keeping his shoes agleam throughout the day, it was interesting to note that he didn't wash his hands in the bathroom after using the head. Slapping me on the back as I washed mine, he merely said, "I'll go warm up the car," and out he went.

The thought that I'd surely be enduring some light jazz or a selection of Buddhist monk chants after lunch set me up for one of my more interesting discoveries. In his passenger side door compartment lay the unthinkable: an old cassette of Metallica's debut album, *Kill Em All*. The man looked to be the antithesis of a metalhead, but what did I know. Our conversations up to that point were limited to the basics: Do you like the business? How long have you been in the business? What new products do you have? Are you from the area?

Naturally, I was curious.

"Metallica, huh?" I said, inspecting the scratched up tape. Ed looked over and smiled.

"Yeah. How about that?"

"You a big fan?" I asked.

"Who isn't?" he said.

Clever response. He had me there.

"I just didn't really picture you as—"

At this moment, Ed's phone rang. Smiling once again, he gently held up his hand, motioning for me to hold on. The phone was mounted on his dashboard alongside a Darryl Strawberry bobble head doll. Staring down at the number flashing on the screen, he waited a few rings before casually responding. I could hear yelling on the other end of the line, but Ed gave a series of smooth, short answers that seemed to dilute the screams to a low mumble before long. He spoke only for a minute or so and ended with a somewhat reassuring good-bye.

"This job is really something," he sighed, placing the phone back on its mount.

"Ed, show me the way of the Force" is what I wanted to say, but all I got out was, "Yeah. Totally."

I was impressed, if not a tad awestricken. Never before had I seen a salesman continually exhibit such control, with such grace under fire. I quietly put the tape down, and for some unexplainable reason, never inquired any further than that. Maybe I just wanted to leave this man in peace, or maybe I just unconsciously conceded that he was, in fact, the Enlightened One.

In the end we had a decent day, but nothing that would offer me any relief in improving my sales numbers. The boss called later in the afternoon and wanted a full report of the two days on the Island. For what, I had no idea. The place was fucking dead. Who goes to a summer resort town in single digit weather? In any event, I whipped up something to keep him off my back when I returned to the hotel. The remainder of the night was spent lying on my bed, staring boorishly at the TV. There was absolutely nothing on, and by the time I had decided on which terrible reality show to watch I had already missed most of what some would call a plot.

Before I fell asleep, a fax came through on the work desk in the corner. My end-of-the-month numbers: Down 18 percent. Goddamn it.

3. As Goes the Alternating Merge, So Goes Society

*"Y*ou *ever live anywhere besides Jersey, Gus?"*
We were smoking cigarettes on the front stoop one morning before heading off to work. Gus was also drinking a beer, which I found kind of amusing at this time of day.

"Besides the war ... no, I don't think I have. Born and raised here in Jersey."

"You ever want to live anywhere else?"

"Uh ... not really. I mean, where else would I go? I got everything I need right here."

"Yeah, but you never wanted to go to Europe or California or something? Just for a few months or whatever?"

"Nope."

"That's seems crazy to me."

He took a drag off his smoke and shrugged his shoulders. "A friend of mine at work told me the same thing a few years back. 'You're afraid that you might find something better.' Or something like that. Well, he's wrong. And you know why?"

"Why?"

"Because I'm not looking for any place better."

"If it ain't broke, don't fix it, right?"

He raised his beer and smiled.

"Breakfast of champions. Good work, Gus."

"Hey, if I want beer for breakfast and pancakes for dinner, who's to say I can't? This is America. Rules are made to be broken."

"Records."

"Huh?"

"It's 'records are made to be broken.'"

"Yeah, those too," he said.

It was an overcast Tuesday afternoon in mid-February that I worked with a salesman named Pete Taylor, who—by his own admission—was God's gift to both wine sales and women. Every blessed second this guy was pulling me into the front entrance of some swanky bar telling me that he banged some cute hostess or used to date this chick or that chick. Pete's married, of course, but referenced his boat and beach house so many times that he must use them as part of some escape plan from his supposed "suburban palace" in Westchester.

While his personality and hedonistic nature ran wild, his sales technique was simple: Deal with everyone like they were your best friend. And I mean *deal*. The opportunity to assist a sale along with some free "off-the-record" goods wasn't just something he threw around blindly; these were strategically placed strikes that could take weeks to build up. They were his bread and butter, and he used them whenever possible. Sure enough, they worked. And quite well, I might add.

Pete's route stretched across every inch of Manhattan: The Village, the Upper West Side, the Lower East Side, SoHo, NoHo, and all points within the city limits. He wore a navy blue suit over a striped shirt and a skinny orange tie; his black hair slicked back and his graying sideburns adorned by a pair of thin wire-rimmed glasses. He was a tall man, I'd say about six foot three or so, and had a way of completely taking control of the room. The guy had a story for everyone.

At our first stop in the East Village, Pete immediately went to work, talking to the manager about doing a shark feeding at the bottom of the ocean outside of Jamaica last fall on a scuba expedition. After twenty minutes of this maniacal story concerning flesh-eating tiger sharks and bloodstained water, he turned to me and said, "So anyway, this is Chet with Bunglewood Vineyards." It felt like I was in some part-time garage band following Led Zeppelin on stage. I lasted about two painful minutes. Right before I began to wrap up—more like fade away—Pete leaned onto the table and looked sternly into the manager's face.

"We're willing to work with you on this."

The manager stood up straight and raised his eyebrows; the last comment surely getting his attention.

"Well," he said, "what would you give me on, say, ten cases of the Chardonnay?"

Pete turned to me with a look of pure concentration, his brain shifting into next gear trying to access the situation. It was serious now.

"What do you think, Chet ... one (free) case on ten?"

Although I hadn't up to that point done many under-the-table deals (it was completely frowned upon by the vineyard and actually illegal), I slowly nodded yes, before looking back at the manager.

"Yeah, I think we could do one on ten."

And that was that. He took the order, we thanked him for the business, and we were on our way.

"That guy can tell you more deep-sea stories than anyone," Pete said outside on the street, lighting up a cigarette. "You gotta get to know these guys, Chet. Down to the bone. After that, give them a deal, take the order, and get the fuck out," he added. "*That's* how you do business, my friend."

We made our way over to the West Side, where the giveaways continued at some old tavern in midtown. Immediately upon entering the place, Pete walked behind the bar and started juggling some whiskey bottles like Tom Cruise in *Cocktail*, flipping them over and around his back in all sorts of intricate patterns. After a minute or so of this, he stopped, poured himself a shot, and hammered it back. Slamming the glass down on the bar, I thought the lone man in the back was about to have a heart attack, but he simply clapped, adding, "You still got it, Pete."

"Damn right, I still got it," he said, wiping his chin on his sleeve and burping. "How are ya, Pauley?"

The three of us sat down at the empty bar that was covered in wall-to-wall sports memorabilia for a good half-hour, talking about the current Yankee pitching woes and whether Yogi Berra or Thurman Munson, in their prime, was the better catcher. Although I considered myself to be a pretty darn good authority on the subject, Pete's knowledge of the team could rival anyone I had met before or since. Little details such as how many balls and strikes there were during each of Munson's at-bats throughout the entire '78 World Series were talked about as fluently as if he were reading off an old scorecard. "Tommy John threw him a slider on a 3-2 count that I swear was dead center. But Munson leaned into it, nearly looking the ball into Yeager's glove, and got the call. I tell ya, I'll never forget that smirk he wore as he trotted down to first base …" How much of whatever Pete said was actually true, I don't know, but the way he told a story made everyone a believer.

There came a point, though, when I began to notice him slowly drift out of the conversation, merely nodding or smiling at whatever the two of us had to say. I could see his concentration had moved on to something else and I knew then that he had sensed it was time to get into his zone. His transition into wine products came smoothly, and before long we were knee-deep into a discussion about deals and long-term buying programs. We ended up giving this guy a free case of Chard on top of the five cases of both Merlot and Cab he ordered, along with a box of corkscrews because, as Pete put it, "Pauley and me go way back."

It didn't take much to see how this all worked out, and soon enough I was left wondering why anyone *wouldn't* buy from him? He was basically giving them the wine for the lowest price, so why not? I knew a lot of salesmen out there that would've said it took nothing to more or less bribe these guys, but I didn't think it was that easy. Pete played the "buddy-buddy" part so well it was hard to tell if he was being completely honest or if he was simply a master bullshit artist. My thoughts on this could have swung either way, really. One thing was for certain: these buyers trusted him. And Pete knew it. There wasn't the slightest suspicion of doubt when it came to every single story, decision, and emotion that he presented. Contrived act or not, he got their attention and kept them interested.

Right from the start, I knew this clever attitude had a lot to do with his ability to sidestep any trouble, but I still questioned the downside. How could he get away with doing this so often and so blatantly? When I asked him about the possibilities of getting reported for dealing illegally, he laughed.

"Who would report me? They all know I give them the best deals. It'd be like sabotaging their own business."

Indeed. Unless some of these buyers wanted to lose a good thing by contacting the State Liquor Authority, there was no reason to complain. Besides, he was their friend. They were all genuinely glad to see him. It wasn't like some wine geek coming in and giving a programmed speech about vintages and ratings. It was real, at least in their minds.

Our path across the city continued on. After stopping for lunch at an old jazz club (Pete took the time to flex his saxophone chops, with the owner on drums) and hitting another sports bar (childhood friend of his—played in city league basketball with the guy) we stopped off at a coffee shop near Gramercy Park, so he could flirt with one of the waitresses while he checked his voicemail. Throughout the early part of the afternoon, I got the feeling Pete was trying to impress a young buck like myself with his attitude, style, and sexual conquests, and as the day progressed he was continually asking me questions about my own life: college, girls, where I'd been, what I'd done, etc. Every city I mentioned he would ask what bars were "cool" and would reminisce about some old places that he used to hang out at. Each spot had a different girl from a different era. "Betty Miles ... wow, what a little hottie she was. Best legs in the state of Georgia. Back then they were a dime a dozen down there, Chet. You ever been to a place called The Glass Slipper? I remember this one night there in the summer of '79 ..."

I couldn't help but think this guy was either going through a late midlife crisis or was desperately searching for clues to what the "youth" of today were into. As he blabbered on and on about these types of things, I pictured him telling the same triumphant stories to every new sales rep he worked with. It was really depressing shit when I thought about it. An aging playboy.

We saw three or four more accounts the rest of the afternoon, with Pete doling out free cases of wine like they were Halloween candy. Before calling it a day, we agreed that I would pull the free goods for him at the warehouse under the orders that they were for "sampling purposes" as part of a tasting event they were running at the stores. This was the easiest way to write off any cases that might come under question, Pete said.

"It's only natural that we take care of this as soon as possible," he added. "The quicker the paperwork gets processed, the quicker we can get these deals completed. The last thing we need is for anybody to question our business. Or, for that matter, question our *friendship.*"

While the chess match between salesman and buyer had come to an end, another game was about to begin. Traffic. Holland Tunnel. Five thirty.

The guy in the car next to me wore dark sunglasses. It was drizzling rain and the grey skies atop the city were becoming more and more threatening by the minute, and this guy had on dark goddamn sunglasses. In between the six or so inches we moved every ten minutes, his red sports car sounded like it was on the verge of a tantrum, scooting up violently before breaking heavily with a screech. This had been going on for more or less a solid hour.

I had to focus on him, not because of the beauty of his turbo-charged vehicle, but because of the leering eyes of the guy to my left, whose blinker had been flashing since Tenth Street. I refused to acknowledge that I'd seen him, his van or, most importantly, his blinker. I pretended not to hear his horn either, which had been blasting on one continuous honk for the last several minutes. The girl driving the small silver hatchback in front of me got the last of my generous wave-ins back at Fourteenth Street. I'd done my part. Please take your heat-seeking stare elsewhere.

Several green lights came and went, but the traffic wasn't moving. Was there an accident? Construction? A stalled '82 Datsun with rusty bumpers and plastic seat covers? I didn't see any police lights or hear any fire engines, so it couldn't have been anything major. I tried to motion to one of the police officers standing in the street, but instead drew the attention of a hot dog vendor. Walking over toward my car, he held up various finger signs and yelled, "What you want? You want drink? You want hot dog?" After I frantically shook my head and waved my hand "no," he slunk back to his stand, mouth agape, his head turning like a pigeon at every horn, conversation, and passing glance. I'm sorry, but I wasn't about to give up a spot in line so I could squeeze packets of mustard and relish on a grubby hot dog. There was no time for that. One person jumps in front of you at the light and traffic could back up an extra twenty minutes. Not that I was in a rush to get home. I had no kids, no girlfriend, and no single friends. I didn't even have a plant. But the more time I could sit in front of the TV and do nothing, the better. It was my motivation. My past life of being a slacker needed to be fed, and I would not deny it.

During the vendor confrontation, I must have missed the van sneaking in a car behind me. It brought a sigh of relief. Loosening up my tie and checking the mirrors, I fumbled around my glove compartment for some music. Sports talk radio was about all I could stand at that point in the day, but they were in commercial and the sounds of some techno bullshit that came from the red sports car was killing me. The coffee ran right through me this morning, which cost me valuable minutes sitting on the throne, so once again I was scrambling to get on the road in time. The selections I had made were not properly thought through. Looked like some Skynyrd or an old Public Enemy mix. Clicking around the FM dial, everyone else was in commercial, too, so I opted for the Skynyrd.

Silver hatchback was pressing her luck. She was already stuck past the white line and in the middle of the cross street. Through my mirror, I noticed some of the lights behind me beginning to switch to red. There was no way the traffic would be moving up. She was screwed. Making one last attempt and hoping that her lane would give way, she drove up about one car length and, as the light turned red above us, got stranded right in the middle of the oncoming cross street of traffic. Cars converged all around her, honking crazily, as the eyes of the traffic world behind us looked on in disappointment.

Leading the pack was a man in an old grey sedan who was crouching forward and squinting through his thick glasses, unable to comprehend the situation. Laying heavily on his horn, his face screamed mental breakdown, and looked to be on the verge of tears. Even from the distance of about twenty yards, I could see the veins bulging on his neck. The lady behind him was smoking a cigarette with one hand and waving her fist with the other, her big hair flopping recklessly about the vehicle. Although she rode alone, I could see her lips moving, obviously mounting a platform of obscenities for anyone who cared to listen. Silver hatchback's failure was not limited to the automotive crowd either, as noted by the ten-year-old boy who rode by on his bike and promptly gave her the finger. Looking at the girl through her back window, she had her hands clenched tightly around the wheel and was trying her hardest not to flinch an inch one way or the other. White knuckles, forearm tendons pulsating, sweaty palms.

I glanced over at the guy in the red sports car. He was still wearing sunglasses, though nighttime had definitely fallen, and was staring straight ahead. The music emanating from his car produced an unrelenting beat that even got me hypnotically nodding to it, yet he remained frozen, eyes fixated on the scene in front of us. Signs of a true professional.

The traffic moved up a bit, and right before our light turned green, silver hatchback inched up and out of the way, leaving only a few seconds for the crosstown cars to chaotically try and get across. Slowly creeping forward, I cautiously waited for the right moment to make my move. If I went too soon, I ran the risk of getting blocked in, with no room to angle around. If I went too late, traffic from the left would get the run of the lane, causing infinite amounts of vulgar comments to be thrown my way for not defending our position against the line-cutters.

After a few seconds, I saw the hole beginning to open up and I quickly gunned it around the last crosstown car before swerving gently back up to the bumper of the silver hatchback, hence maintaining my position. I could see the plastic dividers beginning up the next block up, knowing that they would ease the situation, for once I hit them it was all smooth sailing from there on out. Unless some monster truck wanted to run them over—which could happen—the dividers signaled the end of the line-cutting stretch down Seventh Avenue and the beginning of the flow toward the tunnel. A beautiful sight indeed. To my dismay, though, the traffic didn't seem to be letting up much. By the next red light my car was out of the way of oncoming traffic but in the middle of the pedestrian crosswalk.

I could have cared less about the whining old ladies that looked at me in amazement that I'd taken up their area to walk in. I'd left about a two-foot space, people. That was plenty. As if the glaring looks weren't enough, the black limo breathing down my neck behind me still found it necessary to lay unforgivingly on the horn to move up. Unwilling to accept the fact that I couldn't possibly move up any further, the limo jerked to the right looking for space to blend into the next lane. The guy in the red sports car was right on top of that, though, and rebutted this move by edging up steadily, coming within a hair of the car in front of him. Still looking straight ahead in his dark sunglasses, I took it as a quiet act of traffic defense, although I envisioned him waving his finger and saying, "Not in my house."

Ten after seven, and the mix into the final turn before the tunnel had begun. So far no one had gone outside the laws of one of the strictest rules in the traffic book: The Alternating Merge. One by one, the two lanes converged as we calmly wove together. Blue Honda, tan Mazda, silver hatchback, yellow taxi ... well done. Coming behind the taxi, my lane was set to follow the pattern. But red sports car wasn't slowing down. I quickly started to panic and looked over, abruptly keeping pace with him. "I'm next, asshole! I'm next!" I yelled, as he began to rev up closer to the taxi. Then, staring straight ahead and with no remorse, he pushed forward and made a quick move to the inside. Sounding my horn, I stretched my head out the window and screamed, "Alternate Merge! *Alternate Meeeeerge!*"

To the sounds of an Afro-Cuban beat shaking the change in my cup holder, he nearly clipped my front end before settling into the single lane ahead of me.

As he passed, the glare of a street light illuminated his sunglasses, and like that, he was gone.

4. The Waiting Really is the Hardest Part

*T*he idea that connections—and a little bit of under-the-table greasing—made the sale, was something an old pro like Pete Taylor demonstrated quite clearly. Although I personally hadn't made any friendly business contacts during my short time on the job, I did in fact have one from my previous life as a normal, non-sales person. So the following week I decided to head down to SoHo to pay a visit to an old high school buddy, who recently opened one of those bar/lounge/clubs that seemed to be multiplying by the second all over lower Manhattan. Why I didn't go check out his place the day construction finished, I don't know, but now seemed like as good a time as any.

Mike Paterson was, and still is, a good friend from my adolescent days growing up in Jersey. While the majority of us languished in the area, doing bong hits in our parent's basements listening to Ween albums (still some of my fondest memories), Mike sacrificed summers full of irresponsibility and good times for unpaid internships and managerial training. By his mid-twenties, he'd already gotten in tight with several investors, working at a collection of underground nightclubs in Brooklyn, and was able to round up the monetary base needed to open up a place of his own last fall. Through it all we always remained close, but as with most of the old crew, time—and the fact that none of us had any of it—became a major factor in the two of us not seeing so much of each other over the past few years. It basically boiled down to weddings and funerals.

The mixture of rain and snow held off on this day, and with the sun creeping out every now and then, it made the walk around the city a decent one. When I finally got down to the spot, a pack of teenage hipsters were sitting outside, leaning up against a side wall covered in fresh graffiti. Underneath long shaggy hair, thick-framed glasses, and denim, one of them asked me if I had any extra tickets to some concert around the corner at the Mercury Lounge. I shook my head and told him no.

As I passed, I heard one of them say, "Fucking narc" under his breath.

A hostess was up at the front, staring aimlessly out the window when I walked in. She was unbelievably attractive, with short, straggly brown hair, bright blue eyes, and a petite, yet voluptuous frame.

She looked right through me when I came up to her.

"Hi. I'm here to see Mike."

"Is he expecting you?"

"Yeah, just tell him it's Chet."

"What company are you from, Chet?"

"Oh, he'll know ... I'm an old friend of his."

She gave me an uninterested glare and tapped a button on the phone. "Hi, there's a guy here that says he knows you ... Chet ... okay." She turned back to me. "He'll be right up."

The place was very minimal in decoration, but was offset by incredible mood lighting of mainly soft orange and reds. With plush circular booths and rows of old spinning bar stools, it mixed hip and futuristic with a bizarre, classic diner feel. A droning beat was pumping loudly from the speakers, and a TV screen over the bar was showing the classic Pacino flick *Dog Day Afternoon*. There were a handful of people throughout, all of them impressively dressed like they had just left a fashion show. A closer look around revealed that many of them were quite attractive in the face as well, so I don't know, maybe they *were* all models. What I do know was that none of them were talking; they were merely leaning back in their booths and sipping their drinks, bobbing slightly to the beat. Think pouting lips and half-closed, shifty eyes. The kind of crowd that made you want to just slap someone. Hard. Just to see if they'd budge. Or fight back.

"*Chesterrrr*, what's up buddy?" Mike said, entering the room and giving me a hug. He wore jeans and a striped black blazer over a vintage Rolling Stones tour shirt. Although it was still wintertime, his face was noticeably tan and his spiked black hair was tipped with blond highlights.

"Nice place," I said with a smile.

"Yeah, not bad, huh? What took you so fucking long?"

He gave me a quick tour and introduced me to several of the other bartenders and hostesses, all of them women and all of them absolutely gorgeous.

"Jesus, dude. Where do you find these chicks?"

He laughed and pulled out a joint, leading me out the back entrance.

"I got twenty more begging me for a job," he said, holding it up. "Come outside and hit this with me."

We went out to the alley and sparked it. He asked about what I'd been up to the last year or so, and I told him all about the job situation. I stressed to him that I wasn't coming here to ask for any favors, but he immediately shrugged it off and said he'd take in a few of the wines.

"Do you want to at least taste them?" I said.

Coughing as he held out the joint, he asked if they were any good.

"Not really."

"Ah, don't worry about it. Keep 'em. I'll tell people the bass player for Radiohead ordered it and we'll be sold out in a week."

We bullshitted for a few minutes and talked about what everyone else was up to. One thing I'd come to realize of late was that the older you got, the less interesting the gossip became. Instead of a story about someone falling onto the field at Yankee Stadium and pissing themselves, it was more like, uh "Greg just got a promotion" or "Dave was transferred to Scranton."

As we walked back inside, my body felt as if it were hovering an inch or two above the ground, yet I was in complete control. For now, at least. I sat down at the bar while Mike excused himself into the office for a phone call. The red tea light above me made it feel like I was in a submarine or, quite possibly, that it was pitch black around me and I had on some intense night vision goggles. One of the bartenders strolled up and I ordered a jack and coke. I was reaching into my wallet when Mike came back.

"Put that away, man," he said, calling over the bartender. "Listen up, this guy doesn't pay for a drink, got it? On the house."

Seldom had I been involved with such an offer. My social and monetary status had immediately been upgraded. For all nightlife purposes, I was now *part of the scene*: those select few who drift on a whim from LA to London to New York in search of the next great party, only to wind up in places like this to drink fourteen-dollar martinis and act famous/bored because there was nothing else to do at four thirty on a Wednesday afternoon. The few employed friends they most likely didn't have were still at work, and it was well proven that shopping anywhere near the brink of rush hour was not the time to cross paths with the upper tier of the elite "in" crowd. So it was here that they sat ... and waited ... for something, *anything*, to happen.

The high I was undergoing at the bar was by now doing strange things to my perception level. A feeling that I was constantly sliding off my barstool was a major part of this problem. I couldn't quite find the right balance. It had been months since I last touched the stuff, and my slow re-adaptation to the drug was also making it difficult to hold down a decent thought of any kind. I needed to focus on something besides the TV screen which was positioned on the opposite side of the room, now showing a collection of strange Japanese cartoons.

While Mike retreated back into his office, I calmly asked the bartender for a drink menu. The look on her face as she placed it in front of me was the look someone might give while hand-feeding a bear.

"Is everything okay?" I asked, unsure of her strange expression.

"That's like the fourth time you've said that to me in the last minute," she said.

"What are you talking about?"

"Uh, look. Forget it. Did you want to order something else or were you gonna just stare at my tits for a little while longer?"

"Excuse me?"

"Let's try this again. Did you want to order something else or were you gonna just stare at the menu for a little while longer?"

"I'll take a Yuengling, please," I answered, quickly folding up the menu and sliding it back across to her. "Everything's gonna be just fine."

"Come again?"

"Fine. Fine. Everything's gonna be just fine."

She rolled her eyes and went to the tap.

Across the room a young Asian lady began laughing hysterically. The sound was terrible, like a child being literally tickled to death. Down the bar and directly in front of me sat a huge black man in a leopard skin jacket, no shirt, and dark wrap-around shades. He was staring straight at me. At the exact moment I noticed him, he very deliberately shook his head. I couldn't tell if he was reacting in disgust to the emotional outburst or if he was signaling for me to get my shit together. The bartender returned with my beer and I quietly shifted down the bar, to the far corner against the wall, and behind some huge metal beam.

From that point on, things get a little blurry. I do remember utilizing Mike's free drink deal on a multitude of Belgian whites and Pennsylvanian lagers, but I don't remember passing out in his office, which is where I wound up, on top of a smelly blue sleeping bag, in my underwear, and under a clock that read 9:55 a.m. It took me a few minutes of patient confusion to make sure I had all my stuff together (wallet, keys, wine bag, suit) and to look for any other signs of what may have occurred here last night. No indication of vomit, broken bottles or shattered picture frames, and from what I could tell, no spilled alcohol on the computer keyboard.

I had no time to comprehend any of this, but I was in better shape than I could have possibly hoped for. For one, I had taken the bus in the day before, so my car wasn't parked on the street completely stripped to the bone with a ticket flapping on the windshield. Secondly, I didn't use any of my samples, so there was no need to scramble back to my apartment in Jersey. Lastly, and most surprisingly, my head appeared to be in decent shape considering I blacked out and was standing half-naked in the office of a fucking bar as I thought this out. No doubt, this was all good news, and I had some investigating to do, but I also had a meeting across town at one of the major steak restaurant chains at eleven. So it was important that I moved on.

I took the 6 train up to Forty-Second Street and transferred onto the crosstown express. The whole ride up I had to fight to keep my rolling wine bag from getting in the way of the bustling crowd. People were kicking it, tripping over it, and basically hating me for holding it. At one point, I think it was at the Union Square stop, some elderly black lady poked me in the chest and told me to pick the damn thing up or get off.

Standing outside a corner deli next to the restaurant, I chugged down a vitamin water and nibbled on a plain bagel, trying to combat the early signs of a hangover. The initial energy and good spirits I had were starting to wear off. My mouth was dry and my brain felt as if it had slowly begun to swell. I only had a few small accounts to see after this meeting, so if I could just make it through this I'd be okay.

At ten to eleven I walked in and let the front desk guy know I was here. He told me to take a seat at the bar and that the manager would be with me shortly. I sat there watching college basketball highlights for a half-hour before the same guy informed me that the manager was still in a meeting and to please be patient. I could barely get out a response—a nasty coughing fit had come over me—but I managed to smile and croak out, "No problem." The only other person in the room with me was a big Irish bartender with perfectly coifed grey hair and a protruding iron chin, who stood frozen, arms folded, watching the screen. His only words to me so far were "What the hell is that smell?" It wasn't me as much as it was the cologne I had found in Mike's office. I thought that it would counterbalance the unshowered effect. Apparently this oaf didn't appreciate my concern.

I was still waiting by the time the power lunch crowd began to arrive. Fake laughter, cigar smoke, and bland, terribly-forced conversations had now filled the room. To make matters worse, the bartender had also switched the channel to some golf tournament down in Argentina. The effect this had on the crowd was staggering. Like a pack of Pavlovian dogs, it ignited a fury of golf talk that took mere seconds to engulf the entire crowd. Golf stories, golf scores, golf tips, golf clubs, golf courses, golf this, golf that. I hated golf, but was forced to ride it out for the possible sale.

Lighting cigarette after cigarette and sipping on a warm beer, I sat in my own world, waiting for this asshole to come taste my cruddy wines. Sometime around one o'clock, with my head seemingly about to crack in half due to a massive headache, and by now completely surrounded by a pack of suit-and-tie golf aficionados, I saw the man from the front desk sifting through the herd in my direction.

"Hi. Mr. Fisher, I'm sorry but my manager is going to be unable to see you today."

"*What?*"

"He's very busy and it's just a crazy time here, as you can see."

"I don't understand. *I have an appointment!*"

"Yeah, again, I'm really sorry. Please do call us back some other time."

The man walked swiftly back into the crowd and through the kitchen doors.

I somehow mustered up enough face and energy to hit a few stores around midtown afterward, but wound up not selling a single bottle. I slept most of the way home on the bus, interrupted only by an automated voice message sent from the vineyard. My end of the month sales totals for February: dead even off last month's numbers but still painfully far behind on my overall goal sheet.

If I was to have any hope of keeping this job, it would need to pick up soon. At least I wasn't falling backwards anymore, though. The key here was to stay positive.

5. Dishonesty Brings Blizzards and Sales

Although I rarely saw her due to my schedule, from time to time I'd catch Gus's wife, Mary, unloading groceries or coming to the door to call him for dinner. A petite lady, with graying hair pulled back in a pony tail, she was every bit as quiet and unassuming as her husband—albeit much more shy—and with a very youthful face, so much so that it appeared ten or fifteen years behind the rest of her body. The two of them were noticeably close, but never to the point of public affection or playful behavior. Let me put it this way: whenever she asked him to help her with something, he always did it with a smile.

Gus would always say, "marriage is funny" over and over, laughing to himself. "What do you mean?" I would ask, which, on cue, brought out a very fatherly remark like "one day, you'll see."

The subject of someone's marriage had never been much interest to me, but I felt intrigued by Gus's. It seemed to work for him. I wanted to ask him questions about their relationship—where they met, what she was like—but it felt awkward even thinking about it. I just couldn't see an old guy like Gus talking deeply about anything even closely related to the subject, and in no way did I want to put my own manhood in question by raising the issue.

One night that winter, we both happened to pull into the parking lot of our apartment complex at the same. Grimacing slightly as he eased himself out of his beat-up Ford pickup truck, he zipped up his coat and plucked a cigarette from his pocket. It was about ten degrees outside, and normally I'd be running headstrong for the warmth of my apartment, but when our eyes met, he held up his pack, offering me one. I nodded yes.

Following a minute of mutually understood silence, wherein I tried my hardest not to show any sign that the brutal realities of the weather were affecting me, my body finally caved in and began to shiver uncontrollably.

"Christ, it's cold," I mumbled.

Gus looked around, somewhat disinterested. "That time of year, I guess."

"Yeah, it's fine in December and January—with the holidays and everything, but man, after that it just gets downright annoying."

Gus laughed. "Hey, if you could change the weather by getting annoyed, I'd have started doing that years ago."

"It doesn't bother you I guess?"

"Bother me? No. Why should it?"

"Because it's fucking freezing, Gus. This sucks."

He laughed again and tossed his cigarette butt into a mound of dirty snow that the plows had formed.

"Besides," he said, "how could I think about that when I got a beautiful lady inside cooking me beef stew?"

I flicked my half-smoked butt and followed him toward the steps.

"You got a good thing going there, Gus."

"Damn right I do," he said, clutching the guardrail and walking carefully up the icy steps.

"March is when the selling season begins, Chet. Take control and seize every opportunity." These words came from my answering machine and were the first ones I heard on that initial morning of the month. It was a damn good thing I did hear them too, because my power went out sometime overnight due to a vicious ice storm and my alarm clock had reset itself. Had the self-assured voice of my boss not come blaring through that ratty machine of mine, I probably would have slept in bed well past noon, undisturbed, and not have headed down the Turnpike at eight a.m. to meet another salesman in another town.

I was scheduled to work in New Jersey the first few days of March, not as part of my normal territory, but to help out our rep here who had recently gone into labor with her first child. My job was to simply "maintain her presence in the field" and to make sure that I "represent the brand to the highest degree." Real militant-type shit.

I had barely made it ten miles outside of my apartment when the weather report on the radio announced that the governor had issued an official state of emergency, predicting long periods of snow and ice to continue throughout the remainder of the morning. They had gone so far as to ask people to not leave your homes if you didn't absolutely have to. Unfortunately this was not an option for a traveling sales rep. Spending any time at home was reserved for Sundays, life-threatening sicknesses, and/or multiple broken limbs and skull fractures. Besides, the salesman I was set to work with had already called me a half-dozen times to see exactly where I was and to be sure that I would make it on time. Due to the wintery mix of weather conditions, the traffic on the Parkway was horrendous, but I made sure to give myself plenty of time. Through it all this guy kept mentioning things like "We're going to have a great day!" and "What do ya say we sell some Bunglewood Vineyards!" in a real giddy, annoying manner. Not once or twice, but multiple times per call. It got to a point where I had to seriously calm him down and let him know that I could see his excitement and that I too was truly ready to sell some Bunglewood Vineyards today.

When I finally arrived in New Brunswick, it was a complete white out. The wind had kicked up so much that it was literally snowing sideways.

I had the Jeep in four wheel drive, which meant virtually nothing on ice; each stop came with a minimum one-foot slide. Inching slowly down Route 27, I saw the shopping center where I was supposed to meet him. His tan sedan was the only car in the lot. On my third attempt, with my wheels spinning furiously, I made it over the short incline and pulled up alongside of him.

"Hey, buddy!" he yelled, rolling down his widow and squinting through the wind. "Why don't you grab your stuff and hop in here. This is a good spot to leave your car."

The second I stepped outside, a strong gust of wind nearly blew my jacket off, and my new phone, which I forgot was on my lap, fell into a six-inch pile of snow. Jumping awkwardly into his car, I threw my bag on the floor between my legs and wiped the slush off my face.

"Heh heh. Some crummy weather, huh?" he said. "Name's Jim."

"Yeah, hey Jim," I said wiping my wet hand on my pants before shaking his.

When I asked him how far away our first stop was, he said this was it. It was snowing so hard that I didn't even notice there was a liquor store here. Neither had anyone else apparently; the whole shopping center was lights out.

"He usually opens up by ten," Jim said, looking rather confused through his driver side mirror at the store. "Maybe I should give him a call."

We spent the entire day in various parking lots discussing the same situation. Not one manager had come into work.

We did happen to find a few stores that were open, but it was usually just some zombie behind the counter who spoke no English, ringing in sales to the few brave alcoholics who needed their vodka fix. Before we went our separate ways, Jim reassured me that he would follow up on all these accounts tomorrow. Interesting. Especially considering that we neither met with anyone nor even opened the bottles. What would he possibly say to these people? Would his explanations of showing up in such weather make him a hard worker in their eyes, or simply insane?

The timeline of this day couldn't have been any further from the one I typically saw. On average, the working hours of this occupation consisted of several interlocking peaks and valleys.

The mornings usually started off quite well. Basic conversations with the salesmen and store owners were still somewhat stimulating due to the effects of the morning caffeine rush and the fresh topics. By the time the caffeine started to fall off, the sample bottles have been opened and the first-drink high took over for the caffeine, much like you would see in tag team wrestling. One buzz tags out and another comes in. How much I threw back would normally determine how long this would last, but I had to be very careful here, because the more I drank the harder I would certainly fall. Maintaining an even balance was an absolute necessity, one that came with the ability to judge my tolerance level on any given day, under any given circumstance.

Timing also played a big role here, because if the lunchtime craving set in too early it would have the mind and body operating on two separate clocks. This could send the second half of the day into a world of confusion and turmoil, with the mental side unable to hack the reality of the remaining hours on the job, and the physical side believing the day was over and looking for a steak at three in the afternoon. I had to train myself to fight the hunger until at least twelve, knowing it would pay off in the long run. When that time did come it was important to remember that while the midday meal did offer a break from the sales race, it was only temporary, and must be taken with caution. Stuffing myself silly because I didn't have the time or money to eat breakfast would most likely leave me in dire need of a nap. So I had to soldier on, and with a little more help from both the caffeine and the sample bottles, combined with the right kind of phony attitude, I could regain a few hours' worth of energy in my step.

What followed after this was no man's land, that space in the day where everything seemed to become useless. And it was at this time, the midafternoon home stretch, where the major problems started to occur. I was tired because the caffeine had lost its impact, I was half-drunk but the buzz was unfriendly, and due to the combination of these two—along with whatever I unfortunately gorged myself with at lunch—my stomach began to make strange, unhuman noises. Speaking was also a problem. The once jolly conversations had now morphed into an uncomfortable silence, forcing a constant mental drumming from my brain to come up with something worthwhile to talk about.

By the time four o'clock rolled around, I'd begun to focus solely on the ride home and on whether or not I could beat the traffic. The ability to show any sort of enthusiasm was long gone, my acting skills had all but dried up, and my hands were badly stained with red wine that had dribbled alongside the bottle from pouring sloppily. Basically, at this point, I was hoping for cancellations—anything to shorten the day.

When the work was finally at an end, it was like crawling out from underneath a train wreck unscathed. All of a sudden my spirits were lifted, I wasn't as tired, my feet didn't hurt, and I was finally alone in the familiar confines of my own car, with all the freedom in the world to let out a day's worth of gas buildup, play Sabbath at full blast, and enjoy the few remaining hours of the day in peace.

Coming on the heels of what could have been quite possibly the single most useless day in the history of wine sales, my second day in New Jersey, oddly enough, came as a crucial turning point in my time on the job. I was working in the northwest corner of the state, Warren and Sussex counties, with a salesman named Lenny. It became apparent early on that Lenny worked completely off the press. The man could rattle off reviews, ratings, and scores like a goddamned fantasy football expert. It was his main selling point, his reassurance to the buyer that someone who knew something about wine happened to love *this* particular wine.

This type of game plan was no secret and had been going on for years in this country. Every week a bunch of so-called classy wine magazines put out lists and lists of information that generated buzz among the industry. It was like any movie or album review: people read it and said, "Oh, look, the paper says the special effects are supposed to be incredible in this film. We *have* to go see it" or "This magazine says Bowie's new album is supposed to be a return to his mid-'70s form. I *gotta* get that." Some stores and restaurants will take in a wine without even tasting it, solely because some famous old-fart critic gave it an esteemed ninety-point rating. In turn, the store will slap a ninety-point tag up on the shelf underneath that bottle, and the consumer will buy it. I'd seen it happen a million times back when I worked in the wine shop. So many people were afraid to ask for help picking out a wine (for many reasons: snob mentality, fear of coming off as stupid, underage, etc.) so they just looked for the scores, assuming again, it must be good. These scores could be absolute gold for shop owners, especially the ones who just wanted to sit behind the counter and read their fucking newspapers all day.

The trouble of course with my wine was that we didn't *have* any reviews. Not even a bad one. Through the first part of the day, I knew I had to solve this problem, and somewhere between the second and third stop it dawned on me: I could make up my own ratings and lavish stories. Immediately my mind went to work. "Oh, yeah, you know, Bruno Battaglia ordered twenty cases of this wine for his daughter's graduation. Who's he? Well, in fact, Mr. Battaglia happens to be the head of the Italian Fine Wine Control Board. It was great news for us, of course, among all the great American wineries for Mr. Battaglia to select *this* wine, but then again that's what Bunglewood is all about."

It sounds a bit shady, I know, but it could work.

The first store we hit after this discovery was a small shop in Newton. I dove into the lies at the first sign of boredom growing in the manager's posture.

"Hearing that Leonardo Lentine used this Cabernet as an example of what he wanted to grow in Tuscany was huge. You saw that article last month in the *Ledger*, right?"

"No … I hadn't," he said, coming out of the fog. Lenny looked up, a bit confused himself.

"Oh, boy. You should have seen the reaction from my boss. It was a great shot of confidence for the whole team. Sales have skyrocketed."

"Really? Who else in the area has it?" he said.

"No one yet. We just got it back in stock a few days ago. Some high-priced stores in LA and Chicago snatched up the initial inventory when the news broke. Small production, you know." I was rolling.

"You've heard of Lentine, right?"

The manager stood up straight and closed his newspaper. "Of course I have," he said bluntly.

"A very important figure in the rebirth of Italian wines," Lenny added.

The guy wound up ordering ten cases of the Cabernet.

"Hey, what does Lentine do again? I mean, you know, specifically," Lenny asked, as we were walking back to the car.

"How the hell should I know?" I said, "I just made it up."

We had equal success in the next two stops. I used the same story on the first one, then switched to a different story for the second (a hot new celebrity chef was now using our Chardonnay on his TV show in London. Heard it may be syndicated for the American audience in the fall). These people never even questioned the validity of these stories, but merely gave an interested look and inquired more deeply about the wine. The manager at one stop even asked to re-taste the wine after I told him the story. The guy literally changed his entire view. Originally he claimed that the Merlot tasted bland

and that the finish was too weak, but was now saying that the wine "is really opening up" and "showed some great fruit and depth."

Every account we hit throughout the afternoon placed multiple case orders, and by the end of the day we wound up selling forty-five cases, a new high for me. I wasn't sure if Lenny agreed with my plan, but it worked. Sometimes I guess it was just hard to argue with good results. More importantly, a lesson in reality had been learned here. The positive power of lying in the business world was a completely manageable approach.

Dishonesty *sells*.

6. The Return to a Bar as a Form of Pleasure

A week later, I was standing in the snow outside my hotel in Rhinebeck when I got the sudden urge to have a drink. It was two thirty in the morning and the entire hotel was out there with me, in their pajamas and winter coasts, because of a chimney fire in the building. The temperature outside was an even zero and I was surrounded by a bunch of crying kids, impatient parents, and annoyed business men, all of whom seemed to have their own idea on how to fix the problem. The three firemen leaning up against their fire truck were visibly less interested, wondering aloud why they were here in full gear for nothing more than a bunch of smoke and a blackened chimney.

I overheard one of them tell a guest that a chimney fire was second only to a cat stuck up in a tree on the "bullshit list."

During this questionable experience, there was an elderly man next to me who had been talking to no one in particular since we got out there. He was wearing an old coonskin cap and was rambling on about how he'd lived in the hotel since 1959 and that this "wasn't the first time the ol' chimney got its nose stuffed up." Strangely, he was also smoking some strong hash out of a wooden pipe that was shaped like an elephant. In between pulling huge rips on this thing, he coughed heavily and went in and out of some meandering story about how the '72 fire was an act of religious warfare or some shit.

"Hey, is there a back door entrance to this place?" I said, cutting him off.

"Ah, well ... yes, there is actually. It's an old carriage house door that leads into the dining room."

"Thanks," I said, trudging off to the opposite side of the hotel from where the fire engine was.

"Where are you going?" he shouted.

"Inside. It's freezing and I'm thirsty."

I scampered along to the back, my ankles becoming numb from the wet snow, and sure enough the door wasn't even locked. There was no one else in there, but the light was on and so was the TV. I made my way around the bar, quietly searched for *SportsCenter* on the set, and poured myself a Jack and coke. It was a good hour before I heard the rest of the hotel guests come creaking back along the old wooden floors, and by then I was four deep.

Outside of this, the first few days up here in the mid-Hudson Valley had gone better than expected. Picking up where I left off in Jersey, I was practically either giving the wine away or lying my way through some epic story to get them to take the bait. If people weren't interested, I made them interested. If people wanted deals, I gave them deals. It was that simple.

And so, for the first time on the job, making a sale had become something of a continual occurrence—a groove of sorts—with my confidence growing stronger with each one. Sure, it had only been a few days worth of positive momentum, but it was nonetheless extremely important. My psyche needed to know that I could achieve success through alternative methods. That in itself was the major obstacle. The results, I hoped, would only continue to play themselves out.

Which led me to my last night up in the area, where I did a small in-store wine tasting a few blocks down the street from my hotel. It was well known throughout the wine community—and maybe sales business in general—that the quickest way to get your customer base to take interest in your product was to just let them have it. In the wine and liquor world these "giveaways" were set up in a number of different forms and varieties, but mainly consisted of a dopey salesman (me) supplying a few bottles of wine (Bunglewood Vineyards) in a store which carried your product (in this case, Mabel's Wine and Spirits) to be sampled by the locals. It was free, it was easy, and it would hopefully attract some people to buy your wine in the future.

Unfortunately, past experiences with this type of promotion had not gone well for me, mainly because the Bunglewood product was quite offensive to those who actually enjoyed drinking wine. So I made the decision to eschew my normal mode of operation and go right for the gut. Literally. This included tossing my typical merchandise (technical sheets, vineyard pictures, and free, cheaply made corkscrews with logos on them) back in the Jeep, in favor of a spread that consisted of mini panini sandwiches, water crackers, Parmigiano-Reggiano cheese, and an assortment of cold antipasto. All of which I expensed on my company account. I felt it was time to spice my act up a bit and go for the pity/nice guy route.

The tasting went from five to nine and was dreadfully slow at first. The owner, an aging former beauty queen, was constantly telling me that it was usually not this bad on a Friday night. "I don't understand it," she'd say, trying to come up with an excuse. "It must be a Jewish holiday or something." Her face was so ravaged by plastic surgery she hardly seemed to show any variation of expression when she spoke. It was as if she was talking through a goddamned Halloween mask.

The only other person working in the store was a small Venezuelan kid who looked about ten but had a moustache and apparently a license, seeing as how he also doubled as the delivery "boy." The two times I went in the back to use the bathroom he was sitting on a wine case, half-asleep, listening to some Spanish talk radio station. I'm almost positive that in the hour or so between these visits he hadn't moved an inch, as both times I noticed that the sandwich that was spread across his lap had only one bite taken out of it. These were the things you picked up on when the clock was working against you.

Over the first two hours I didn't even *pour* anyone wine, never mind sell any. The only pouring I was doing was into my own cup, to help stave off the boredom. It was agonizing having to stand there behind a wobbly makeshift kiddie table, in my suit and tie, with a tray full of untouched food and free wine—so I had no other options. Amidst the easy-going sounds of a Mel Torme tribute that came from the speakers above her vintage stereo system, we stared off into nothing, only occasionally interrupted by the random phone call or underage purchase attempt.

It was sometime around seven o'clock when the crowd picked up and spared me any more of this unspoken torture—although I don't know what was worse, that, or the constant sight of the owner trying to flirt with every barely-out-of-college male customer. Pouting her fake lips and flipping her hair back over a wry smile while she rang in the orders was truly a disgusting thing to witness.

"And there you are, sugar. You have a good night, okay? And don't do anything I wouldn't do—which isn't saying much. Ahahaha."

Her eye contact lingered just long enough to get the "it's here if you want it" message across. Unfortunately for her, there would be no takers on this night.

As for myself, most of the customers I dealt with seemed rather knowledgeable about wine, although there were still a few old ladies holding up the bottles and shouting, "*Is this red?*" You had to learn to take the good with the bad. At least it kept the clock moving. In a way, the smaller tastings were always kind of a drag because you either didn't have time to mess around being you were the only one pouring, or you had too much time and no one to talk to.

By eight forty-five my mental state had gone from bad to worse, figuring I must have drunk a bottle and a half on my own. I sold five or six of them, too—okay considering the atmosphere—but at this point, sales were secondary. I needed to get away from this place while I still had some of my moxie left. But what about these lingering middle-aged customers sipping free Chardonnay and talking about homeowners insurance? And my business commitment to this damaged creature smiling at me from behind the register? Too bad, I thought. I wanted out. So before I could endure any last-chance sexual advance or horrid conversation piece, I seized the opportunity and bolted through the front doors while the owner excused herself to the bathroom.

Stumbling awkwardly around the corner, I plopped myself down on the curb behind a post office drop box and lit a cigarette. Goddamn, I was out of shape. A one block sprint and I was huffing like a fish out of water. As I frigidly clung to my smoke, I discovered something across the street that I hadn't seen before: a small tavern. In the daytime it probably just looked like a simple brick house—which it was—but at night there were a collection of big blue and red neon beer signs in the window, and every time the door flew open the sound of Nirvana's "Rape Me" blasted out into the barren sidewalk. For such a quiet town, it seemed to be full of action, so without hesitation I shuffled my way over the icy pavement and went inside.

The place was a mix of young college students and a few old burnouts. My suit and tie definitely got some weird looks when a waitress carrying a full tray of beers kicked the back of my leg and yelled for me to get out of the way.

At the bar, clusters of people were sandwiched together sideways, trying to make room to simply breathe. The only place I could fit was in the far corner, which took me nearly ten minutes to get to. Along the way I spilled beer on some biker chick, got stuck in the middle of a fraternity toast, and stepped on a dozen toes.

Squeezing in between two guys with their backs to each other, I got one elbow on the bar, with a ten-dollar bill clenched firmly in my hand. I saw only one bartender on duty and she appeared to have her hands full. Stunning in every sense of the word, she wore a pair of tight black pants and a skimpy red tank top, with every curvaceous detail of her figure on full display. With one flip of her sleek black hair, she threw a quick gaze out toward the crowd, bit on her lip, and went back to the register.

As I panned across the bar, all eyes were on her, with a furor of people barking out orders for another drink and frantically waving money in the air.

"Hey honey, when you get a chance, over here!"

"Yo bartender, one more of the same!"

"Can we *please* get another round of shots!"

It was such an unrelenting barrage of demands that, given the circumstances, it would not have been surprising to see anyone in her position break down and start jabbing at these people with the end of a broomstick. But all the while, this woman was operating on some dominant frame of mind. There wasn't a hair out of place or a single bead of sweat on her brow. She was composed, calm, and in complete control. In this modern age of whiners, quitters, and short-tempered hood rats, it was a thing of beauty.

Sadly, though, this act of inspirational hard work left me struggling to even get her attention, which, without being overly annoying, was hard to do. Most of the apparent regulars couldn't have cared less about this and just wanted more beer. For example, the fat, drooling slob who sat a few spots down the bar from me. He wore a Giants jersey two sizes too small for him, and with his eyes closed and head cocked to the side, pounded his fist on the counter screaming, "*Another lager please, another lager please, another lager please!*" monotonously, over and over.

After about fifteen minutes of waiting, she made her way over to my side and gave a quick look out to a swarming pack of eight or nine of us hunched together over the bar. The instant she looked into my eyes I shouted, "Jack and coke!" and without saying anything, she nodded and went over to make it.

Looking back at the other guys, they were already trying to better reposition themselves, and were snarling at one another, each claiming that they were next.

"I was after him, bro!"

"Like hell you were. I've been here for twenty minutes!"

"Bullshit, man. All you a-holes were behind me!"

I didn't say a word. She came back and handed me the drink and change. I got in a quick thank you but it was barely audible over the screaming of the entire place trying to get the next order.

Hiking over to the far side of the bar, I found a seat and watched her work. Hearing a few people call out "Anna," I figured that was her name. The place was too crazy to even attempt trying to talk to her, but in a way, just looking felt good. Something about an attractive female in action could do that. Being on the road all the time, I met a lot of people that I'd most likely never see again, so I learned to just take what I could get. More often than not, names were forgotten and faces became nothing more than a fond memory of some random, insignificant moment. Shit, if I were better looking and no doubt a better conversationalist, I could've probably had a few different girlfriends in a few different towns by this time.

Seated next to me was an older gentleman with a white handlebar moustache and a red bandana around his head. The back of his jacket pledged allegiance to some motorcycle club, but the lettering was so worn I couldn't make out the inscription. Meanwhile, I casually removed my tie, took off my jacket, and rolled up my sleeves.

"This place always this crowded on Thursday night?" I asked, scooting my stool up. The man had his elbows up on the bar and was holding on to his beer with both hands.

"Yeah. Just about," he said, taking a sip. "Somewhere along the line the place became a hotspot for the college kids down the road in Poughkeepsie."

We both turned to see a bunch of frat guys arguing loudly over a dart game.

"What was it before?" I asked.

"Just a regular old watering hole, you know. I guess once those people all starting dying off or getting jobs, the owner must've had to come up with a new idea."

"What was that?"

"Three big screen TVs, a new jukebox, and a biannual wet T-shirt contest."

"Interesting."

"Yeah. Welcome to the real world."

I sat in that spot until closing time. Little by little the few older people left and more college kids came in. For the last two hours I probably had seniority amongst all of them—at the ripe old age of twenty-eight. I couldn't help but feel both nostalgic and beaten at the same time. Even though I wasn't that far removed from this scene, it felt as if I was now on the outside looking in. I was no longer one of them. Between picking up various surrounding conversations and ordering more drinks, I drifted through several thoughts on whether or not I had spent the time of my youth wisely, knowing full well no money or success could ever bring those years back. I distinctly remembered there was a point when I had tried to imagine how an older version of myself would feel. Would I regret not taking more chances? Should I have taken the straight path toward a better education? A better job? Or would I kick myself for not having more fun when I could afford the time to do it?

Last call came around two, and by then my mind was too warped to find a definitive answer to these questions. I guess that was the price you paid for living irresponsibly into your late twenties, one way or the other always wondering "what if?"

Putting on my wrinkled jacket, I walked the two blocks back to my hotel, puked on the bearskin rug in the lobby, and passed out in my suit. In the morning, I pushed my checkout back as far as I could without getting charged an extra night and made the journey back down the New York Thruway into Jersey.

Another week on the road …

7. A Snob Sighting in Midtown

*T*here was one Monday morning, a few days after I got back from being upstate, that I didn't see Gus out front. His truck was there, but no sign of him. To the best of my memory, I couldn't remember him ever calling out sick or even appearing as so—give or take the random smoker's cough. Frankly, I didn't think much of it at the time, but as I was on my way home I began to wonder if he'd be sitting out there when I pulled back into the lot. He was—complete with beer and smoke in hand.

"I guess you didn't call in sick today," I said, pointing at his fresh can.

"No. My son came into town last night. We went and had breakfast this morning and then he dropped me off."

I'd seen his son a few times here and there. If Gus had a complete opposite, it was him. Well built, he stood about six-four and was a few years older than me, maybe thirty-five or thirty-six. Gus didn't talk much about him, but I think he lived in the city and worked on Wall Street or something.

"How's he doing?" I asked.

Gus took a sip of his beer and smiled.

"Good. Good."

"You guys get to catch up?"

"Yeah, we did. He's a great kid, Chet. Reminds me a lot of myself."

I looked at him for a second, waiting for the punch line, but it never came. I just grinned and nodded my head.

"I know what you're thinking. We look nothing alike and all that."

"Well, there is sort of a—"

"It's not that, Chet. It's his spirit, his attitude. When I was his age, I had that same look in my eye. I mean, yeah, we live our lives in different ways, but that look ... it's there all right."

"What kind of look are you talking about?"

"Well ... if anything, I'd say it's part confidence and part knowing you got your whole life at your doorstep."

"Ever wish you could go back?"

"To where? Being young again?"

"Yeah."

"No. I don't think so."

"Not even to change a few things? You know, take a chance on something you wish you had?"

Gus took a deep breath and leaned back against the steps.

"Chet, I've lived my life the way I wanted to live my life," he said. "Maybe I don't have the money my son has or maybe I don't have the home some of the guys at work have. But I lived every day the way I wanted to. So if I went back and did it all over again, it'd just be a repeat. And I hate repeats."

"That's awesome, man. But c'mon, you don't have a favorite episode of something you'd watch over just once more?"

"Well, sure I do. But it's never the same as it was the first time you saw it, is it? I mean, I'd love to go back and revisit some of the times I had when I was your age, but I think I'm better off looking forward at the times I'll have right now."

Gus dusted himself off and tossed his beer can into the garbage bin next to the steps.

"Look, I don't want to come off sounding like some high school guidance counselor, but life is weird, Chet. You make mistakes, you learn from them, and you move forward. I'm not one of these reincarnation kinda guys, so it's my belief that you got one chance to do what you want to do down here. If you wanna be a stockbroker, be a stockbroker. If you wanna climb Mt. Everest, climb Mt. Everest. If you

*wanna be a bum and eat banana peels out of the garbage, be a bum
and eat banana peels out of the garbage. It's up to you."*

My only view of the outside world down onto West Fiftieth
Street was blocked partly by the inset of a brick wall and the
remainder by a massive fire escape. And it felt great.

It was sometime in mid-March that I wound up staying at the
Amsterdam Court Hotel, a few blocks north of Times Square, for
the entire work week. The opportunity was a stroke of pure luck.
Knowing I was scheduled to be in the city, I gave a ring to my buddy
Mike down in SoHo the weekend before, hoping to meet up with
him for a drink one night. Not only did he agree to that, but he also
hooked me up with a bag of some intense weed and a prepaid room
here at the Amsterdam. At first I balked at the offer, but he
explained that he wasn't going to be using it and that money wasn't
an issue. Apparently, his girlfriend's sister was expecting to fly in
from Dubai that week, but had changed her mind at the last second
when she found out it was still bitterly cold here, opting to spend a
week drunk and topless in St. Bart's instead.

The hotel was a decent place, nothing ritzy or anything, with a
newly refurbished bar downstairs and a real old-New York feel to
the rooms—which were quite small, by the way—giving me just
enough room to walk around the bed to get into the bathroom. I
will say this about my first impressions of the hotel staff, though:
very chill folks. My first night here was proof of that. Mike and I
had been watching the Knicks game in my room, smoking this
ridiculous weed out of an old metal pipe, when we heard a loud
knock at the door. It was at that moment that I realized we'd forgotten to crack open the window, leaving the whole place completely
clouded in a dense fog. So thick in fact that I couldn't even make
out Mike's face as he struggled trying to get the window open,
which appeared to be painted shut.

Peeking through the eye hole, I saw one of the bellhops standing in front of the door and another behind him spraying a can of air freshener.

"Yes," I said, peering out the door.

"Hello sir," he said, getting a big whiff. "We've got some complaints of smoke coming through the hallways and into several of the other guest's rooms."

"Oh … is that right?"

"Yeah, uh … look, can you try to keep it a little more … *controlled?*"

He gave me a smile that spoke volumes about his character.

"Absolutely," I said. "And thank you for letting me know. It won't be a problem."

When I walked back into the room, Mike was gone. I found him fully clothed in the bathtub, with his arms folded, and looking straight ahead.

"This shit is too much," he mumbled. "We need to go back to smoking some of that dirt we had in high school."

I continued to stare at him.

"Why are you in the bathtub?"

He laughed with a somewhat sad expression and shook his head.

"I don't know. You see … this is exactly what I'm talking about."

I turned around and walked back into the other room. The Knicks lost.

Not having to deal with the traffic the next morning was something I could have definitely gotten used to. Although my boss afforded me the opportunity to expense hotel rooms when I was further upstate or out on the East End of Long Island, Manhattan was out of the question. My arguments were typically short-lived. "Timing is everything in this job, and naturally this puts me in a more controlled situation. If I have to spend three hours getting in and out of the city because of traffic every day, it's going to eat away at both my preparation, my performance and, most importantly,

my soul." The response I got was simple: millions of people commute daily to get to work. Take the train. End of discussion.
I figured it was worth the shot.

The relaxed, peaceful feelings I had that morning over a nice breakfast didn't last long. At my first stop twenty minutes later, I came within inches of beating a Korean store owner senseless with the butt end of a cheap bottle of Merlot.

I could just feel a problem coming on the moment I entered the account. The tension and anger this man possessed had completely enveloped the place and sucked the good vibes right out of me. The meeting at eleven was to taste him on some of the new vintages we got in, and for some reason, he immediately went ballistic on me because I wouldn't give him a better deal. He basically wanted *more* free shit. The guy didn't know anything about wine and told me that I should somehow feel honored to be represented in his store and that all the other stores in the area got deeper deals. I hadn't even set foot in those other stores, but this guy kept telling me otherwise. "I see the price! I see the price. Don't call me liar!" I don't know why I was even there to begin with. The store was full of big name wines that he obviously took on price alone, but from what the boss told me, I guess he had connections with several other Korean-owned stores in the Lower East Side.

So anyway, as he was screaming in broken English about being robbed of the best price, I just started packing up my wines. Before I left I told him that this was a fine way to run a business, by berating a sales rep who was just trying to help him out. He followed my remark by sipping some of the wine I poured for him earlier and spitting it on the ground at my feet. My first thought was to pummel this wee man (he was only like five foot three) but I quickly regained my composure and simply told him to get his skank wife out here to clean it up. Like a branded bull, he immediately charged in my direction from behind the counter, furious and yelling in Korean—but was intercepted coming around the corner by one of his stock boys.

"You should thank him," I said, waving a bottle in his direction.

The man screamed that he would call the State Liquor Authority on me and I told him to go ahead, I could report him on ten counts of illegal sale orders.

Otherwise, it was a pretty good first day. I went to three fairly upscale steak houses and sold multiple cases of Cab and Merlot. After convincing a long-haired bar manager who said "man" after every sentence ("Nice to meet ya, man." "What's the price, man?" "I thought it was supposed to rain today, man.") that the wines were the only ones on Neil Young's tour bus, I reeled in the last two through the power of some immediate free goods out of the back seat of the Jeep.

The rest of the week, unfortunately, continued to have its ups and downs. When I met Brad, the salesman I was set to work with, outside the Second Avenue Deli the next day, I was surprised to find that he was actually younger than I was. Looking a bit stiff and timed, he wore a fashionable black leather overcoat and had a mid-'60s mod haircut. His voice on the phone was somewhat gruff, giving me the impression he was another weathered veteran of the sales force, but this was not the case. In fact, it was only his third week on the job and his first day working in the field with a winery representative. This was all rather interesting, given it was the first time that the role of experience had been turned in my favor. With that came the opportunity to mold the day into the way *I* saw fit—and the only way I imagined this possible was to start drinking, fast and early. So for the first hour I advised him to reschedule our first meeting until later in the day, so we could sit in the Horseshoe Bar on Seventh and B and sample the goods.

This worked out quite nicely and by lunchtime we hadn't sold anything yet, but we were in good spirits. I remembered what Pete Taylor said to me last month, that this business was built on establishing relationships, and we were certainly doing that. How else can you get someone to support your product if you don't know their girlfriend was a former burlesque dancer on Eleventh Street or that they somehow preferred *Happy Gilmore* over *Caddyshack*? Details such as this paid dividends down the road, or so I was told, and besides, what did I have to lose in trying? My sales numbers had only recently showed signs of steady improvement, so maybe my failures weren't because I had no prior schooling or development in the trade, but because I was trying too hard to transform myself into someone I could never be: a prototypical businessman. Granted, as of late, I had been able to understand the benefits of the double Ds of sales (*D*eception and *D*eals), but deep down I knew there must be a more essential ingredient than mere dirty work.

And as I sat there, staring out on to the cold East Village sidewalks full of unemployed musicians and toothless meth addicts, I began to realize something. The main problem with this job seemed to be more of a difficulty in adapting to a certain businesslike manner than anything else. The actual occupation was perfectly fine, but the way you had to go about everything was what had me struggling to leave behind my own identity. For one, there was a distinct, phony voice used while on the job and I'd yet to master it. I'd gotten the ass-kissing tone, the proper use of language, and fake laugh down, but the credibility wasn't there. I didn't look comfortable trying to pull it off. The sales pitches that I gave at our meetings showed signs of this as well, along with the fact that most of my ideas and presentations were terribly dull and outdated. Even my appearance wasn't fooling anyone; regardless of what suit I was wearing, something was always out of place. Either my pants were too short, my sleeves were too long, or vice versa. Going in to see a tailor would've been nice, but I was convinced my lanky frame and casual upbringing just weren't made for the business suit.

The point of all this was that there was nothing *real* about me … and I knew what had to be done. My personality, or lack of one in the work setting, had to be cracked open immediately and injected deep into the almighty blue vein of this job. I'd seen it work for a few people I knew in the business, so why couldn't it work for me? I mean, was it beyond the realms of possibility that I could actually behave like a *normal human being*, even during working hours? Well … I wasn't quite sure. But if I was going to succeed in this business, I knew I had to succeed on my own and not by some ancient rule of textbook behavior and sales techniques. I simply wasn't cut out for it any other way. That much I was sure of. Now, this didn't mean I was prepared to completely abandon my sales act or that I planned to show up for work in a Motorhead T-shirt the next day, but there were going to have to be some necessary adjustments. I had tried being like them … and now it was time to just be myself.

Maybe it was the one thing that had held me back all along.

"Don't you ever answer that thing?" Brad asked, interrupting my train of thought. My phone had been ringing constantly for the past two hours. I hadn't even bothered to see who it was.

"No," I said, sitting up. "I never risk putting myself on the spot. If it's important, they'll leave a message—damn, I should have left this tie at home."

I'd been struggling with my tie all morning and had grown tired of it, so I just yanked it off and stuffed it inside my bag. Looking over at Brad, I asked him to do the same. He looked at me, confused.

"You should lose that," I said, pointing at it.

"The tie?"

"Yeah, it's gonna throw off my game. You wearing the tie and me not wearing one. We need to get on the same page here."

Fast forward to later that afternoon. We were in a small store on the East Side, talking about the wines, when a man walked in wearing a pinstriped business suit and shoes so agleam they made reflective light marks on the ceiling like a disco ball.

"Can I help you?" the manager said, motioning for me to shut up. Looking around, the man answered, rather smugly, "I don't know. Let me see if you have anything interesting first." I looked over at the manager, who turned to me with the same "who is this guy?" expression.

"All righty then. Just ... let me know."

The guy paced around for a bit glancing at some bottles more specifically than others, with his hands gently placed behind his back.

After a few minutes, he grabbed a bottle from the Bordeaux section and, tilting his head back behind his black-rimmed glasses, looked at it like it was a Picasso painting.

"Do you have the '95 vintage in this Chateau Beychevelle?"

The manager walked over and scanned the shelves.

"I already looked there," the man huffed impatiently. "I meant do you have any in some sort of bin room or something?"

"Whatever's here is here," the manager said. The guy slammed the bottle back on the shelf and let out a long, gentle moan. Perusing the aisles he squinted and winced at nearly every item, and on occasion, even flashed a look of disgust.

"Where are your Brunello's? I don't see any."

The manager gestured to his assistant to show him, but the young man ignored him, pretending to stock check items on the computer, which, from the look of it, he quite obviously had no idea how to use.

"They're right over here next to the Chianti's," the manager told him.

"Ewww, these are all '99s. Don't you have any '96s?"

This went on for the next half-hour. In the California section they didn't have the right appellation. "I only drink *Alexander Valley* Reserves." In Germany they didn't have the correct producer. "You must have *something* from Darting." In Spain they were an absolute failure. "You don't have *any* Ribera del Duero's? Are you *serious*?" It was unbelievable. Somewhere in the middle of all this, I asked him if he had ever tried a certain wine from a Chilean producer that had been getting a lot of publicity of late.

"I had dinner with the owner last year at Nobu. Never cared much for his wines, though," he said. "Have you ever eaten there? You really should. It's fabulous."

In the end, the guy wound up taking a liter of vodka. "Give me your most expensive bottle," he said, tossing his credit card on the counter. "And have it gift wrapped."

After we left, I asked Brad if he'd ever seen a wine snob up close and he shook his head.

"I only thought they appeared at tastings," he said. "That was quite a showing."

We ended up only hitting three stores total before calling it a day. My plan to drink ourselves into selling mode went somewhat awry. In short, we both got shit-faced. The communication was definitely there; it was just that we spent it on subjects having no resemblance to selling wine. What started as simply talking about the Knicks' lack of defense of late, wove its way into a deep discussion about the important hip-hop albums of the early '90s and then somehow into the downfall of network programming as a whole.

The afternoon was not a total loss, though. At the last place— some upscale lounge in SoHo that wasn't on his list—we saw a famous model sitting with a friend at the bar. Unfortunately, just getting a glimpse of a real live supermodel wasn't enough for Brad, who walked up to her, staggering drunk, and told her that he really loved her work and thought she was "like, one of the most beautiful girls in the world." The two of them stared at him for a moment, as he wavered like a boat in difficult waters, before moving down to the other side of the bar. Seeing this made me laugh so hard I shot wine out my nose, to which Brad responded by howling rambunctiously and pumping his fist in the air.

The bartender escorted us out immediately, as the supermodel and her friend were consoled in a corner booth by the manager and given cosmopolitans at no charge.

The rain fell hard the following morning in the city, a day in which I may have stretched the relationship factor out a bit too far once again. The result: working the Lower East Side nearly ended in blows for the second time this week.

The morning showed no signs of what was to come. In fact, things started off quite nicely. Over a well-received breakfast consisting of a pork roll, egg and cheese sandwich (a rarity outside of Jersey, and no doubt a pleasant surprise), the salesman I was working with began to break down our schedule for the day. A few stores here, a few stores there, more or less the usual routine.

"What's the first stop like? Nice guy or what?" I asked.

The salesman, an uppity kind of fellow, laughed and said something to the likes of "Wait 'till you meet him. A real character."

"What do you mean?"

"Well …" he said, "the guy has a real appetite for tasting wines. Know what I'm saying?"

Indeed I did. And I immediately knew what I had to do: give the man what he wanted. Feed his happiness.

So we got to the store, and, to no surprise, it was a truly old-fashioned setup. I say this because the majority of store owners with an affection for boozing rarely tinkered with such things as technology or modern culture. That was something wine snobs and giddy young entrepreneurs did. In places like this, it was more of a time warp than anything. Several dimly lit rows of wooden racks, a few dusty black and white photographs of Joe DiMaggio and Rocky Marciano, and a distant sound of doo-wop music being played softly on the radio. To further set the vibe, a large sheepdog was asleep/dead in front of the cash register, and a number of old, yellowing posters of items that I'd never seen or heard of were running along the walls: Pappy's Rock and Rye, Mr. Teagles Gin, and Rolling Thunder Blackberry Schnapps.

When we found the owner in his office, he was sitting in a large reclining chair, smoking a cigar, and playing solitaire on his computer. A rather plump, stocky man, he had a smile so big that his eyes squinted shut when he grinned.

"Vinny!" he yelled. "Come get these guys some chairs and glasses."

Looking around his office, I noticed several newspaper clippings tacked to the wall, including one from when the Yankees won the Series in '96. We sat there for about fifteen minutes talking about that season (we both went to the Game One slaughter by the Braves) and about the current team. It was a very comfortable setting for a change.

And it was at that moment, where the controversy began.

Now, keep in mind, these were *my* samples, so it was completely up to me how we would use them during the day. Having said that, this, in essence, *was* our day. We never left the place.

After I poured him small, normal-sized glasses of all five wines (Cab, Merlot, Chard, Pinot Noir, and Zinfandel), things started moving along quite well. He liked the wines and liked the prices. More wine was poured. We started talking about the wine business in general. More wine was poured. He told me about some of his favorite wines. More wine was poured. We talked about the Yankees, the Jets, the Knicks, the Rangers, the Stones, the Beatles. We ordered a pizza. More wine was poured.

This whole time, I had it in my mind that I was making a connection with this guy. We agreed on almost everything, including that the salesman I was working with—who had by now resorted to talking on his cell phone out in the storeroom—was a complete prick.

Hours passed like minutes, and by three thirty we'd polished off all the wine. Two people, five bottles. I'd almost forgotten about the job, but as I was saying good-bye, the owner told me that he was cleaning out most of his old stuff and wanted all my products once he had the open space. I thought the salesman had actually left hours ago, but when I went outside, he was standing underneath an umbrella, still on the phone.

"Listen, he just came out, call you later," he said hastily.

"What the hell is your problem?" he yelled. "Is this how you wanted to waste my time? I've been on the phone all day apologizing to all the other stores!"

"What are you talking about?" I said, stepping up in his face. "I just set a bond for life with that guy! He wants to take in the whole line!"

"Did he place an order?"

"He said he was cleaning out some old vintages. Then he would call *you* for the order."

The salesman shook his head and simply started walking away.

"Hey! What's the deal here?" I yelled.

He stopped and turned around.

"He just wanted the free booze, asshole. He says that to everyone."

"Bullshit. I can go in their right now and—"

"Congratulations," he said, turning back around, "you've just spent the whole day being duped by the happy drunk of Manhattan store owners."

I didn't say anything else … as I stood in the rain, watching him cross the street and disappear around the corner.

Although this signaled the end of my work week in New York, a friend of mine was getting married the next day in the Village, so I decided to stay in the city an extra night.

My memories of this evening were a little hazy, but my feelings aren't. Looking around the reception, it amazed me that it had only been ten years since we all were in high school. Throughout the discussions going around the bar, across the walls of the room, and out amidst the balcony of smokers, it seemed as if we'd all been somehow transformed into our parents. The night was a continuing cycle of conversations centered around the newest golf equipment, profiles of company performance, and opinionated political views. Girls that I once remember skinny dipping and passing joints with were now mothers themselves, showing baby pictures to women they'd never met before.

A lot of my friends had since moved back to the area, not in with their folks again, but with families of their own, hoping to raise their kids in the same place where we had grown up. Though most of us were still in contact with each other, sitting back and taking this all in through the backdrop of a wedding seemed to amplify the feeling of youth slipping away. Or maybe it was just that experience of being able to start a sentence out with: "Do you remember twenty years ago when …"

When I got back to my apartment the next day, I spent a solid hour looking at an old high school yearbook and wondering what all the hot girls in my class were doing for a living.

And if they'd gotten fat yet.

8. Personality Breakdown of a Beast Woman

O ver time, the conversations between Gus and I became sort of a regular thing. It was interesting to me, because we would be there talking every morning, night, or whatever, but we'd always leave it at that. There were times when we'd both go inside our apartments to watch the same game or TV show, but never once was it even suggested that we could actually hang out together.

His life wasn't without friendships, but I never saw him with anyone besides his wife or son. There were plenty of stories, though, and from time to time he would look back on different events and friends in a very glowing manner. One person in particular he often spoke of was a man named Clint, who used to work with him, but had since retired. One morning we were discussing the outlook of the Yankees batting lineup and he got into a story about sneaking in to see games when he was in high school. Clint was always his sidekick.

"Any time the Tigers or the Twins, the good pitching clubs, came into town, we went. Just to see how Mickey and the boys would hold up. Great battles. Mind games, all that."

I thought I'd seen the guy in town, walking his dog or reading the paper on some of the benches near the park, but I couldn't be sure.

"Is Clint the guy with the long white hair, who wears the flat cap? Walks the black lab?"

"Yeah, that's Clint all right. Heh heh."

"You guys still friends?"

"Yeah."

"Sorry, I wasn't sure."

"Well, we're not hitting up the bars anymore or whatever, but I know where he's at, and he knows where I'm at."

I looked at my watch and saw that I was running a bit late. Gus grinned and stood up from the stoop.

"Better get going. Wouldn't want you to lose that fancy job of yours," he joked.

I smiled and said good-bye. As I turned to walk to my car, Gus said, "Hey, Chet. Friends come and go, you know. Sure, you keep a few close, but life is kinda funny the way we view our reliance on them."

I remember thinking that "reliance" was a strange word to use.

"You can't expect to have the same relationship with anyone—your parents, your friends, your wife—that you had when you were young," *he said, stretching out his back and looking off in the distance. "But hey, that's not a bad thing, you know."*

"'Castaway' Clint Daniels. Heh heh ..." *he laughed to himself, before shaking his head and walking back inside.*

Connecticut, several days later. Once again I found myself thrust into a territory not my own, and once again it was at the request of my boss, this time for personal reasons.

The call came on a Sunday morning, in between a second round of both coffee and *SportsCenter*.

"Chet, I have a special assignment for you."

"It's Sunday."

"Listen," he muttered, "what are your plans this week?"

"I have a few appointments and salesmen to work with scattered throughout the city—"

"Reschedule them. I want you to ride around with Nora."

Nora. Our Northeast manager. Goal-orientated, determined, frank. Her idea of a fun time was the annual corporate sales meeting. A machine.

"We think it would do you some good to see how she works out in the field."

And that's how it went down. Short and to the point. I tried desperately to whip up a story regarding a church meeting I couldn't miss, but he wasn't buying it. I was given no choice but to comply. This, of course, completely blew my entire week. Not only did I have to spend my one day of freedom rounding up the usual hotel reservations, clean business attire, and directions, but I also had to postpone several new ideas that I wanted to try out. The six-pound, whole chicken that I got from my neighborhood butcher in exchange for two bottles of Cabernet would have to wait another week for its promotional debut. Not sure what I was actually going to do with the damn thing, but for some reason I thought it could work. People love chicken. I also had a bunch of phony ad schemes, a crystal decanter I stole from an antique sale, and a pair of Knicks tickets that I got from my uncle. Certain buyers nearly fell to their knees when you dangled free Knicks tickets in front of them. It was the ultimate wild card when you were in desperate need of a sale and the tide was turned against you. Sort of like leading a loose puppy back inside the house with a biscuit. Gold.

But all that was behind me at the moment, and I had to focus on the present. Unfortunately, the journey up to meet Nora the next morning didn't go as smoothly as I had hoped for. A high-speed pursuit of a stolen vehicle ended up as a ten-car pileup and had the northbound section of I-95 down to one lane. The radio said the car was jacked outside of a Jersey City apartment complex by a twelve-year-old boy, who apparently lost control of it when he tried crossing a tight space between two trucks going 120 mph. Remnants of the stolen car, as well as bits and pieces of others, were scattered over a half-mile stretch of the road.

The trouble continued on the Hutchinson River Parkway. When I finally got onto it, I got off the wrong exit and wound up lost on what I believed to be the outskirts of New Haven. From there a pack of high school kids at a gas station gave me directions that led me down a dirt road and into a graveyard. A confused, toothless digger told me I was nowhere near the parkway and went into a long ramble about how he remembered when there was no parkway and how some guy named Henry made the best sausage and peppers down on Wooster Street. Cringing at the idea of phoning Nora, I ended up calling Information on my phone instead. After ten minutes of being transferred to a half-dozen different departments, I was eventually able to be directed out. The operator laughed when I told her I was from New Jersey—commenting on how much harder it was to get around there—but what could I say, it was only my second time ever in the state of Connecticut and the last time was several years earlier for a Phish concert at Hartford Meadows. Summer tour, July 2000. I made the mistake of buying mushrooms from a black guy in a Raiders jersey and by the time the band ended the first set with an epic version of "Split Open and Melt," I was already curled up in the fetal position and behind a trash can, covered with vomit.

In that instance, I was in no shape to even describe what color my car was, never mind how I actually got there.

When I finally got to the meeting spot, Nora was leaning up against her caravan, cradling a phone between her shoulder and ear, with some kind of pocket computer in each hand and a notebook under her arm.

The second I got out of my car I tried to apologize.

"Jesus, sorry I'm late. There was a huge—"

"What's the price of the Bunglewood Pinot in New York?" she barked, with a bizarre salivating glare.

"Uh … Eighty-eight front line."

"Eighty-eight, uh huh … best discount?"

"Eighty on two cases."

"Eighty on two cases," she relayed, giving me the thumbs up. "Great. Thanks again, Sal."

"Hop in," she said. "We'll do the meet-and-greet on the road."

Nora wore a rather drab, dark blue women's pant suit, no visible makeup, and had long frizzy red hair tied back in a pony tail. She drove with both hands firmly clenched on the wheel, except at stop lights to drink her never-ending bottles of water. Although countless electronic devices of hers were going off all around the car, she didn't like to be bothered by such things as music or talk radio. And she spoke nonstop *business*. No filler, no interesting comments about the area, just business. It was a veritable question and answer session that reminded me of an oral grade school test.

"How do you see the growth of Pinot Noir affecting the consumer?"

"What, in your mind, is the most important aspect of Bunglewood Vineyards that you try to instill into the buyer?"

"Where do you find the most difficulty in the sale of Bunglewood products?"

She followed this with her own ideas and beliefs, dictated in a laborious fashion that suited her competitive approach to sales. I couldn't recall much of what she was saying, but soon enough she was delving into her endless bag of tricks, beginning sentences like she was giving a seminar: "Here's what I do" and "For example" and "Let me show you something interesting."

Her tactics and strategic devices had an ill effect on me. It sent a mixed signal that this was possibly how the vineyard wanted *me* to act, which, when broken down, came out like some mechanical warthog spitting out uninteresting stats in frightening detail. I'd barely been in the car for more than a half-hour, and I knew the only way I could survive this impending horrible experience was to put on the acting shoes. So I did, complete with my best just-out-of Harvard, pretty boy accent.

"Frankly, I find that method a bit ... safe. *If I may say so*," I'd point out.

"Safe?"

"Yes. When selling such products, I like to get to know the person I'm dealing with. Find out where he lives, how he breathes, if he's ever knelt down and smelt the rocky soil of the Rhone Valley of France."

Nora's reaction to answers such as these proved to be confusing for her. I don't believe she was able to grasp exactly what I was trying to say. And neither did I for that matter. It was very much a two-person, one-sided conversation; she continued to ramble on over several hundred topics, and I gave her my thoughts, none of which she replied to. At one point, she asked if I had ever attended a certain prestigious wine class in Manhattan, to which I responded, "I don't believe in them. Conditioning someone to smell and taste properly is the closest thing to dog training for humans."

Silence.

Because of this weird mode of conversation, the first day with Nora turned out to be kind of fun—in a methodical sort of way. We drove relentlessly throughout the southern part of the state, spoke to each other like robots, and promptly stopped into several big accounts at the precise moment she had scheduled. (I know this because I was given a printout of the day's agenda. It was color-coordinated with several pages of information on each account concerning buying history, product placement, and year-to-date sales from the past ten years.)

At each place, I was instructed to "observe how I handle this situation," but sadly the only thing I was observing was that this lady had no life outside of her job. I don't think I heard her mention one single comment that resembled something personal in regards to her life or to anyone else's for that matter. Even during lunch, she was crunching numbers, taking notes, and talking about the intricacies of selling various types of wine. I thought I might be able to piece a few things together through some careful observations inside her car, but there were no clues anywhere of anything that would even suggest the slightest hint of a hobby. No magazines on the back seat, no sand on the floorboards, no empty CD cases, no bumper stickers, no bike racks, no ski racks, nothing. It was downright depressing.

One occasion in particular could sum up the entire "Nora experience." We were in a wine shop out in Fairfield, talking with the owner, when Nora began to go over a list of items she thought could work in the shop. As she monotonously read aloud the dreadfully long catalog of wines, prices, and discounts, I looked up to see the owner looking back at me. The man rolled his eyes and made an expression like he was falling asleep. We exchanged brief smiles while Nora unknowingly continued to pore over the list.

For all that she could accomplish in terms of preparation and efficiency, she had the aura of a rigid schoolteacher. And these managers couldn't wait till the bell rang.

By the end of the day I didn't even have the heart to ask if she had dinner plans. There wasn't a ring on her finger, so I doubted she had a family to go home to. Certainly not a happy one with this lifestyle. My brain couldn't withstand anymore of her, anyway. The best thing for me to do was to get a six-pack of really cheap beer and watch *Animal House* a few times in a row to return my psychological balance back to normal.

"Pick you up here tomorrow morning at seven thirty," she smiled. "We'll go over the day's strategy over breakfast."

"Fantastic," I said, with an intense grin. "I look forward to another productive day."

"Me, too. I'm just gonna call in some orders here in the parking lot for a bit."

"Sounds awesome. I'm gonna go score some low grade heroin and put a gun to my head."

"What?"

I smiled again and left with an exaggerated wave.

Eight a.m. the next morning. Good news had arrived. For the first time in months, I got a call from my boss that didn't involve either a lecture or a request. He actually called to tell me that my sales numbers were already up 75 percent over the last month. At first I didn't know quite how to respond to this. Genuine confusion and giddiness is one way to put it.

"Gee, that's, uh, that's good news. Thanks for the update."

"No need to thank me," he said. "I should be thanking you."

Thanking me. Okay.

"I only wish I had this information a few days ago, before I sent you up to work with Nora," he added. "Our reports show you've made some serious sales out there."

"Oh ... is that right?"

"Yeah, let's see ... I've got a number of cases sold in several sports bars in Manhattan ..."

Deals.

"... a wide range of stuff sold in some nightclub ..."

Connections.

"... some great numbers coming out of Jersey ..."

Lies.

"... and what else ... Oh, I see you've had a few very productive days up in the Mid-Hudson Valley as well."

Deals and *lies.*

I'm fairly sure we talked for a few minutes longer, but it remained a huge blur of unconnected sentences and unconscious responses. All I could remember thinking was "Amazing. Something must be working here ..."

Needless to say, I was rather pleased to start this cold, late winter day on such a good note. Even Nora's vigorous detail of the game plan seemed to roll right over me. She got nothing but nods and smiles over my sausage and biscuits sandwich as my brain wandered effortlessly, dipping in and out of various ideas and reflections. Above all, I knew that whatever changes I had made were now beginning to pay off. And I knew that they had nothing to do with anything I could possibly learn from this beast-woman who sat across from me.

Throughout the first half of the day, I tried to diffuse any sort of mental breakdown in regards to Nora. In order to get through this, I had to keep my head straight, play the part. In my mind I knew that if I could just get through a few more hours, I could go back to doing my own thing.

"You see, when I go into an account, Chet, I know exactly what I'm going to try to get them to take. I know every single wine they have in the store, that way I don't bother them if, say, they have too many Merlots or too many Chardonnays. That would be a waste of their time, and mine as well. Do you understand?"

"Completely."

"The growth of the consumer's mind as a whole is rapidly changing for the better in this country. We are no longer selling eight or nine types of wines. We are selling literally hundreds. People are excited to try new wines today. And they are learning, Chet. They are learning and they want to learn. Do you see that in New York?"

"Every day."

"We are coming into an age where people want to get the most out of any price. With value wines coming in by the boatload from Australia and Chile and New Zealand, the need to produce at a lower price point has never been higher in this country. That is what Bunglewood is all about. Give the customer their money's worth, whether we make a large profit or not. Don't you agree?"

"One hundred percent."

"When I started in this business, we didn't have the technology. We just didn't, Chet. Now I'm able to track exactly who took what and when. All at the touch of a button. Buying history, cycles, prices—it's all here. I find that the quicker I can get information to and from the accounts, the quicker I can move on to the next project, and in turn, the more I can get done. Isn't that the point of our job?"

"Absolutely."

This was more or less how the whole morning went. I'd gotten her speech patterns down to the point where I wasn't even listening anymore. I figured out when to respond solely from either the length of her pauses in between ideas or the intonation of her voice when she was proposing a question. Whether or not my responses made any sense didn't matter, she wasn't interested anyway. It was a trick worth saving, so I pulled out my unused pad of paper and made a note of it. From the big, dopey smile on her face, Nora probably thought I was taking down one of her priceless bits of information, reassuring herself that she was, in her mind, a living legend in the sales world.

In all likelihood she went home that night and spent quality time mulling over a future in motivational speaking or quite possibly a celebrated career as an author.

Just when everything appeared to be going smoothly, Nora mentioned something that threw my daydreaming world into chaos: We had to cancel lunch in order to hit another account that just opened up.

"This is great news, Chet, great news! I've been waiting to see this guy for months. You're gonna love his new store!"

The unpleasant feeling of skipping lunch was something that I should have prepared for, but somehow, I overlooked it. Goddamn it. I should have known she would try to pull something like this. Act like it was an unplanned event, when she probably knew it all along. It was an obvious attempt again to try and show me how hard you have to work in order to achieve whatever status she had attained.

My brain immediately started to fizzle. I didn't want to listen to her babble on and on about this shit anymore. Quickly, my whole attitude began to change. Had I underestimated her intuition? Christ, did she see a weakness in me? How could she, I thought, I was practically skin and bones. It wasn't in my physical makeup to be hungry.

I tried to regain my composure, repeatedly telling myself to snap out of it, but it was to no avail. As a nauseous feeling slowly began to build in my stomach, I noticed a McDonald's up the road, a few traffic lights away. I calmly asked her to pull into it, but she told me that we didn't have time, that it was essential that we get to this store by two, and that we were still forty-five minutes to an hour away, depending on traffic.

"I have to use the bathroom, Nora. Please pull into that McDonalds."

She agreed to make the stop, but insisted that I be quick. Instead, I got in line and ordered a number one special with an orange drink.

Getting my food, I took a seat in an open booth. Nora stormed in a few minutes later and looked around like a scared chicken.

"What are you doing?" she screamed upon seeing me, throwing her hands up in the air. I was in the middle of a huge bite.

"I told you we don't have time for this! We have a meeting set for two o'clock!"

Still chewing …

"Didn't you understand what I said?"

Still chewing …

"*Answer me!*"

"*Don't you know it's rude to talk with your mouth full?*" I yelled, before washing down my burger with a sip of the orange drink. "Sit down and stop whining like a little girl."

She stood there in shock and looked as if she was in the early stages of a seizure. I had no remorse for her.

"I was asked by the head of Bunglewood Vineyards to share my knowledge of this business. If you think for a second that I don't have better things to do—"

"Well, you can either sit here or wait for me in the car. It's your choice," I told her. "It's lunchtime and I'm having my lunch. I'll only be five minutes, so calm down."

She didn't speak another word to me. Fucking baby. All the business expertise in the world, but not one single cell of adult social behavior.

Over the next few hours, we went to the rest of her stops as planned. Nora continued to conduct business in her typically stiff manner at each account, this time around barely acknowledging my existence. It had the tension and uncomfortable ambience of a recently divorced couple at a chance dinner party. A truly terrible vibe that transformed her once-unabashed confidence into an impending feeling of failure. I could tell she was beyond frustrated. The long deep breaths, the restrained expressions, the fist tapping of the steering wheel. My presence and attitude had totally infected her … and for some sadistic reason I loved every second of it.

While I was rather delighted at the prospect of not hearing her speak another word, I felt the need to end this stand-off before we parted ways, so on the ride back to the hotel I broke the silence.

"Nora, what do you like to do for fun?"

"Excuse me?"

"What do you like to do, you know, for fun?"

"You mean, besides work? Well, uh, you know … all sorts of things," she said, acting almost embarrassed.

"Yeah? Like what?"

She laughed and shook her head.

"Gee, well, let's see … oh I don't know. This is kinda on the spot. Heh heh."

I waited for her answer, but it never came. Was it possible that she actually didn't have a life outside of work? Were there other Noras out there, living solely through a never-ending cycle of expense reports, focus meetings, and business lingo? It was a staggering thought. To think that people were roaming their short time on Earth in this way.

What a waste.

9. Mother Nature Takes a Dump on Syracuse

*T*hree-quarters of the way up Interstate 81 I got a call from our distributor's office that the meeting I was headed up to in Syracuse had been canceled.

"We apologize for any inconvenience, but due to the effects of this snow storm, we will be rescheduling our meeting for next Friday."

Christ. I'd already been on the road for five hours in this mess, and, of course, I get the call an hour outside of the place.

"Why do you have to cancel it? There's been three feet of snow on the ground for the past five months!"

"Yes, I'm aware of that, sir. But we've had reports of too many flights being cancelled across the country. Not enough people can make it."

"What about those of us who've been on the road all day trying to get up here?" I yelled.

At first there was no response, then came a quick, uninterested remark. "Look. I'm really sorry."

Click.

I pulled off at the nearest rest stop to reassess the situation. In between a tear of some beef jerky and a swig of Mountain Dew, I realized that I should probably wait until tomorrow to inform the boss that the meeting had been cancelled. The logic was simple. If I said anything too early, he might just be cheap enough to cancel my hotel reservations and arrange a backup plan for work the following morning back down in the city. And there was no way I was doing that. Not after an entirely useless day that could have been wasted in a much better fashion. So, under the watchful eye of the Indian store clerk, I refilled my tank and continued the trek up.

The grey skies had faded into darkness by the time I finally got to the hotel, and my back was killing me from being in the Jeep all day. The ride up had been an absolute bore. The only thing that kept me going was playing road games with all these assholes who felt the need to ride my tail going 120 mph and flash their lights, just because I was taking up valuable seconds in the fast lane. My game was simple: Don't let them pass.

First, I would pull up even in the left lane to a slow-moving truck in the right lane. Outside of using the shoulder or perhaps the grassy median, it left the impatient highway racer with no legal means of getting around on a two-lane highway. Their only reaction was to ride up as close to my bumper as possible and shimmy back and forth like an Indy car, all the while laying heavily on the horn as they continually flashed their high beams. Looking in the rear view mirror, I could just about feel their frustration mounting with each second. The pounding and wrenching of the wheel, the reddening in the face, and the constant, jerking of the head to see if there was any room to squeeze around the side. In the event the person felt the need to be a particular nuisance, I'd sometimes run my windshield wiper fluid on the back window. This was significant only for the fact that I'd rigged the fluid to shoot straight up in the air instead of down on the glass.

After about ten minutes of this, I could usually sense they were about ready to lose total concentration due to road rage. At this precise moment, I'd make my move and floor it past the sluggish truck. Darting as quickly as possible up to the next slow vehicle in the right lane, it would hopefully give them no time to cut around and in front. Then I'd start the whole thing over again.

With a bit of luck this could go on for miles and miles. Good times.

When I walked up to the front desk, there was a huge man-child sweating heavily over a nervous smile and saying "Hello, hello" over and over. I didn't see anyone else around.

"Hello, hello."

"Hi. Uh … is this where I check in?"

"Hello, hello."

"Yeah, hi …"

"Hello, hello!"

"Is there someone else working here?"

"Hello, hello!"

After a few minutes of this, a young girl with terrible acne and a blonde ponytail came out.

"I got it from here, Rodney, thanks. Can I help you?"

"Hello, hello …"

The hotel turned out to be in no way up to any of even the slightest standards that I had hoped for. For one, the pool was closed. There were also no movie channels on the TV, the ice machine was broken, and the only items in the vending machine were packages of nuts and raisins. My bathroom also had no shower curtain, and there were massive red stains all over the carpet. It looked as if a murder had taken place here the night before, which could probably explain the "discount rate" I was given minutes earlier. I immediately called downstairs demanding to switch rooms, but my claims fell on deaf ears. I was informed that the place was booked full, and that some guy named Larry would be upstairs in a few minutes to put up a new curtain. My brain was too tired to get behind complaining any further, so I simply hung up. Fuck it. All I wanted to do was relax and maybe do some casual drinking, anyway. Smoke a joint and watch sports. Whatever.

I went back out to my car and grabbed two bottles of wine, but was snake bitten when I got back to the room and realized I had no corkscrew to open them.

The girl at the front desk offered me no help.

"Yeah, we don't have a bar here or a restaurant for that matter, so maybe, hmm … I don't know. What about a gas station?"

Retreating back to my room once more, I figured I should just get the hell out of here. Minus the beef jerky, I hadn't eaten all day and I wasn't drunk, lazy, or stupid enough to try and shatter the necks off the top of these bottles. So a few blocks away, with the snow coming down hard, I found a twenty-four-hour diner.

A little bell above the door jingled as I entered, transporting me to a scene straight out of an old Rockwell painting. A business man wearing a loose tie sat alone at the counter reading a newspaper, while a bored middle-aged waitress with her hands on her hips blew bubbles and stared off into the quiet, snow-covered streets. In a far booth, a few teenagers were giggling, possibly at me, as Johnny Cash's "One Piece at a Time" played distantly on the jukebox. A very cliché setting, to say the least. Either that, or all of these diners began to look identical to a traveling salesman after a while. Interesting. One of the reasons I took this job in the first place was to escape the doldrums of working in the same, boring location every day. Now, virtually everywhere I went was beginning to look as strangely and disappointingly similar as the last.

Brushing the snow off my head, I smiled and politely asked the hostess if I could borrow a corkscrew. She bluntly told me "No." I made it clear I would gladly get something to eat and not drink the wine inside, but she refused to budge, telling me it was against the law or something.

"Ma'am, look … I'm in the wine industry. Here, see. I have a solicitor's license."

She carelessly inspected the card.

"Sir, if you don't believe me, maybe you'd like to talk to the cops sitting over there in the corner."

"The cops? Are you joking?"

"No, I'm not. And honestly, I don't appreciate your tone."

"Tone? *What?* Look, all I want to do is borrow a corkscrew. Jesus. Forget it already."

I moved past her and took a seat up at the counter. Tossing my wet coat on the back of the stool next to me, I slammed my keys on the counter and yelled to the waitress for a beer. The gentleman reading the newspaper looked up over his bifocals and frowned, before turning slightly away from me. When the waitress came back with the beer I threw a crumpled-up ten on the counter and told her to keep them coming.

Slugging down half the first one in a single gulp, I saw out of the corner of my eye the gentlemen once again looking at me over his glasses. I immediately asked if he happened to know if there was a liquor store in the area still open.

"Excuse me?"

"A liquor store. Do you know if there is one around here?"

He adjusted his glasses and gave me a long glare.

"You're asking the wrong person," he said, turning back toward his paper, "but to my knowledge I don't think so. You'd have to head back toward the college."

Defeated, I sat back in my chair. Looked like I'd be paying for my booze on this night. Probably for the better, I thought, seeing as how these bottles were part of my last batch of samples. It was the notion of a failed, simple mission that hurt I guess. One measly corkscrew away from complimentary salvation.

I thought about going home the next morning, but there was nothing for me to do there. My apartment was basically just a bed for me to sleep on over the weekends. In addition, this rare free pass from Mother Nature afforded me the luxury of having an excuse *not* to get any work done. With the snow piling up two inches on the hour, I had almost no reason to even get out of bed. And had this been any sort of a decent hotel, I probably wouldn't have needed to, but I missed the only available meal (a continental breakfast of toast, mixed fruit, and a choice of coffee or orange juice) and had to get out to find something to eat. So, I headed back to the diner and sat in a window booth for most of the afternoon, watching the snow outside and ordering rounds of both beer and coffee from the lone waitress on duty.

Over the next few hours, a handful of other people came in, mainly truckers, but for the most part I was her only patron. During this time my phone rang constantly, but I refused to answer it. Turning it off completely would have attracted suspicion, so conscious ignorance was my only way out. Every question and complaint about new vintages, price adjustments, and shipment dates from salesmen and managers throughout the state went straight to voice mail. They would get their answers, but not on this day.

For a brief moment, I remember having this amazing flashback of a "snow day" when I was in grade school. Nothing was more exciting as a kid than waking up in the morning to find out that school had been canceled, leaving the whole day to do absolutely nothing and absolutely everything. Although it brought a smile to my face, I quickly shook away the memories before it had me thinking back any further. Strange. You grow up through life in such a hurry to get older, and then you hit an age that has you wishing you could go back, or at the very least, hit the pause button.

When I finally got home the next day, there was a package waiting on my front door. Two weeks earlier I got a message from the vineyard instructing every sales rep to update their business card information and fax a proof sheet to the card company. At the time I decided to do this, I was savagely drunk, coming back from an all-night binge at the local watering hole in town where I'd somehow ripped off all the lighting structures and was thrown out trying to pour my own drinks behind the bar. I'd forgotten all about the cards, and more importantly, what I had requested. When I opened the box I was rather tickled at what they read. Somehow I'd promoted myself from "Winery Representative" to "Director of Sales, Eastern Division." Two thousand of them.

After spending much of the ensuing week zipping up to Albany for a restaurant meeting, rushing to Buffalo for a sales blitz, and heading back down to Westchester to work with a salesman, I was home only a few hours before I was back putting on my fake smile and pouring wine. In an exchange with an old friend for the original Led Zeppelin box set, I had agreed to set up a table at his sister's art exhibit down in the quiet river town of Stockton.

The place was chock-full of young artists, many of who looked to be just out of high school. Their dress was a combination of bohemian hipster and early '70s British guitar hero which, come to think of it, was more or less the same thing. Fitted jeans, scuffed cowboy boots, a throwback tour shirt of a band no one actually liked, scarves, and an overabundance of tribal jewelry. Straw fedora or woolen flat cap optional. My immediate thought upon entering was that I should have changed into something more casual. The pleated slacks and polo shirt I had on made me feel like a chaperone at a grade school dance. Maybe I'm letting my mind get the best of me here, but I could've sworn I saw one kid put out a cigarette just because our eyes met.

Turns out it didn't matter one way or the other anyway. My presence on this night would be strictly as a servant. The artwork rightfully took most of the attention, which left the majority of guests ignoring me to the point of barely looking in my direction for more wine. They opted instead to simply hold out their glasses, some in midsentence, when they were ready to be refilled. Any hesitation on my part usually got a little shake of the glass, just to punctuate the fact that they were waiting.

In a situation such as this, it was impossible not to pick up on the surrounding conversation. Bottom line, there was not much else to do. In hindsight, what I should have done was just opened the wines and went the fuck home. Instead I found myself standing quietly behind the table, numbly immersed in their deep discussions of the paintings—which, based on the local river country atmosphere, were either of an old barn or grazing cattle. Although objective and often highly critical, the feeling among the crowd was anything but hostile. In fact most of the guests seemed to be enamored with conversations based on how the paintings made them *feel*, as in, "I'm getting a warm sense of a forgotten playground here … one that brought a lot of joy to someone." After one such comment, I even saw a couple hug, looking at what appeared to me as just some abandoned farm with a major weed problem.

I'll admit, at first it all seemed a tad silly. But as the night progressed, I think I became somewhat jealous of their cultured lifestyle. That freedom of being able to enjoy life and the peaceful existence of creating something tangible. It made perfect sense when I thought about it, as it was basically the opposite position that I found myself in. Usually surrounded by industry executives, wine snobs, bullheaded customers, and stressed-out salesmen, it was no doubt a nice change. I remember thinking that wine could be taken in a more artistic setting, but the business aspect of it would never settle for that. For every one person who talked about the beauty of a certain wine and why they simply *liked* it, there were a thousand others who would rather talk about the price, the deals, and who *had* it.

Interestingly enough, toward the end of the night, a few people had stumbled up to me and asked if I actually did this for a living.

"Like, do you get paid to do wine tastings?"

"Yeah, that's part of it I guess."

"Wow. So you get paid to drink wine? That's pretty cool, man."

I had on occasion gotten this same kind of response. Many people found it to be a rather neat job to have. They saw the wine tastings and the free samples and joked, "Damn, I'd love to drink wine all day and get paid for it." But laid-back tastings such as this were a far cry from the reality of the job. Staying in different hotels, logging thousands of miles, and drinking alcohol nonstop every week *was* pretty damn cool … if you were a rock star. There's a difference between traveling two hours to Brooklyn to play in front of adoring fans and traveling two hours to Brooklyn to get belittled by some crude store manager named Donny, who thought what you were selling was absolute shit, and who wasn't afraid to tell you in those exact words.

Another one I got a lot was, "Do you enjoy working in the wine business?" Most people asked this question smiling through the expectation that you were going to obviously say "Yes." It's like when someone gets married, the first thing you're inclined to say to them is "So, how's married life?" How many people actually come right out and tell you something other than "Great" if they don't mean it?

"Oh, married life? It's absolutely terrible. Worst decision of my life."

No one says that. It's just easier to give people what they want to hear, regardless of whether it's true or not. Anything else just entices them to proceed with further questioning, and who wants that?

Shit. If I knew whether or not this job was going to work out, I could've truthfully answered that question. Any negativity or disregard toward being in sales had been predominantly based around the fact that this wasn't where I had envisioned my life going. A lot of times I simply found it hard to show any real emotion or grit for that reason alone. Similar situations had always been a problem for me, dating back to when I was in grade school. My mother used to yell at me constantly, saying things like, "Why can't you show the same determination and heart in your homework that you show in playing baseball or skateboarding?"

But everyone knows the answer to that. The only difference being, at twenty-eight, I was old enough to realize a change in attitude—as hard and forceful as it may have seemed—could potentially lead to bigger and better things. Which was the entire point of trying to hold on to this job in the first place. Not necessarily because I wanted to, but because of what I could learn about myself, as well as what I could learn about life in the apparent "real world." Sure, on one hand I had to be thankful that I even *had* a job, especially one that provided free meals and alcohol several nights a week. Yet on the other hand, the bullshit factor was similar to any other sales job. Some people were just born to put up with the acting routine, the long hours, the never-ending travel, and greed, all for the paycheck. But being born with ice in your veins was one thing, accepting it as an alternative was another.

So anyway, to answer the question of whether I liked working in the business, I usually just went with "Yeah. It beats selling copy machines," followed by a killer fake laugh. Nobody really cared, but so what? Play the game.

10. No Help for the Questionable and Unproven

*I*t wasn't always constructive thinking between Gus and I. Hardly the case at all. In fact, most of the discussions we had, had nothing even remotely insightful to reflect on. Unless, of course, you could find deep meaning in something like Derek Jeter's on-base percentage or Roger Clemens' strikeout-to-walk ratio. But conversations such as those aren't the ones I tend to remember. What I do remember is that I'd often come home from work to find Gus sitting in the same exact spot I saw him earlier in the day. Only dirtier. While I limped back to my apartment with a disgusted look on my face and a partially untucked dress shirt flapping in the wind, he always seemed totally at peace. Can of beer in one hand, cigarette in the other, and just looking out into the tree-lined edge of the complex down the street.

Gus rarely spoke about work. He liked to say that when he punched out, he punched out mentally, too. But every so often we'd dip into the subject.

"How long have you been in the construction business?" I asked him once.

"Since birth, it seems."

"Ever grow tired of it?" I said, taking a cigarette out of my front pocket.

He leaned over and flicked open his lighter. "Sometimes. But what am I supposed to do about it?"

"Quit and look for a new job."

He laughed and shook his head.

"What's so funny?"

"You kids take work so seriously."

"I thought it was the other way around. My generation doesn't take work seriously enough."

"No. What I mean is that it's just a job. I go to work, perform to the best of my capabilities, and that's that. I don't go beyond it."

"Yeah, but it takes up the majority of your day, Gus. Doesn't that account for something?"

"In the summer I get home in time to watch the Yankees and have dinner with my wife," he said, stubbing out his cigarette. "So my two priorities are covered."

"That's it? That's what gets you through?"

"Hey, when you got what you need, who's to complain? Don't bite the man that feeds you, Chet."

"Hand."

"Right, right. Don't bite the hand. You know what I mean."

Back to Scarsdale, this time around for our distributor's first quarter meeting and review. My plan was to go up the day before and expense a room at one of the local carbon-copy commuter hotels. Knowing this again might be a problem when I turned in my monthly expense reports, I made a preliminary call to the Bunglewood offices of my intent, basically stating to the boss that in order for me to be completely prepared for such an important meeting, I needed a good nights rest. Getting up at the crack of dawn, sitting in traffic on the Tappan Zee Bridge, and shoveling shitty gas station coffee down my throat the entire drive was not the way to get focused to speak to the sales force. This time he was willing to listen. Following a barrage of ridiculously in-depth examples of how this had damaged my psyche in the past, I casually mentioned the two fifty-case sales I made at a warehouse-sized discount store the day before—just to let him know who he was dealing with here. A man on the rise.

This proved to be the clincher, so yeah, I got the hotel.

Having only one appointment scheduled in the morning, I made the trip up in the early afternoon. The next day would be a mob scene trying to get samples, so I figured I'd get a head start on the swarms of salesmen and reps that would be infiltrating the area. It was my intent to get three times as many this time, for nothing more than to give away as part of any on-the-spot deals I might encounter over the next month. But when I got up there, the warehouse manager had no record of my request, so I had to venture inside the office and square out the details with one of the ladies in the order board.

This was by no means an easy thing to come to grips with. Most of these endlessly bored individuals spoke through a ghetto Spanglish dialect and tipped the scales at a cool three hundo each. Their big waistlines were matched only by their big attitudes. On several previous encounters where I had to merely explain a similar problem, I'd been insulted for challenging their intelligence, accused of trying to sabotage their job, laughed at for no apparent reason, and informed that I was gonna have my balls ripped off if I didn't leave immediately. One even took a swing at me for insinuating that she may have gotten a single code number wrong.

Now I knew for a fact that I put this particular order in, but that didn't matter. Whatever the circumstance may be, it was always your fault. Arguing would only get you in deeper trouble, so I typically just tried to reintroduce the information as calmly as possible and pray for the best. It was no secret that most of the sales force agreed with this view. Horror stories of run-ins with these ladies have been passed down like urban legends. Nonetheless, I needed those samples.

The sound of my shoes on the cold, marble floors echoed throughout the entrance hall as I tried to focus on what lay ahead. While the distribution company had several offices throughout the state—Buffalo, Albany, Syracuse, Rochester—the Scarsdale office was no doubt the big daddy of them all, the main headquarters.

With five floors of newly renovated space, it had the look and feel of every other corporate building I'd ever been in: stale, unoriginal, and with a distinct aura of high-class arrogance.

The front lobby was set in a huge open area with towering, end to end glass windows and several black leather couches scattered along the sides. Toward the center sat a metallic front desk, accompanied by three young female secretaries with headsets on.

"Hi. I need to talk to someone in the order board."

"Are they expecting you?" one of them said.

"No, I just need to double-check something."

She looked at the other two and laughed, as I stood there silent, staring straight ahead.

"Wait, are you serious? Oh, uh, all right … Just take the hallway on the right to the elevators, go up to the third floor, turn around the corner, and head down the hallway. The order board is straight ahead."

I thanked her and walked around the desk. Just before I entered the hallway, I heard one of the others call out to me. I looked over to see her standing up with her arms at her side. "Good luck" was all she said.

I nodded and turned back toward the hallway. Her concern for a perfect stranger said it all, and as I made my way up, I tried to tell myself that everything was going to be fine.

But hard-thought self-assurance can only get you so far. When I entered the department room, I quickly realized this day would be no different.

"Jackie, hold on one second. Yes … *Can I help you?*"

"Hi. Chet Fisher with Bunglewood Vineyards. I put in a request for some samples early—"

"Second desk on the right," she blurted. "Jackie? Okay … What? I dunno, some guy …"

I was confused. There was no desk on her right or mine.

"Uh, excuse me. I don't under—"

"Jackie, hold on. *Sir, second desk on the right!*" she yelled, pointing behind her. "Do you *see* a sign that says Place Orders Here? No, you do not!"

Picking up her phone, she let out a big laugh. "Oooh, girl. I don't mess around! Ha ha!"

I was given more attitude at the next three areas I was directed to. One lady screamed through a mouth full of chili cheese fries, "Can't you see I'm on my lunch break? What are you, *a Nazi?*" while another simply ignored me for ten minutes, talking softly on the phone to her boyfriend, before shooing me away with her hand like I was a bee buzzing around her head. The third one attempted to help me out, but after about five minutes of searching for the information on her computer, simply gave up and told me that she was getting a headache.

There was only one other lady in the immediate area at the time. I looked over at her, and was about to ask for help, when she warned me to not even think about it.

"Look, all I need is for someone to tell me if—"

Before I could even finish, she got up out of her chair and started charging toward me, belly fat spilling everywhere and nostrils flaring. I turned and nearly fell over a chair trying to get out, but I did, eventually losing her in the one place I knew she couldn't handle, the stairwell.

Turns out the warehouse guys had it all along. They "overlooked" it is what I was told. Fifteen cases with my name in big black marker written on it, sitting ten feet from the entrance, overlooked. When I sighed and told the warehouse manager that he could've saved me a lot of time and frustration, he told me that he could save me a lot more with a punch to the face.

The comment didn't faze me the slightest, but it may have fueled the fire for what happened next. After filling the Jeep to the brim with the wine cases, I walked back inside the office and swiped all the donuts and chips from the kitchen. Barreling down the hallways with a bear hug around the pile of snacks, I made it past the front desk girls, around several confused salesmen, and out the doors untouched. It was the least I could do. Nothing would hurt these bitches more than to take away their life support of glazed jellies and barbecue flavored Fritos.

Once I got back to the hotel, I sat in the far corner of the bar trying to devise a plan of attack for the following day's meeting. Earlier in the week, I had gotten a call from the boss offering some suggestions on how to handle it. We discussed several options of what might get the sales team behind me, but none of them seemed right. "You need to give them an incentive to sell our product," he said. "Come up with something that will serve as a goal, a prize of sorts at the end of the tunnel." But these guys didn't want any more restaurant vouchers or vineyard tours. I knew I needed something different, something that wasn't another conventional attempt at trying to act the part. Several ideas ran through my head during the night, some worthy of writing down on the back of a beer coaster, and some not. One thing was for sure: I had to connect with the younger salesmen. There was no sense in trying to relate to the elder family man with a shore house and a boat. I had nothing to offer them, and they weren't going to listen to me anyway. It just wasn't the American way. If I'd learned anything up to this point, it was that listening to someone twenty or thirty years younger than you was almost taboo in the business world. Even suggesting it looked unprofessional.

I stayed at the bar until closing, annoying the rest of the patrons by playing twenty-seven straight Steely Dan songs on the jukebox, and continuing to jot down any ideas that came to mind.

While the generic atmosphere of a hotel bar may not be the ideal place for strategic thinking to flourish, sometimes it took the most mundane setting to spring the most unusual thoughts. This notion came to me the following morning when I found myself seated among a dozen or so other commuters in a small breakfast nook, staring up at a tiny TV perched in the corner of the room. The main restaurant of the hotel must have been under construction, because all that was being offered was a continental breakfast in what appeared to be an old boardroom in the basement. The selection was slim: rubbery bagels, watered-down orange juice, some strange raisin bread, and an assortment of single-serving brand X cereal boxes. Besides the sounds of white America coming from a preppie morning show on the TV, the room stood frozen in dead silence. I don't think anyone was even paying attention to the two overly cheerful hosts on the screen, but felt the need to just fixate their eyes on something to help fight off the morning letdown phase. Which was precisely the reason I had been watching.

So anyway, in the middle of a spoonful of corn flakes, I happened to take a look around at the room. One glimpse at all the trance-like faces staring up at the set gave me an immediate and ominous case of goose bumps. It felt like a scene straight out of one of those futuristic horror movies where aliens take over the world, and all humans are rendered as mindless, robotic slaves. Hunched over, mouth agape, eyes wide open and not blinking, focused on the medium. I couldn't be sure of any drool, but it was possible.

I remained still during this so as to not disturb such a moment. But shifting my eyes over at the clock several minutes in told me I needed to get a move on. The meetings started at nine, and I hadn't yet decided on a final plan, nor did I know what time I was scheduled to speak. As I quietly stood up and scooted my chair back, not as much as a finger budged throughout the room. So without thinking, I bent over and slammed both my fists hard on the table. Several people jumped in shock, like they were being woken up in the middle of the night with a bullhorn, but no one said anything. They just simultaneously looked at their watches and straightened their ties.

Gathering up my plastic plate and utensils, I smiled and casually walked toward the exit. What a shame, I thought. Not for what I saw but that I didn't have a camera to capture it. It could have truly been one for the textbooks a hundred years from now. A "downfall of society" type of thing, I'd imagine.

I pulled into the distributor office about a half-hour later. It felt more like a car dealership. Moving slowly through the parking lot in search of an empty space, I saw three separate instances of the same car model parked four wide. Life had apparently come down to two choices: BMW's or Hummers.

The rest of the morning was spent standing with a few other salesmen, in a loose circle, around one of the guy's new car. The man was awfully proud of his new vehicle and showed it by running down all the options he got on it, one by one: self-adjusting tint, automatic climate zone control systems, hill descent stabilizers, etc. Every time he'd mention one of these things he'd always follow by saying, "Nobody has this yet." As this was going on, everyone else was complementing him and giving him high fives and all that shit. I looked at the guy next to me, who nodded his head and chimed in, "Pretty impressive, Bill. You really hit the jackpot with this baby." He was wearing a hat from some golf course that looked like it read "Dogfucker."

"What does that say?" I asked, squinting at it in confusion.

He mentioned the name. It sounded like Donn-hoff-ner or something.

"I got it from our last trip out to Germany. Absolutely wonderful course. Have you played it?"

"No."

"You really should. It has the most challenging back nine I've seen in the Rhine. We should go out there together. What's your name? Do you have a card? What company do you represent? Is that your X9 convertible?"

I looked blankly at him for a second, then turned and headed straight for the front entrance.

The meetings were just getting underway. After checking the presentation timetable, I quickly tried to score an empty chair in the lobby before things got crazy. But it was too late. In a span of what seemed like seconds, every spare inch on the first floor had become flooded with a collection of the industry's finest. Vineyard reps in thousand dollar suits were hunched in group circles going over game plans, salesmen were darting in and out of the doorways, and an orchestra of a hundred different cell phone ringers were constantly abuzz throughout every crowded corridor.

Now, originally I had been scheduled to go on at quarter to eleven, but the meetings were delayed when a shoving match between two Italian winemakers spilled into one of the main offices, knocking the president of the distributor headfirst into a steel filing cabinet. Out cold. It was an hour before the bleeding had stopped and he was conscious enough for the meetings to continue.

I then got stuck waiting around even longer when, at twelve thirty, it was announced that the sales force was getting cranky and needed to break for lunch. It would have been nice to get out of there before all of this, but I knew I was better off. Nobody wanted to be that guy who held several hundred half-drunk salesmen from pizza and cigarettes. In the meantime I sat in my car, sipping wine out of a used coffee container, and listening to a sports radio station talk about the upcoming baseball season, trying to take the edge off my mounting nerves.

At least I knew what would be awaiting me. The basic make-up of these things changed little from one to the next. For one, the seating inside the actual meeting room was very similar to what you'd find in high school or college. The first two rows were typically filled with the younger, more eager-to-move-up crowd, looking very attentive, or maybe more accurately, *acting* very attentive. Constantly taking notes, head up, nodding in approval, and laughing at all the dumb jokes were key points to playing this role. Toward the back and in stark contrast were the old-timers. With nothing to prove or gain, and seemingly half-asleep, they sat slumped in their chairs, arms folded, and hadn't given thought to even opening their briefcases, never mind take notes. Their heads were not nodding in approval, but rather, nodding *out* in pure boredom. And who could blame them? There was only so much the mind could take before it turned to mush and began operating in some sort of comatose state.

Time would be easy to pin as the main culprit here, but not so. What became even more frustrating was that there was almost no difference between each presentation. Like the monotonous drip of the Chinese water torture, it was eerie how every single winery rep up at the podium, no matter if they were from Spain or from Long Island, had the same exact speech. "This is our new product … It has a really great price … This is our plan for the summer … We really need to focus on this … Blah, blah, blah." It was as if there was some sort of stale guideline to what you could or should say. A fill-in-the-blank blueprint of repeated information. How anyone can possibly be instructed to endure seven or eight hours of this was beyond me. Frankly, I thought it was borderline cruel. Though I shouldn't be one to complain. My awareness of the dying creativity in this industry hadn't allowed me to escape falling prey to it as well. Hopefully that was all about to change.

The meeting room was still bustling from the break when I was announced as the next speaker. I doubt a handful of them even heard my name and fewer probably even cared if they had. Looking up at the podium from my crumpled page of notes, I caught the eyes of several hundred uninterested salesmen, slouched in their chairs, boorishly awaiting what I had to say. Right before I could start, someone in the back yelled, "Nice tie!" which I guess was supposed to be funny because I wasn't wearing one. Nor was I wearing a suit, or even slacks. I had on a wrinkled pair of brown corduroy pants, brown shoes, and a sweater that looked like I bought it from the sale bin at a ski lodge. I'd planned to go with something a bit more hip and personable, but the shirt and pants I was thinking about hadn't been washed since the last time I wore them. They smelled like beer and cigarettes, and were badly stained with barbecue sauce. With no money to go buy something new, and with my suits at the cleaners, I was left with nothing else besides a pile of ripped jeans and faded T-shirts.

Brushing off the sarcastic remark, I dove right into describing several new products that we would be releasing in the upcoming month as well as some of our new pricing. It was real technical shit, but I had to get it out of the way early before I got too carried away and lost whatever attention I still had. Once this was finished, it was time for the incentive. Clearing my throat, I confidently raised my voice and immediately offered the sales force something I thought might spark some interest. What I got instead was a round of confused laughter, several hoots and hollers, and a quick exit, escorted by the vice president himself.

Apparently offering three free lap dances at the strip club of your choice, male or female, for every fifty cases sold wasn't what the boss had in mind when he told me to come up with something to get the sales team behind us. Although I'm sure there were many that disagreed with my decision (I didn't stick around long enough to see) I must say I did receive phone calls into the wee hours of the night from dozens of young members of the sales force, men *and* women, asking if I was indeed going to be true to my word. I assured them I would … and, for once, I meant it.

My travels for work brought me back to the city for the last few days of March. It would have been great to end the month on a high note, but instead it turned out to be a lesson in both humility and reality. I was scheduled to pour my wine at several big name restaurants that week as part of a five-day, citywide event, but I came down with a horrible cold after the first day that left me stricken to my bed. *Happily* stricken, I might add, because it was the only legitimate time off I'd had in years.

Everything was going fine on Monday morning when I showed up at my scheduled stop, a major steakhouse in midtown, sometime around ten thirty. Due to the surprising lack of traffic on this morning—the alternating merge into the tunnel was as beautifully executed as it gets—I arrived in the city much earlier than expected. Having already eaten and not wanting to waste money in a diner just to kill time until the event started, I figured the restaurant would let me hang around a bit; you know, maybe just sit at the bar and read a newspaper. Not the case.

Glancing inside, I caught the eyes of several staff members who tried their best to ignore me. Knocking on the locked glass door, I was frantically waving my corkscrew and pointing to the wine week promotional sign, but it was no use. Normally this wouldn't have been much of a problem, but it was an utterly cold morning for late March, with temperatures hovering around twenty degrees. To make matters worse, I hadn't bothered wearing my winter coat or gloves, thinking that I'd be only outside for the short time to and from my car.

After about thirty minutes of frigidly standing in the doorway trying to get either someone's attention or sympathy, one of the managers walked up behind me with a pair of keys.

"Excuse me," he smiled, opening the door.

"Thank god," I said. "My face is frozen solid."

"I'm sorry, sir, but we don't open until eleven thirty."

Stunned, I quickly told him I was working as a wine pourer today.

"I'm sorry, but you'll have to come back at eleven thirty."

"But it's freezing out here! Can't I just sit inside?"

"Sir, we're really busy."

And then he simply put the key in the door and locked me back outside.

I could have gone across the street into one of the jewelry stores to warm up, but decided to stand there, shivering violently, and staring down anyone who looked my way.

By the time eleven thirty finally came, the bar manager strolled up and opened the door. I immediately asked to use the bathroom. My hands were completely numb by then, and I wanted to run them under some warm water. The guy told me they'd just finished cleaning up and to be careful of the wet floors. Once inside, I made them even wetter by pissing on every square inch I could reach.

11. Blue Balled in the City

*M*y numbers continued to climb through the end of March, and for the first time ever I found myself out of the cellar position in our company standings. In my wake were Tim from the Midwest, Barb from the Carolinas, and Jerry from Utah/Nevada. I was confident that by the middle of summer I could be in the top five, then begin my assault on Nora, who currently stood as the eight-time reigning sales champion.

Nora. The soulless machine. A day after we all received the monthly newsletter and sales numbers, she sent me an e-mail congratulating me on my recent spike upward. All I sent her in return was a picture of a leopard sinking its teeth into the neck of a wide-eyed antelope.

Subliminal messages aside, the month of April started off in grand style with a massive portfolio tasting at the Marriot Marquis. Several hundred wineries all lined up at end to end tables, catering to an onslaught of consumers that came in all shapes and sizes. The tasting was a beastly six hours long, and all vineyard reps were instructed to be there several hours before to make sure their wines got there safely and that they were opened and ready to go. I arrived around eleven in case our winemaker, who'd flown in the previous night from California, happened to get there ahead of me. The scene was by then already in bloom with the sound of corks being popped, tables screeching across the floor, and a steady hum of voices that seemed to be mounting by the second.

At the entrance to the event sat a table of four or five women checking credentials. After giving my name, rank, and affiliation, I was handed an identity badge, a program the size of a phone book, and a free tasting glass. "You're going to be at table 135," I was told. "Please use only that glass for sampling."

Utilizing the map on the inside cover of the program, I was able to navigate over to my spot in a relatively short amount of time. As I sifted my way through the legions of industry folk, however, it became increasingly apparent to me that I was largely unprepared for this type of gig. The degree to which the majority of the other reps had gone to in order to transform their table display into something more than just a few wine bottles on a white tablecloth was ridiculous. I saw everything from topographical vineyard diagrams, giant poster boards of reviews, and hi-def video screens to grapevine trellises, Hungarian oak barrels, and full service bar counters.

The only thing I was packing was a crumpled up brown bag of plastic corkscrews. Pathetic.

I checked underneath the table to make sure all the correct wines were there, and then began lining them up in the preferred drinking order, from white to red, lightest to fullest. Gazing curiously around the room as I did this, I noticed many of the same people that I'd seen at other tastings. I never remembered their names, and I doubt they remembered mine, but it was basically the same faces in the same suits pouring the same product; all of them busy setting up their tables in their own pregame ritual. While a few stood around looking as if they hadn't slept in days (probably those entertaining the Australians in town—crazy fuckers), most had the intent expression of a head football coach on the sidelines before a big game. Their actions were very much the same—going over the game plan, assessing the opposition, and making sure all the right plays were in order—but in this case, the headset was a cell phone and the play book was a collection of product notes.

Every now and then I'd catch the eye of someone that recognized me and they'd flash a smile or wave, implying the universal notion of "How have you been?" "How's business?" and "Here we go again." Albeit brief and sometimes nothing more than that very look, there was a feeling of community out among the reps, a reassuring sense that other people were doing the same thing out there each day.

After popping open two bottles of each wine and checking to see if they were drinkable, I took the elevator back down to the lobby and crashed on one of the couches. Unless you wanted to sit on the floor upstairs—there was no other choice, because they never supplied us with a chair behind the tables at these events. It promotes laziness.

There was no sign of our winemaker yet. I made a quick call out to the vineyard to make sure he got in all right. Our secretary Betty said he left word this morning that he had changed hotels after finding out his bedding was made of a non-hypoallergenic polyester blend. "Other than that he said everything else was on schedule for today." Which it wasn't, because he should have been here by now. Not that I couldn't handle the show by myself, but since he was now "out of his territory" it was my responsibility to look after him. Winemakers were very uneasy when put out of their natural element. They seemed to have trouble adapting to urban development and things like crosswalks and middle-aged hookers.

This concern lasted only momentarily. After a rather unamusing half-hour or so of people watching, I decided to hell with waiting around. I was getting hungry. So I went back upstairs to grab something to eat from the smorgasbord of food that was being laid out.

To my astonishment, I was immediately denied by one of the hotel's servers, who told me that the food was not to be eaten until the consumers were let in.

"But I'm working here today. You see Table 135? That's me."

"Sir, at one o'clock you can help yourself."

"But at one o'clock I'm going to be working."

"I'm sorry. Rules are rules."

The second he turned around, I began to stockpile a huge plate of bread, salami, and assorted cheeses.

"*Hey! What did I just tell you?*" he screamed, looking back from the other end of the table. As he rushed in my direction, I began to make several loud squawking noises for some reason.

"*RAAAA! RAAAAA! RAAAAAAAA!*"

He cautiously tried to grab the plate from me, but I continued with the squawks until he backed away and took off swiftly for the exit doors. The scene got the attention of the entire showroom. A few people began to sporadically clap, while most simply looked at me in horrified amusement.

At around twelve thirty, our winemaker finally strolled in. He looked like a cross between peaceful and lost. Standing about six foot four, his long blond hair (always tied back in a pony tail) was coupled with the burnt, beady eyes of an old hippie and the tan, leathery face of a crocodile hunter. Impossible to miss in a crowd of ties and slacks as it is, he topped this off by wearing a buckskin vest, a cowboy hat, and blue jeans.

He was in the middle of the floor, staring off into nothing, when I approached him a few minutes later.

"Hey, Paul."

"Hey, how are you?" he said, rapidly turning around like I had just woken him up. "Nice to meet you."

I'd met him at least three or four times over the past year.

"It's Chet ... I help represent Bunglewood in New York. Remember?"

We looked blankly at each other for a second before a tiny light bulb went on inside his head.

"Oh yeah, right! Gee ... sorry man," he laughed, slapping his forehead. "How's it going?"

As I led him over to the table, he asked if there was any info he should know about. I told him no, and with that he quietly walked away. I didn't see him again for three hours.

By a quarter to one a long line of consumers had assembled, stretching around several corridors and back down toward the elevators. All the reps were at their positions behind their tables, periodically glancing at their watches and curiously awaiting the first signs of outside life. The initial wave of people that would hit us would be the geeks and snobs, that much was clear. Equipping themselves with their own notebooks and wine glasses, they already had a detailed route of which tables they would visit and when. It was like the beginning of a treasure hunt.

While there would be plenty of the lesser known wine to go around the entire night, the higher end and more famous vineyards would be out of their top level stuff by the end of the first hour. Even the consumers who didn't know a red wine from a white looked in the program and checked for one thing: the price. If they knew it was expensive, they wanted to taste it first. This, of course, bothered the snobs, who got extremely grumpy when they saw "novices" drinking wine they couldn't possibly understand the value of. Besides these fine specimens, you also had the old socialites, the wanna-be-famous twenty-somethings, and the cranky store owners. Quite a scene.

A garbled announcement came across the PA at one o'clock sharp, and the headstrong stampede of drinkers infiltrated the area like ants on a fumbled spare rib. The show was on.

Besides the occasional geek passing by saying "There's nothing here," I didn't have much foot traffic the first hour. The only reason I eventually had a few return consumers was because I was giving full glasses of wine, instead of the typical sip. I felt this would build a strong fan base among the alcoholics. And it did. In fact, they usually came staggering back with friends in tow, telling them they gotta taste this wine and that I was a cool guy and all. In a way, I kinda liked this setup. A strong collection of the same dozen or so drunks hovering around my station, blabbering about last night's Knicks game and summer vacation plans, while the snobs and geeks ran around spitting their wine into buckets and taking notes. Of course, limiting myself to a confined fan base probably wasn't the best way to help maximize future business. But crowds attracted attention, so who knows, maybe the American obsession with popularity would help lure some people over to see what all the commotion was about. After all, well-known commodities and success went hand in hand.

As I was contemplating this idea, a man wearing a pin-striped, skinny blue suit pulled me aside and whispered with a smile, "Please don't give them full glasses. Only enough to taste."

"I wouldn't worry about it," I told him, friendly. "Why don't you do your job and I'll do mine."

"This *is* my job!" he screamed. "I'm running this tasting! We can't have dozens of drunk people wandering around after the first *hour!*"

He had a point, I guess, but I didn't care. I wasn't going to go through all my wine anyway, so I continued to pour big and have my own little party at table 135.

There were a few exceptions to the heavy drinker, though, and as the day rolled on I had my unfortunate share of visits from both the snob community and the high society. Most of the snobs were portly, balding men, horribly dressed in moth-ridden plaid blazers and sweating over thick notebooks full of dangling flyers and pamphlets. They would ask questions like what kind of dirt the vineyards were planted in and what the average rainfall was in June last year. I gave them as much information as I could, which of course, was never enough.

Once they were ready to actually taste the wine, they would commonly enter some sort of evaluation phase, which included standing there for a few seconds, eyes closed and motionless, swirling the wine in their mouth, before spitting it into the bin and quickly writing down a flurry of notes. What followed was a long-winded explanation of what they "got" from the wine in terms of the overall composition. "I'm picking up a slight aroma of dill and asparagus on the nose. The wine could be a tad off. Have you checked it? It reminds me of something I had last week in Provence. Shoddy table wine at best. As far as body goes, I'm not finding much here, which is surprising, since the wine rests on a tart, black-cherry flavor. Very unbalanced. The aftertaste is something less desirable. Yes. I'm unfortunately beginning to pick up a faint trace of some stewed green tomatoes and perhaps a touch of rotten crab apple. When was the fruit harvested? Did you use *any* French oak? What is the percentage of alcohol?"

The high society crowd, on the other hand, was much different. They didn't want any information whatsoever. In fact, even suggesting that they might not be aware of something was completely off limits. Ditto correcting them when they were wrong. In their mind, you were there to serve them and that was it. To no surprise, their review of the wine was typically negative, but I couldn't have given two shits about whether they liked it or not. Actually, right before Paul made it back, one well-to-do lady almost gagged on the wine, spitting it quickly into the bucket and yelling, "Ugh! This wine is terrible! I think there's something wrong with it! Dump this immediately before someone else drinks it. Ackk!"

"It's an unfiltered Merlot, ma'am. It has some sediment in it … ah … due to it not being filtered."

"I know what it means!" she screamed, acting like she'd just been poisoned. "There's something wrong with it!"

I didn't bother asking where Paul had been, but I told him I needed a break and asked him to man the table. After two and a half steady hours of saying the same thing every thirty seconds, my brain deserved a rest. The acting was killing me. "Hi. Would you like to try some wine? Yes? Great! Well, I have a Sauvignon Blanc, a Chardonnay, a Merlot, and a Cabernet … Our Chardonnay is only aged about seven months in oak, so the crisp fruit really comes out … This Cabernet comes predominantly from the Sonoma Valley

and has about 13 percent Merlot blended in to soften the back end
… Isn't that nice? And it's only ten dollars retail, Sir. Yes, we've had
a great response this year. Thank you."

How or why I continued to put on this front, I couldn't be sure.
But like a flick of the switch, it just happened. The system.

I walked outside to the smell of burnt pretzels and bummed a
cigarette from a crowd of well-dressed Frenchmen. The street noise
somehow felt serene in comparison to the event inside.

As I was lighting up against a wall, with a hand cupped around
to combat a swift moving breeze, someone bear-hugged me from
behind, causing me to drop my cigarette in a puddle of dog piss. It
was a salesman named Tommy that I'd worked with in the past. I
hadn't seen him in a few months, and as he handed me a new cigarette he told me he was now in business with a winery group from
Oregon, representing them from New York to Massachusetts. It
should be noted that besides being a brilliant salesman, Tommy was
also a complete maniac, quickly amassing a solid career of legend-
ary carousing and drunken mayhem. He was one of the few people
my age in this business that wasn't all about the money, more about
having as much fun as he could get away with. As I have stated
before, this was an extremely rare attitude for someone in his late
twenties to take. With cameras, personality tests, drug tests, strict
performance guidelines, and egos now common in the workplace,
there was a lot to jeopardize for being original and true to yourself.

Yet for whatever reason, Tommy seemed to get away with it. In
fact, most people loved the guy. Just a week earlier, I'd overheard
someone telling a story about how Tommy picked off a billy goat
with an old Remington 700 rifle from 220 yards out, on a bet, just
to sell a case of wine. The crowd of four or five guys howled in
laughter, each claiming they were close personal friends, and each
eager to tell their own Tommy story.

Anyway, after a few minutes or so of catching up, he asked if I
was doing anything later.

"Nothing planned."

"Good. We're goin' out tonight. I know a few spots down in the Village afterwards where some of these chicks here are headed. We'll rage."

He took a final drag off his cigarette, stomped it on the ground, and slapped me on the arm.

"I'll come by your table after the show. Later."

When I got back upstairs, Paul had drifted off again.

"I saw him over at the Bliss Mountain table, talking with their owner," the guy at the table next to me said. "Is he your wine-maker?"

"Yeah."

"Shit, man. That guy is weird."

The last few hours of the tasting crept along at an incredibly slow pace. The time between consumers got increasingly longer as the night progressed, and I was running out of things to talk about with the neighboring reps. I think I asked the lady to my left if she lived here in the city at least three different times. It was terrible. Constantly pouring myself glasses of wine in the hopes that my heightened drunkenness would make this night more interesting were of no use, either. At that point it was just silence and the occasional delusional feeling of being stranded. "Why am I still here? Who would notice if I just left? I can't feel my legs …" Just stare straight ahead and smile, I told myself repeatedly. It will all be over soon.

By this time of the night, even the drunks had become annoying, especially since most of the jolly, light-hearted ones had already left or passed out. What remained were the pompous idiots with nothing better to do than act cool at a wine tasting. Like this one guy who walked up with these two blondes, talking obnoxiously loud and wearing dark sunglasses—inside a dimly lit room, mind you, as night was beginning to fall. He sported a dark blue corduroy blazer over a black T-shirt and ripped jeans, while the girls had their hands full trying to keep the straps to their flimsy flower dresses from falling off, seemingly in more amazement to them than anyone else.

"Okay, ah ha ha ... Now, what do we have here ... Ahem," the guy said, trying to clear his mind up to act in a civilized manner.

"These are all wines from California. I have a Sauvignon Blanc, a—"

"Hold them up, man! I can't see them down there," he said, laughing out loud as the two girls giggled beside him.

"*All right*," I sighed, lifting up the bottles. "I have a Sauvignon Blanc, a ..."

The guy was looking around the room and hardly paying attention as I ran through them, just occasionally saying things like "Uh-huh," "Yeah, okay" or "Right, right." Halfway through my routine, he simply blurted out, "Hey, enough with the talking, man. How about some wine? This is a wine *tasting*, right? What is this one here?"

"Dude, why don't you take off your fucking sunglasses and then maybe you could see them," I said, pouring one of the girls some. She was staring through me with glazed eyes that screamed drunken whore, all the while awkwardly swaying side to side.

"Excuse me?" he said, standing up straight. One of the girls tried to calm him down, as his face wrinkled up in confusion. "No, I'm cool, I'm cool ... I think this guy is trying to step to me."

They quickly pushed him over to the next table, as he turned and mumbled something unintelligible back at me. I grinned and shook my head. There were dozens more like him at every one of these things.

At quarter to seven, Tommy came by and we got the hell out of there. I don't know if Paul had stayed the whole time or what, but I wasn't about to wait around for him. We were scheduled to be together the following night for a winemaker dinner, so I left him a quick message on his answering machine at the hotel as a reminder, in case he thought about drifting somewhere else.

As I was packing up my stuff, several members of the drunken zombie crew must have sensed my departure and quickly surrounded the table asking for any unused bottles of wine. I told them that once I left, whatever was on the table was fair game. "But you didn't hear that from me." They immediately started arguing over who got to take what. Fucking scavengers.

Meanwhile, Tommy and I hopped on the subway and made our way over to his hotel in Union Square. The second we got inside his room, he popped open a bottle of Pinot Noir, chopped up some lines, and sparked a joint. Not sure about the cocaine, but the wine and weed were clearly of high quality. I could barely feel my face.

We sat up there for about an hour, watching part of the Knicks-Cavs game and listening to the Stones' *Exile on Main Street*, before we were back out on the streets looking for a good spot to grab some beers. Each place we walked by was packed. Weekend drunks and bridge-and-tunnel hipsters everywhere. Under the combination of substances going through my veins, I could've settled with just about anything short of an alleyway with decent lighting. But Tommy insisted we find the right place, with the right women. The weather was, for once, in compliance with this plan. It was still cool out, but compared to the past few months of freezing temperatures and blizzards, fifty degrees at night felt almost tropical.

We eventually wound up meeting a few girls that Tommy knew from the tasting over at the Belmont Lounge on East Fifteenth. There were about five or six of them, and they were all quite attractive, but it wasn't long before Tommy mentioned we should go somewhere else.

"These girls know me to well," he said. "They ain't gonna party late night. Too much at risk. What we need to do is find the *international girls.*"

It only took him a few minutes of rummaging through a stack of business cards to do so. Contacting some Italian girl he met earlier had us headed back on the subway toward the Upper West Side.

When we got to the place (I can't recall the name of it) there were two gorgeous women sitting in the back booth. Their eyes immediately looked over in our direction.

"That's them," Tommy whispered.

Impossible, I thought. These two wanted nothing to do with us. But before I knew it, Tommy was coolly greeting both of them, and introducing me as the winemaker for Bunglewood vineyards. "In fact, Chet here also *owns* the home vineyard in Sonoma Valley." At first, all I could do was smile. These girls were no joke. Sexy doesn't even scratch the surface. I'm talking statuesque models here, to a tee: long legs, erotic facial bone structure, perfectly sculpted hair, and silk dresses that barely draped over all the necessary parts. How I didn't notice them the entire time I was at the tasting was beyond me. They were probably so far out of my range that my mind didn't even register them as actual human beings.

Which wasn't the case at all. As it turned out, they were very much down to earth. And human. It was horrible that this had to be refreshing and strange news, but let's be honest here: If all beautiful women were approachable and kind, life would be much different. As far as a social hierarchy was concerned, everything as we knew it in America would be tossed upside down. For one, the nerds would cease to exist, as no true nerd could ever possibly have a supermodel connection. The ability to cut through the holier-than-thou fog would be too difficult. That only happened in teen movies and intimate daydreaming—not in real life. Unless, of course, you were a *rich* nerd. But even then, you had gone above and beyond your own stereotype and into something entirely different. Which could be a whole separate discussion altogether ... so let's move on.

We talked broken English for a while, behind a solid lineup of high-end Cabernets and single malts. Although they seemed practical enough for a few domestic lagers, Tommy was taking no chances. Our conversation centered mainly around touristy shit they wanted to see, as well as the core differences between the

American and Italian people. The stressed, strict life of America had no allure to them, and in between constant drags off their cigarettes they happily spoke of the simple lives the Italian people led in comparison. Their nonchalant views on clothing—or lack of it—and drinking were of particular interest. I must have drunkenly said I was moving there a dozen times.

After repeatedly being told by the bar manager—rather nicely I might add—that the girls couldn't smoke inside, Tommy mentioned that we should go back to his place and take in some of his party favors. The girls were up for it, and we wasted no time ushering them out the door and into a cab. When we got back to the hotel, Tommy spread out all the goods on the table, ripped open the window curtains to expose a spectacular view of the great city at night, and popped in a Prince mix, mainly stuff off *1999* and *Dirty Mind*, to set the mood.

Unfortunately, this was where the fun ended for me. Carmella, the girl I was with, somehow got violently ill, and I spent the next two hours in the bathroom with her as she vomited nonstop. The only reason I didn't bolt the second this happened was because she was constantly crying for me to stay with her. The Italian accent must have tricked my mind, allowing the karma to sneak in and take over.

If that wasn't enough, the sound of Tommy and Angelina (I think that was her name) banging away on the other side of the wall stood as a constant reminder of the good times I *should've* been having. Every thirty minutes or so, after they stopped to do another round of lines, Angelina would casually walk in, topless, asking if everything was all right. The sight of this hovering over me as I attended to her sick friend was enough to make a case for the strongest set of blue balls in the history of my life. I almost didn't want to look at her. How sad is that?

Although I felt I had sobered up quickly by the time her first round of vomit hit the toilet, my body had other ideas, and I woke up on the floor the next morning with an epic hangover. My brain felt as if it was on some sort of two-second delay, thumping like a human heart in one of those old science movies you see in high school. My stomach wasn't in such great shape either, gurgling so loud that it continually woke me up every ten minutes. It took the help of one of the front desk guys (who ran across the street and got me a half dozen bottles of Gatorade and a bottle of aspirin), along with four hot showers, before I was able to pull myself together enough to face the outside world. Thankfully, I'd already been in contact with Paul, who called me around seven that morning, asking if I wanted to go do yoga with him in Central Park. I politely told him no and said I'd see him at the restaurant at four to help set up.

At first glance, the old Italian restaurant had the look and feel of a place my grandfather and his buddies would have frequented to smoke cheap cigars and talk about bare-knuckle boxing. There was little decoration aside from a few dimly lit candle lights and some timeworn prints of the motherland. Very classic. Think lots of wood and brass rails. Strangely enough they even had a bocce pit downstairs. Paul thought it was some kind of meditative sand garden and spent most of the afternoon sitting cross-legged, drawing patterns in the dirt, while I ran around upstairs trying to get everything ready.

Shortly after five o'clock, the paid guests began to arrive for the meet and greet cocktail hour. If there was one thing I had to admire about the boss, it was his ability to bring together a group of people who normally wouldn't be caught dead drinking cheap American wine. The majority on this night had clearly come from a wealthy background, as evidenced from their luxury cars, Park Avenue mailing addresses, and extensive plastic surgery. Yet there was something peculiar about them. It wasn't long before I got the unmistakable sense that they were trying hard to dress down for this occasion. And I mean *hard*. Bad sweaters, khaki pants, and boat shoes were the norm for the guys; drab blouses, ill-fitting capri pants, and penny loafers for the ladies. They were acting strange, too, laying abnormally heavy on the polite introductions and fake laughter, to a point where I actually thought there might be a nitrous tank stashed behind the bar. It all looked so ... out of order.

Slowly, as I watched them mingle about, I began to realize something: that this type of gathering was what wine geeks must think of as a "party." A time to let loose and be *casual.* No doubt, the night had all the signs of a fantasy camp for them: A five-course meal with each course accompanied by a specific wine, hand selected by the winemaker himself, who, naturally, was present to speak about them in full detail. Although Paul didn't have the clout of some big-name winemakers, it didn't seem to matter. He was from California, he made the wine, and people got off on it. I, on the other hand, was of minimal entertainment value and made myself useful by helping the wait staff pour drinks.

An hour later we ushered "the party" into the dining room, where a table was stretched long enough to fit the eighteen guests with us. The conversations going around the room were not uncommon for a group of people who had just paid a hefty price to be here. This included discussions about various wine collections, who's got what in their cellar, what vineyards in the world everyone had been to, and that sort of thing.

Although I was the one in the business, it was obvious that I was also the one with the least amount of experience with any of these. Besides the samples for work, I didn't have a single bottle in my apartment that was being saved for any reason except to be finished whenever I got home. And as far as actual vineyard experience, I'd been to a grand total of two, both of which were in Long Island, and both of which I'd been kindly asked to leave. The first for drunkenly trying to get a crowd of senior citizens in the tasting room to join me in a "Sweet Caroline" chorus, and the second for causing a near riot when I flicked a cigarette butt among the vines. Bad idea. My immediate thought on the latter was that if there were mounds of dog shit lying around everywhere, what harm could a butt impose?

That's when I learned that dog shit in the street was much different from dog shit in a vineyard, where it was considered "part of nature and nutritious." Excuse me for being urban.

That said, I spent most of the dinner doing one of two things: smiling through dumb questions ("Do you get tired of drinking wine all day? Ahahaha.") and acting interested in stories that went nowhere ("Fran and I just got back from Sardinia and let me tell you, they have the most *amazing* shellfish.")

The night dragged on until a little bit after nine, when the last of the tipsy winos summoned for their car to be brought up front. I thought about asking Paul if he wanted to come outside and smoke—I knew there had to be a little Deadhead left in that melted brain of his—but he disappeared before I could. Nonetheless, it was a nice night out again, so I decided to take my time and walk the thirty or so blocks back to the hotel, where Tommy had left me a spare key.

I don't remember much of the walk (good weed will do that) but at one point I did stop to write something on the back of a napkin. It reads: "Each passing street is a socioeconomic snapshot of a world going in two separate directions. It makes you feel good to be somewhere in the middle. Lost ... yet comfortable." It also reads "Cactus plant megaphone" on the other side, but I didn't know what I meant by that.

When I got to the hotel room, all that remained of Tommy was a note saying he flew to Italy with the girls and to enjoy the room on him. There was a lipstick kiss on the bottom of the paper with an arrow pointing to it that said "from Carmella."

I threw the note back on the table and turned the TV on. Some of us were just born with it, I guess ...

Per his request, I took Paul around to several key accounts throughout the city the following day. It basically amounted to him talking for an hour here and there about technical shit like Malo-Lactic fermentation and pH levels. I was hardly necessary, nor was I acknowledged as actually being there. This, of course, was to be expected. But what really gnawed at me was that these were the very same accounts that had refused on several occasions to even see me. It wasn't until our glorious winemaker accompanied me that they were even remotely interested in the product.

The fact of the matter was that salesmen and reps simply did not get any respect. None. Zip. Zilch. Nada. It's like we went around selling and promoting this stuff night and day, and the only people whoever got any love and attention were the winemakers or the goddamn owners. It was bullshit, and I didn't know how those of us who worked in this cesspool of attitude we called the tri-state area stood for it. In retrospect, maybe I should have started a revolution to blacklist these accounts ... or, I don't know, maybe I should have just quit whining and done my job.

Anyway, after I dropped Paul off at LaGuardia, I had to sit in three hours of traffic just to get to Route 78 in Jersey, where I was late for another wedding. Yippee.

12. The Abundant Flesh of Atlantic City

Underneath the classy, corporate image of some of these large-scale wine tastings, there ever so quietly beat a heart of playful seduction. This became rather clear to me in Atlantic City in mid-April, when I walked up to the grand showroom at the Borgata Hotel & Casino and a whole crowd of scantily clad, barely twenty-year-old models turned in unison to look at me. There must have been at least fifty of them; it was like taking a secret portal to a mythical land of unattainable women.

The sight of this paralyzed me for a moment, my immediate thought being that a porn convention was in town, or at the very least, a European car show. I soon came to the realization that these girls were in fact being hired to work behind the wine tables and that my appearance had merely interrupted an instructional discussion on how to properly conduct themselves. The basic concept of this strange phenomenon was something I had seen before, in and around various trade shows in the city, but never on a grand scale such as this. It made me laugh. After years of trying to find ways to appeal to the younger generation, the wine industry finally gave in to the one sure-fire method: sex.

The whole reason I walked up there in the first place, three hours before the show began, was to simply get a look at the room. I'd heard great things, and wanted to see for myself what was in store for the two-day event. After discovering this collection of beautiful women, though, there was no need to see anything else.

I immediately called the boss in California.

"You want what?"

"I want you to call the head people here at the Borgata and ask them to supply me with the two hottest girls they got."

He seemed to think I was kidding.

"Look, we've never done anything like this, I don't think—"

"I know. Listen, you've been to these things. You know how it works. I'll be here to explain the wines and everything. I just want the attraction."

It took a few more minutes of discussion (equal parts persuasion and compromise), but he came around. The call was put in and an hour later I was back up at the registration booths, talking to the manager of the company supplying the models. The deal was solidified in the end with an old "hundred-dollar bill handshake" slipped in courtesy of Bunglewood Vineyards. The cash was my idea, but it was nonetheless a necessary means of doing business and would be accounted for under Miscellaneous Promotional Items in my expense report.

After having some down time to unwind and play a bit of black-jack, I got to my table about forty-five minutes before the tasting was set to begin. My barren space and lack of materials were almost comical compared to the surrounding setups. I found it perfectly fitting that the guy directly across the aisle from me had a giant waterfall built in behind him, with a sixty-inch high definition TV showing soaring images of the vineyards shot from what I suspect to have been a military helicopter. Normally, this would have made me feel a bit small, but not on this day. Let him have his lavish agricultural exhibition, I thought. Just give me the girls.

Over the next half-hour or so, I methodically uncorked and sampled my bottles, trying to keep my patience at an even keel. "You never know what's going to happen in Atlantic City," the guy next to me said, when I asked him what the scene was like. "It's part of the attraction." Indeed. I hadn't been guaranteed anything at this point except that I'd given a hundred-dollar bill to a stranger in a brown leisure suit, who apparently was the head of a modeling agency but could have easily passed for an off-track betting enthusiast.

It must have been around quarter to six, as I was lining up my rows of wine, that the sight of two girls walking down the lane caught my attention. They were looking at the numbers on the tables as they strutted their way toward me, leaving a slew of turned heads in their wake.

"Number forty-two," one said to the other, giggling a bit as she walked up to me. "Hey, is this Bunglewood Vineyards?"

I gratefully extended my hand and introduced myself.

"All right, we get a young one this time," the other said, laughing. "You don't know how many times we get stuck with some perverted old dude."

Their names were Katie and Candi (I shit you not) and they were both stunning. Katie stood about as tall as me (six feet), had long wavy brown hair, and wore a revealing red dress that was cut straight down to her belly button. She looked like a classic '50s pinup, like Ava Gardner or Jane Russell. Candi was a complete— pardon the cliché—Barbie doll, right down to the bright blonde hair, a very short, flowered silk dress, a constant carefree giggle, and what appeared to be an impressive boob job.

The deal was legit.

Lo and behold, the first hour of the tasting came and went without much changeover from my usual number of visitors. I banked this on the fact that most wine snobs did not fall much for the allure of live sexual attractions. They seemed to be hardly thrown off by the two girls beside me, and passed on the lack of merits that my wines contained. Snobs were quite nomadic in that way. Oftentimes too rude and selfish to maintain any sort of friendship, they traveled alone and were hardly social. They were once thought to be completely territorial to European soils, but from the information that I'd gathered over the previous few months, it seemed as if they were multiplying rapidly here in the States. I'd even heard a rumor that swarms of them were migrating elsewhere, including parts of New Zealand and Australia. Because their sole mission was to seek the wines they desire and all-knowingly critique them, my table had nothing to offer in terms of the execution of this plan.

It was around seven thirty when the tides began to turn in my favor. The second wave of consumers had shifted from those who wanted to taste to those who wanted to *drink*, and heavily. As the average age dropped, the temperature in the room heated up. And it was at this point that the scene down in A.C. had transformed into something completely different from the big New York City tastings. The crowd here was in general much younger and, partly inspired by the obvious surroundings, much more fun and free-spirited. There were literally hundreds of people who looked like they had just walked out of a nightclub mixed among the upper elitists of the wine community.

This type of atmosphere made for a most entertaining night. The younger sect came strong, and it seemed as if the night would easily reach the forbidden wine tasting level of "rowdy." And had it not been for the mature, well-behaved community—who were by no means backing down—it surely would have. Counterattacking over-exuberant laughter and "indecent" attire the only way they knew how, the elders formed tight barriers around the high-end tables and unleashed a storm of over-the-shoulder rolled eyes and head shakes. It was like a "battle of the superheroes" cartoon. I could only imagine what Vegas must be like at these things.

As all this was going on, Katie and Candi were on the verge of taking over the entire bottom left wing of the showroom. These girls were by no means novices in the field of public approval. They instantly recognized how to tailor to each clique specifically. Take, for example, the differences shown between two totally separate consumers: the frat boy and the older married gentleman. The younger and more susceptible frat boy received overbearing attention, flirty eyes, and an assortment of playful banter. Any drunk, single man will always think they have a shot if this was executed correctly, which in itself, *was* the trap. Done deal.

On the other hand, the older married gentleman had no realistic use for the possibilities of "hooking up" later on, as this would merely be seen as—with wife in tow—a cruel tease. No, they just wanted the attraction. Accordingly, this meant a long, lean-in pour, the slight contact via a hand on the arm, and, of course, the tractor beam naughty stare. [*To note: positioning of cleavage was a key element in both cases, as adjustments for a full bra-less view were made in terms of both height and angle of the consumer.*] It was a bit like fishing. You could have the most expensive, perfect lure in the world, but unless you knew how to use it, you might as well be casting your line into an empty bathtub.

Naturally speaking, this was all very interesting, but what impressed me the most was that their obvious mastery over the mindset of this crowd wasn't limited solely to men. Hardly the case at all. Compliments on jewelry, hair, and dresses were thrown in every direction to any female who hadn't initially turned their head in disgust or jealousy. Confidence was installed in these women, leaving them feeling as if they were part of what Katie and Candi exuded—*pure sexiness*—and it was going to pay off for many a married man later on in the evening.

An absolute beautiful sight indeed. I only wish I could've taken the two of them on the road with me.

By nine, my table had become ground zero for the young and hip. No suits here. Even the snobs were forced to go around a different lane because of all the commotion. During the last forty-five minutes there must have been a crowd of nearly seventy people gathered around me, guzzling wine at an enormous pace and conversing about where the next stop would be on the A.C. drunk train. Word had been passed down from the event committee to cease pouring full glasses immediately, but it was too late. There was no stopping me at this point. Standing back and taking it all in, I felt I had made a great decision. Not only had I lured the attention of the public, but I even got the attention of an official magazine photographer. Seeping his way in through the crowd, he asked to take a picture of the three of us in front of the Bunglewood Vineyards logo that had been positioned behind the table. With the girls flanking me on both sides, they posed with their bodies leaned in, each exposing a long leg in front of me, with one hand on their hips and the other draped around my back, as I held up a bottle of our ten-dollar Cabernet. The crowd roared in approval.

Before I could bask in the glow of my accomplishments much longer, the lights in the showroom flickered on and off, and a low booming voice came over the PA announcing that it was now ten o'clock, and that the tasting was officially over. A slight boo went up from the crowd, who turned and filed like cattle toward the exit doors.

As for myself, it meant I had to *un*happily (for once) start packing it in. This included, among other things, counting the number of bottles left and marking them for the distributor as per Jersey law. While I was taking care of this, I told the girls they could go, and they did, not before giving me a peck on the cheek and saying they'd be back tomorrow.

They were off to a private party somewhere with a few of the other models, leaving me to only imagine what that was like.

While most of the reps were on their way to relax back down in the casino, the night was not over for me in regards to work. As part of an agreement with the boss in exchange for the ladies, I was to meet up with a few key account people at the Tropicana for dinner at Carmine's. These individuals were managers of some of the better stores in the tri-state area; major players within the retail community. Not a bad deal for me, really. I'd always been a big fan of the Carmine's in Manhattan, but especially because it was on the vineyard's tab. The only drawback was that I had a few offers to go hang out with some people I'd met earlier in the night, all of whom guaranteed an assortment of recreational drugs and single women.

Dwelling on the missed possibilities of such things only induces regret, so I quickly put this behind me. After a run up to my room to hit half a joint and take a leak, I hailed a cab and made it over to the Tropicana in time to meet the group. They were waiting at the bar when I arrived, talking loudly about various wine products and looking as enthusiastic as a bunch of anxious travelers in line at an airport gate.

Now, in my mind, the first thing to do upon entering a bar is to order a drink. But when I mentioned this to these people they looked at me as if this was the most outrageous thing they'd heard in decades.

"Oh my," one lady said to me, giggling, "I don't know ... I really shouldn't. I have to get up early, and well, I don't know if this is the right time to ..."

She quickly turned to the woman on her left and asked if she was going to have a drink, and then to the man next to her and asked him the same. Her nervous excitement echoed throughout the group, while a few just shook their heads in embarrassment as if I was offering them an underage nymphomaniac. Of course, they had just come from a five-hour wine tasting—but that was strictly business. Apparently, drinking in a social atmosphere no longer registered as a viable form of entertainment.

Following a few minutes of stale conversation at the bar, we were escorted to our table. Besides the short amount of time it took to order food, they spent most of the night interrogating me on what inside information I might have coming from the production side of the business. Their tone was serious, and I had no choice but to put on my polite act and answer all their questions pertaining to the upcoming forecast of trends in the industry. "Yes, I believe we will see an overall decrease in oak aging for Chardonnay; in fact, this year we will only be putting ours in the barrel for roughly six months ... Our winemaker is very pleased so far with this year's vintage. He's even made projections that it could be the next '97 ... Consumers are starting to accept Pinot Noir as a major grape in this country. We've already bought two new vineyards in Carneros solely for it ... The cost of California Cabernet is certainly a problem, one that unfortunately doesn't have an end in sight."

While I was babbling on about this kind of stuff, they looked at me with an intense gaze, accompanied by a continuous slight nod of the head. For whatever reason, they seemed interested. *Too* interested. In the middle of one particular discussion on the fate of Merlot, I even caught one fellow scribbling some information down on a napkin by using the end of a straw and some red wine. With my words trailing off in confusion as I looked at him, he soon realized his actions were being observed. Slowly leaning back, he secretly crumpled up the napkin in his hand before stuffing it in his coat pocket. I couldn't be sure if he was taking notes on what I had to say, but even the thought of it seemed entirely ridiculous. I had as much knowledge on the wine industry as some part-time field worker spraying pesticides out in the vineyards. But to them, I guess, I was just another source they could tap for inside information. So without much delay I launched into a string of bizarre announcements, claiming the Napa Valley was now 90 percent lesbian and that a new indigenous pink grape called Star-tron would revolutionize the market by next fall. Just to see if they'd take the bait.

As much as I didn't care for their conversation or their business attitude, they were nice people I guess. But after five hours or so of drinking and talking about wine at the show, you'd think they might want to discuss something else. I mean, there was a war going on somewhere, baseball season had just started, and as far as I know past experiments in procreation could have yielded a few children to talk about. It made me wonder if bickering in extensive detail about pricing, products, and promotions was actually fun for them. Was there a science to it? Is science *fun*? Maybe I'd been missing out.

Sitting there in between a whirlwind of occupational dialogue, I tried to suppress any feeling that this kind of behavior was the end result of living a life in sales business. People succumbing to the pressure of living solely through their jobs because of the fear that there was always someone waiting in line after them. That "If I don't do it, someone else will" attitude that scared people into working overtime seven days a week. But as much as I tried to make it into something else, I knew full well it was the truth. If you wanted to make it, you had to make it your life.

No one in this country remembers who finished in second place.

After dinner I went back to the Borgata. It took an hour of observant laps around the gaming floor before I was finally able to score an empty seat at a ten-dollar blackjack table—the cheapest I could find. In about a quarter of the time it took me to do that, I was already down to my last few chips. Nine straight hands of defeat. Amazing. I needed a big hand to bail me out, and I got it: a miraculous three-way split of eights against an eventual dealer bust. It laid the groundwork for a nice little run, and I wound up playing until four in the morning. Sure, I lost a hundred bucks in the end, but it felt good to have a bit of careless energy running through me. If that was possible for someone who had nothing to spare but his stock Jeep stereo and a Gibson SG guitar that he never learned to play.

By noon the next day, the good feelings were long gone. What remained was a solid headache, a lingering taste of rum, and a random collection of thoughts on how I was going to make up the lost dough, which would surely handicap me for the remainder of the month. It took a relentless hour-long attack on the snooze button to get me out of bed, and by the time I did I barely had the time to hop in the shower and get dressed for the second day of the event.

Skipping a much-needed breakfast and with my hair still wet, I was able to make it down to the showroom with about twenty minutes to set up. Unfortunately, when I got to my table I realized I didn't have the one thing I needed: a corkscrew. During the rush it must have slipped my mind, so instead of running all the way back upstairs I figured I'd just borrow one from one of the other tables. Wasn't happening. My neighboring winery reps turned out to be a bunch of selfish pricks, as they each had an excuse for not lending me one. The French guy two tables down shrugged his shoulders and told me, "This is my only one," even though I pointed out that he had a whole basket of them sitting right in front of him. "Oh, those are for the consumers," he said smugly. Others tried to plead the same story, while some simply shook their heads.

I did have one person who at least seemed willing to let me borrow one, but she made such a scene I thought she was going to ask for a deposit for the damn thing. "Please, please, *pleeeease*, whatever you do, remember to bring it back. You have no idea how many times people just walk off with them. Where is your table? When do you think you'll be done with it? Do you need it the whole night? Can I have your business card, just in case? Here, let me take your cell phone number down." Her whiny Brooklyn accent was doing terrible things to my brain, so I just threw it back on the table and walked away.

Moments later, Katie and Candi arrived, and I told them why I was staring at a table full of unopened bottles. Katie went over to the same French guy who denied me and got a corkscrew from his basket. The guy smiled and waved her off like it was no problem.

The tasting on this day was packed from start to finish. Split into two separate times, the first three hours were strictly for retailers, restaurateurs, and other VIP's, and the last three were open to the public. The first half was a blur. It got so swamped with industry people that the only time I put a bottle down was to grab another full one. Guys left and right were doing double takes looking at the girls, spilling drinks on the unsuspecting people in front of them. It got to the point where some felt it easier to just camp out a few feet away and stare at them like they were in a zoo.

In between the times, it was announced over the PA system that the reps should take the opportunity to have a break and enjoy some of the food. It was very much needed. My right hand was stained completely red from the wine that kept dribbling down the bottles, and the girls were so hungry they were practically crying.

After grabbing something to eat, the three of us reconvened back at the table. It was over a plate full of cheese and crackers that the bomb dropped between the girls and I.

"You guys are what?"

"Exotic dancers," Katie mumbled through a mouthful of crackers.

"Both of you?"

"Yup. A lot of the girls here are."

"Bullshit."

"You think we make enough money doing these kind of shows? Here's our manager's card."

They brushed it off like it was nothing, and maybe it was for them. Damn, a couple of good-looking girls like that could make some serious money in this town. But as for me, it momentarily sparked an outpouring of erotic visions, as one could imagine.

Coming back down into reality, I asked if they worked in the area. Katie explained they mainly performed locally, for bachelor parties and stuff like that.

As they coyly smiled back at me, I felt a little embarrassed.

"What?" Katie said.

"Nothing."

"Just say it."

"Well, it's nothing ... I was just wondering what you guys make in a night. That's all."

"It depends. How many people, how long, that sort of thing. Our manager usually does the deal."

Taking this in and continuing to nibble on some crackers, I looked around the room and got an idea.

"I don't know if this is rude or anything, but, ah, are you girls working tonight?"

They looked at each other and shook their heads. "No. Why?"

Eleven p.m. sharp. My hotel room was filled with a dozen of the best retailers from the New York/New Jersey area. While a hat full of hundred-dollar bills rested on the dresser, the girls were stripped down to the bare necessities, gyrating every inch of their immaculately toned bodies one by one across the laps of these men, who were seated next to each other on the edges of the bed. For the next hour, a hundred dollars apiece got them two things: a top-of-the-line private strip show and a never-ending glass of Bunglewood wine. Chalk it up as a relationship builder. Genius.

Besides a few initial awkward moments, rounding up the crew was much easier than I thought. These guys weren't has-beens or recent inductees to loner status—these were full-time employees. You could just see it in the way they acted at the wine tables: the nervous look in their eyes as they waited their turn, the bashfully low tone of voice, and the constant shuffling of their feet in fear of getting in other people's way. They were going to spend the evening alone, whether it was at the slots or in bed with hotel porn.

It wasn't in their personality to go to one of the strip clubs—but deep down *they wanted to*, and I basically brought it to them. The wine was no problem, either. I simply informed the event staff with a half hour to go that I'd used up everything, then just took the remainder with me as I left. If the distributor ever asked about the missing bottles, I'd merely tell them some drunken hooligans must have raided the table when I wasn't looking. "There was no way to keep track of everything. They were everywhere. My threats of police action were useless against them."

When the night came to a close, the guys left my hotel room looking as if they had the adrenalin of teenagers, shaking their heads in disbelief and patting each other on the back in laughter.

As they walked down the hall, I heard one of them shout, "What do ya say we all go down to the bar for a few drinks!"

Pumping their fists in approval, they moved confidently toward the elevators.

My journey into Brooklyn and Queens the next week turned out to be a riot. The stripper idea paid off tenfold. I didn't really know what would come from that—besides a free viewing for myself, but when I went back to see these guys, all of them took twenty-five to fifty case orders. It was a joke. I didn't have to explain anything or even taste them on any specific wines. Nothing. They acted like I was an old friend, or even better, an old *college* friend. On my last day in Queens, for example, this one Pakistani guy named Rafi showed me a picture he took that night, giggling like a school boy with his arm around me, while his wife sat in the back office eating a tuna fish sandwich. In cases like this, one idea had instantly transformed a typical cold shoulder into a warm embrace.

All in all, I must have sold two hundred cases by noon that day, enough to spend the rest of it driving around in a young salesman's Hummer, smoking some schwag herb, and listening to an obscure hip hop bootleg he got on Canal Street. The boss saw the numbers and didn't know what to make of it. He thought I was running some sort of buyer incentive program.

However he saw it, it didn't matter. And why should it? As the month of April came to a close I'd shot up to sixth place on the sales rep depth chart, even outselling the almighty Nora during the four-week stretch. Everything that I'd hoped to accomplish was finally coming together, and more importantly I was doing it my way. No corporate interference, no dated ad campaigns or hokey sales gimmicks, and no ass-kissing. Just sheer modern abuse of whatever it took to get things done. I'd found the light through underground deals, misleading stories, and strippers, and I was going to follow it to the end. If nothing else it guaranteed that *I* was back in control ... and being in control was a much more fun approach than anything else that I'd experimented with.

Where it would lead, of course, was anyone's guess. But whether it be in a penthouse suite on Central Park West or in a ditch in North Bergen didn't concern me at that point. I was flying high in more ways than one, and to look back now would have been an obvious sign of weakness and doubt. So it was critical that I continued on while the going was still good.

At least … that was the plan.

Part Two

13. Getting Burned, and the Peeling of the Skin that Followed

*B*efore I go any further, I should at least warn you that what happens next, happens rather abruptly. You see, at a desk job things can go unchanged for decades. In my mind it is very much a controlled setting that rarely allows any noticeable, out-of-the-ordinary behavior or tactics to fester for very long. When you're on the road and in command of yourself, though, it's an entirely different story. This isolation from management can cause a simple problem to get completely out of control in a relatively short amount of time.

Which is exactly what happened to me.

It was around early May that I began to undergo a transformation that could only be explained as an addiction to selling. As it creeped over me like a rabid disease, I found myself in a world that had nothing to do with anything else but selling. I had entered *the zone*. Once those big deals started rolling in, I couldn't help but keep them rolling. It became too easy. I cheated, lied, and pushed my way into every store I could. It was a blur, a black hole of sorts that remains hazy at best. The warehouse payoffs in Rochester, the phony winemaker dinners in Saratoga, and the unmarked delivery programs in the Bronx. I was flying high all right—too high, and if I had any common sense whatsoever I would have felt the burn just before I flew straight into the sun.

But being in such a state—overconfident, inexperienced, drunk—I rarely picked up on these things. And so it took a letter from the State Liquor Authority the third week in June, explaining that I'd been caught doing illegal business, to bring this desperate and undisciplined plan of attack to an end. It was just a warning (these under-the-table deals were done every day; it's getting caught that's a sign of an amateur), but I was officially put on notice. One more infraction and it would mean the end of my job, a criminal stain on my record, as well as possible legal action against the vineyard.

Although it may appear to be nothing more than a slap on the wrist, the effect this had on my sales routine was immeasurable. No deals … no love. Unable to utilize any of the unconventional methods that once triggered a historic resurgence in my short sales career had reduced me to an entirely different person almost instantly. It was like a dramatic scene in a war movie when an officer gets his badges of rank torn off. I had been reset to my starting position, with no tools in which to work with and not an ounce of pride to rest on.

Sadly, this was only part of the problem. Whereas initially I had difficulty in just selling the product, I was now dealing with the aftershock of going around to some of these accounts a second time, *after* they had bought big quantities. The more recent inconvenience: no *customers* were buying it. I was basically being handcuffed by my own product.

The response I got from these account managers varied little from place to place. It usually went something like this: "Listen, young man. I already took in your wine. But for Christ's sake, now I got fifteen cases of shit that I can't sell that's been sitting here since the last time I saw you. What on Earth makes you think I would want more? *I can't sell a single fucking bottle!*"

It was better than them not having it; the original sale still counted. But word traveled quickly among the various shop owners and restaurant managers, and my product was now being labeled as a "dead brand." Which was a shame, really, because there were thousands of other wines just like it for the same price, and those brands did just fine. But like I've said, no one had ever heard of mine, and that was a problem. No billboard ads, no appearances on the tables of popular TV shows or rap videos, nothing. I thought I could undercut the competition a few dollars by giving away free cases on top of each order, but the stores never lowered the price. They kept it the same, giving them a higher profit. Which does make sense—but only if you were actually selling it. The few times I'd mentioned lowering the price to help generate sales, they looked at me like I was trying to pawn off one of their children. So naturally *I* had to help sell it, and the only way to do this was by going in and doing an in-store tasting or restaurant promotion at every single one of these accounts.

For the next two months I was booked solid every Saturday. Good-bye, summer.

The demand for help started immediately and appropriately on the Fourth of July. No holiday for me. No sir. Instead I worked a tasting as a favor to some guy out on the East End of Long Island. He ordered fifty-six cases over the phone back in April and had sold a grand total of three bottles to date. Why he had me there on Independence Day was beyond me. It's typically a beer holiday. Punishment, I guess.

Located a block off the water's edge, the store was in the center of what appeared to be an old fishing town. Oars, seagulls, a distant smell of raw fish, the whole bit. I was set to start the tasting around four, but having gotten there a bit early I figured I'd stroll around and take in some of the sights. With the sun out and the early signs of humidity nowhere to be found, it made for an absolutely perfect day to do so. No doubt the coastline businesses were pleased to see the weather hold up. Due to the amount of income these holidays generate, a washed out, rainy Fourth of July and Labor Day could spell doom for the entire summer. Whatever happened in between them, I'd been told, was often secondary.

Unfortunately, the main street area *here* turned out to be nothing more than a few rundown bait shacks and a bank. Thinking the docks may hold something slightly more interesting, I crossed over the desolate street and headed south. Barely visible from the street, and tucked around the corner of an alleyway, I came upon a tiny seafood restaurant. It was a dingy little place, but the smell of fresh chowder was too much for me to resist, so I scraped up some change and bought a bowl to go.

Walking down to the waterfront I found a bench in the shade, where I sat and watched as a few boats gently passed in the distance. The only other signs of human life were a handful of little kids running along one of the loading docks. They were swinging plastic swords furiously at every pole, chair, and boat that stood in their path. As I sat there eating, I wondered how many of them wanted to grow up to be a salesman just like me. Well, none probably. But it was still amusing to imagine one of them telling his classmates of such aspirations.

I think I wanted to be one of the guys on *The Dukes of Hazzard*. Or an astronaut.

The store itself was a nice change from the bland supermarket style that had become all too familiar on the road. In keeping with the fishing town theme, the walls were covered in weathered wood and decorated with a countless number of related seaside items. This included, among other things, a pair of stuffed pelicans, several various-sized wooden seagulls, a handful of antique rods, and a few old pictures of big game fish and local boats. Very cozy.

The manager was a bearded fellow named Jim, who looked every bit like an old fisherman himself. When I got there, he explained to me that he would be taking off in a few minutes to go to the Mets game, and that his son would be working the register with his younger sister. "If you could, please make sure he keeps the classical music on" was his only instruction. The son, a tall, skinny teenager who was sitting, arms crossed, and staring out the window, turned and gave me the finger, while his sister, dressed in a tight powder blue velvet jumpsuit rolled her eyes.

Sure enough, the second the little bells rang above the door signaling the manager's exit, the music was immediately changed to some hip hop station. Before I could even say anything, the son looked at me and said, "If you don't like it, you can fucking leave." I thought about mentioning the dozens of P.E. and Tribe shows I attended before he even knew what hip hop was, but instead, just turned the music even louder until he walked away. The only other time I saw him was when I passed through the back office to use the bathroom and caught him looking at porn on a laptop computer. His sister ran the register throughout the night and spent the entire time on the phone talking about some bitch named Samantha, why Taylor was going out with that skank Monique, and some new full service salon down in Southampton that did the best color.

I wound up selling only one bottle of Chardonnay. No excuses, no story to tell, just a downright sad display of salesmanship. Most of the people that came in just smiled and headed straight to the fridge for cases of Corona or whatever other kind of beer you could put a lime in. My sudden demotion back to ordinary goon status was now official. I had no game.

Just get to the hotel, I told myself, walking back to my car. Get to the hotel and get a beer. Maybe a few. And some shots.

The place I was staying at on this night was located right off the Long Island Expressway, in a large nondescript structure that looked like a mental institution, or one of those medical corporation buildings. No artistic intent whatsoever. The central location was ideal, though, and it proved to be quite popular among the business commuter crowd, as there were literally hundreds of them milling about when I walked into the lobby. It left me wondering whether or not a suit and tie were prerequisites to even check in. Either way, it didn't matter. I wasn't going anywhere near the registration desk. Instead I made a beeline to the bar, where I promptly ordered three baskets of french fries, a pitcher of beer, and a double shot of Jack. All I wanted was to sit there and get drunk in peace.

But that, of course, would have been too easy. So within minutes, this plan was foiled by a gentleman sitting to my left who was hell-bent on telling me the story of his horrible life and deflating marriage. I should have gotten up and moved immediately, but I thought he'd wear himself out after a few minutes. Besides, it was no secret that I had the best seat in the bar. TV to my front, jukebox to my back.

Wearing a grey suit with a loosened tie and nursing a pint of beer with both hands, the man sat hunched low over the bar. Staring across the way at a couple of semi-attractive, middle-aged businesswomen, he meandered through several unrelated topics concerning his single days, before trailing off into some deep thought. "Boy, we had some good times back in Colorado. Use to have a whole garage full of bikes, guns, you name it. I was probably about your age. What are you, twenty-five? Twenty-six? Doesn't matter, fella. Girls left and right. And pretty ones too, boy. Whoowee. I tell ya, I woulda had *both* them two sittin' across the way. Goddamn right I woulda …"

I tried to ignore him at first, but the beer was going down fast, and the more I drank, the more I fell into the conversation. Before I knew it we were exchanging business cards and discussing the idea of going to some strip club down the road. But like the two pretty ladies and the six or seven other patrons (mainly older men sipping whiskey on the rocks), he soon tired out and called it a night.

During the last few minutes, he was barely able to keep his head up, and kept repeating the phrase, "You win some, you lose some."

I hung around for about an hour after everyone else had left, watching the game and slugging down more beer, with the occasional daydream of being in the shoes of whoever was playing on the jukebox. Mick, Pete, Jimi, Jerry …

At some point the bartender came up to me and asked if I'd like to charge it to the room or pay now. I didn't know I was ready to stop but she said they couldn't serve me any more alcohol.

"I can see it in your eyes. You're done," she sneered.

I paid and walked out.

On my way down toward the front desk, I checked to see if the pool was still open. Not sure what was more strange: that it was at midnight or that there were two dozen Mexican kids running around screaming. I didn't bother to ask. After checking in I grabbed a bottle of wine out of my car and spent the remainder of the night watching Australian Rules football in my room until the sun came up.

Crammed in between this tasting and the next one was one hell of a week on the road. And I don't mean that in any gratifying, reflective way, either. Just a sheer sense of actual living hell on the road.

It was a week full of meetings, strategically placed throughout the state of New York to help inject some spirit into the summer months. Each one was dreadful in its own special way. In Albany I introduced the new "Chardonnay for Summer" program and was rewarded with a flat tire in the parking lot, a lost hotel confirmation, and had my CD case stolen at a McDonalds. In Buffalo I got sick on a plate of hot wings (go figure, of all things), missed the meeting completely, and wound up vomiting in my Jeep as I tried to make it back to the hotel. Rochester saw me actually get booed by the sales force after I said their numbers were down, and in Scarsdale I did the same and got a round of complete silence, punctuated in the end by a single, yet sadly audible "Fuck you." Enough said.

Immediately following this, I had to haul ass down the Thruway and across the LIE at speeds between 85 and 105 mph—the latter pushing the limits of the old Jeep—to make it on time to a tasting out in Montauk. Even at five o'clock it was another unbearably hot day on the road. I had to stick half my body out the window for the last hour, trying to filter the wind through my shirt to help combat the gobs of sweat that were forming around each square inch of fabric. Although the prospect of both embarrassment and a rash loomed, I had to be thankful the traffic had been moving at a steady pace throughout the late afternoon.

In spite of this stroke of luck in regards to traffic, these long summer drives made it incredibly hard to be upbeat about traveling around for work. Passing countless numbers of cars filled with half-naked teenagers heading from the beaches and lakes were inevitable and quite depressing. Their happy, carefree faces, wearing dark sunglasses and bobbing to the beat of a blaring stereo, dotted every stretch of road. Guys in tank tops, their arms covered in tattoos and dangling outside of rolled-down windows, raced by and flicked you off, while the girls with their youthful flesh spilling out all over the place, laughed and blew you kisses. It was a sure sign that you were now a responsible adult and had no life during the week.

"Thought you weren't going to show" were the first words I got from the burly store manager upon entering. I was dripping sweat, wearing khaki pants and a white polo shirt, while holding a black bag of wine bottles and a melting bag of ice.

"It's ten to seven. I thought I was scheduled to be here at seven o'clock?"

"You are."

"So ..."

"So nothing. Get your wines out and start pouring. The customers are already waiting."

I dropped the bag of ice on the floor, placed my wines on the cruddy little table set up with a paper towel cloth, and walked back toward the front door.

"I'll be back in, let's see ... eight minutes. At seven o'clock," I said, looking at the wall clock. "I'm going to smoke a cigarette. *I'm early.*"

It wasn't until I began to walk out that I quickly realized that the entire store was full of what looked to be a life's worth of Boston Red Sox memorabilia. Signed balls, autographed eight-by-ten glossies, game-used bats, wrinkled ticket stubs, clocks, cereal boxes, etc. This being New York, it was not only surprising, but through the eyes of a die-hard Yankee fan such as myself, also completely distasteful. Being surrounded by the likes of Big Papi, Yaz, and Teddy Ballgame made my already bitter feelings toward this man blossom into pure hatred. Silly? Maybe. But to those of us who considered the Yanks to be a source of one of the only consistently enjoyable things in life, it was serious business. You could trace my family's allegiance back three generations for proof.

I went outside to have my smoke. During that two-minute excursion, I was interrupted by three different old ladies who asked if they could try the wine. I told them I'd be inside in a second.

"But we have dinner plans at seven thirty," one of them said, tugging on my shirt sleeve. "Can't you just come inside real quick?"

I pretended to not hear them and continued to enjoy my cigarette.

Back inside I was positioned underneath a gigantic painting of Carlton Fisk waving the damn ball over the Green Monster in Game 6 of the '75 Series. Luckily for me the place was crowded enough to take my mind off this sight. The customers, on the other hand, seemed to not even notice. And at that they shouldn't. This was Mets territory. They couldn't have given a damn about the Red Sox or the Yankees. It was also a vacation crowd, a noticeably goofy collection of out-of-towners dressed to disappoint. Legions of flabby, pasty white bodies barely concealed by a bright yellow tank top infested this area every summer. They were among the many waves of people to hit the Island as a refuge from their cubicle-induced days of midmorning memos and focus meetings, and they were in no mood for anything but sun and booze.

This type of atmosphere, combined with a week's worth of bad vibes, gave me all the inspiration I needed to get completely plastered. For every customer that I poured a cup of wine, I poured one for myself, growing more and more ridiculous by the minute. I was a drunken fool. A sweating, laughing, socially adept drunken fool. Every so often the manager would shift his eyes over his bifocals toward me with a look of disapproval, as I blabbered and slurred my way through tales of imaginary ratings and bogus awards. There wasn't much he could say … I was on a roll.

My inebriated state seemed amusing to these people, and while they weren't buying it by the case, they were at least looking interested in the wine. In between my spiel about volcanic soil and aromas of bing cherries, I made sure to switch up the conversation to more leisurely topics: offshore fishing with the guys, celebrity gossip for the ladies, and timeless jokes for the kiddies. Throw in a pat on the back, a few high fives, and I was golden. For the next few hours I would become a pleasant, distant memory to a score of summer travelers as "that nice, wasted salesman at that wine tasting on the Island."

Just as the daylight faded into night, so did the customers. By nine thirty the crowd had thinned out considerably, give or take a few vacationers who were in it for the long haul and needed a restocking of alcohol before closing. As for myself, I was running out of steam. Wearily leaning up against the Fisk Shrine and staring off into space, the week had finally caught up to me. I gave a tired glance over to the manager, who looked at his watch and, with a backhanded wave, told me I could go.

As I gathered up my materials and slowly stumbled toward the door, I came upon this horribly annoying framed picture of Pedro Martinez on the wall. Twenty minutes later I would use that very picture frame as firewood on the beach, where I polished off the remaining bottles from the tasting and sat looking at the moonlit waves until I fell asleep.

That is, until I was awakened by police, who told me it was a private beach, and to please leave immediately, or they would charge me with trespassing.

14. The Gathering of the Tribes

*D*ue in part to the obscene rise and fall of my sales career the pre-vious few months, I didn't see much of Gus over this period of time. We'd cross paths every now and then, but the conversations were usually whittled down to a few on-the-run comments on the Yankees or the weather. More often than not, it was merely a wave and a smile.

It wasn't until a few weeks after I'd been reported by the state and upon returning from my debauched wine tasting in Long Island that I once again sat down with the man on the front steps.

"I don't mean any disrespect, but you don't look so good," he said, giving me a perplexed look. This coming from a man who weighed a buck-twenty, tops, had hardly any teeth, and looked like he'd slept the night in a trash can. It made me laugh.

"Yeah, it's been a rough few weeks, Gus. Don't know if I'm cut out for it all."

"Problems at work, I presume. What did I tell you about getting all worked up over it?"

"I know. I know. But I was doing really well there for a while. I got caught up in the moment."

"Then what?"

"The short cut I took went in the wrong direction."

"Well … sometimes they work and sometimes they don't. You've got to know when to use them."

I looked over at him with an empty stare.

"Gus, how can you possibly predict that?"

"Shortcuts only work with confidence, Chet. Faking it gets you nowhere."

"But I've cheated or whatever at a lot of things on a whim, and they've worked out sometimes."

"Well, now you're talking about luck, which is an entirely different thing altogether. I can go walk through highway traffic right now and I might not get hit. That doesn't make me Superman. That just makes me one lucky son of a bitch."

"Yeah, I guess you're right. I don't know."

"There's no right or wrong here, compadre. You should be glad that it wasn't in your blood to take the easy path in this situation. There's nothing more dangerous than fooling yourself. God knows how easy it can be to fool others and just look at the problems that causes."

We both turned and watched as a group of teenagers came through the lot on skateboards. One of them tried to ollie over the sidewalk partition, but clipped his wheel on the curb and tumbled awkwardly into a bush. I chuckled a bit, while Gus just shook his head in amusement.

"Gus, dinner will be ready in a few minutes," his wife said gently through the screen door behind us.

"Turkey pot-roast, woo-hoo!" he cried out with a big smile, springing up to his feet. He followed this with some kind of weird old-man jig. It looked like a chicken tap dancing.

"Enjoy the rest of your evening, Gus."

"I always do, Chet, I always do."

The timing of my recent troubles couldn't have been any worse. There were certain windows of opportunity in which to sell wine and liquor, and the last rays of hope for making any summer wine lists were by now growing dim. Most restaurant managers were well into coasting on their set choices and would rather not even look at a single winery rep until after Labor Day. Unless you had an "in," you were simply not welcome. Nevertheless, the boss had me back on the southern shores of Long Island hoping for any midseason adjustments that might be there for the taking.

While actual sales during this time of year proved to be hard enough, the powers that be felt it necessary to add insult to injury. Traffic on the Island—which had escalated to Absolute Gridlock Status—was one of the chief reasons, as the already harrowing morning rush was now melding with the vaunted summer beach crowd. There was no more helpless feeling for a man of the road than to be at the mercy of a congested traffic route. You start playing mind games with the clock and the surrounding landmarks, saying things to yourself like, "If I can get to that third light pole by 8:20 I can still make it." After an optimistic hour or so of this, your awareness of the problem and expectations of its defeat fizzle amid a sinking feeling of despair. And then you just go blank. Although I found this to be a much calmer (if not psychotic) stage of stress, the results were not always so friendly. My Jeep experienced this firsthand one morning, when in a tired state of frustration, I zoned out and rammed the front end of it into a produce truck, snapping off both fog lights and denting the grill.

Other reasons were often something entirely different. Not as torturous or costly by any means, but in many ways even more nauseating.

One event in particular occurred on the very same morning as the accident. Due to the traffic delay, I didn't have the opportunity to assess the damage immediately, and was racing the final stretch of the way to be on time to meet a salesman in Suffolk County. The commuter parking lot I was instructed to be at was right off the expressway, on the north side of the exit overpass. The salesman told me he would be driving his wife's red Fiat and would be parked in the south-west end. But as I entered the lot and made my way over there, I saw no sign of him. When I called to see if I was at the right place, he told me I was, but added that he'd strangely been in a minor accident himself and would be running a bit late.

"Not a problem," I said, tilting my seat back. "I'll be here getting my materials together. Tan Jeep. See you then."

At the time, I felt relieved. Coincidence had finally worked out in my favor. What happened next, though, was something that would no doubt scar my view of the average, seemingly peaceful parking lot forever.

The initial signs of confusion arose as I was listening to some sports radio and feeling a bit sleepy. Staring off out of my driver side window, I began to notice the same four or five cars circling around the area. At first I really didn't think much of it, but as it went on, I became curious. What I found strange was that they weren't moving in any set pattern or speed, like a procession or race of some kind, but more like they were having trouble finding a spot. Which didn't make any sense. There were plenty of open spaces. Maybe, I thought, they were just looking to meet up with someone for work, like I was. Could be. I've certainly had to do that from time to time. But after about fifteen minutes, it didn't let up. As they continued to circle, I grew more and more suspicious. Something didn't feel right.

Just as I was about to start up my car and move to another spot, a black truck pulled up and rolled down its window.

"How's it goin?" a man said. Bald with a graying moustache, I'd put his age in the late forties.

"Fine."

"What's your name?"

Puzzled, I became a bit defensive.

"What? *What's your fucking name?*"

The man laughed and asked if everything was all right. I looked around and couldn't understand what he was getting at.

"Do you know what's going on here?" he said.

"What's going on here? No. I'm just waiting to meet a guy for work."

He smiled and slowly pulled away. I sat there for another few minutes, watching him circle around the lot once more. For a second I thought he might be an undercover cop and quickly looked around for any loose seeds or empty baggies.

Coming up to my driver side, he again rolled his window down.

"You really don't know what's going on here, do you?"

"No. I don't."

"Wanna know why you see all these cars driving around you?"

"Not really."

"Blow jobs, man. You're fresh young meat."

Disgusted, I cringed in disbelief.

"You interested?" he said.

I couldn't believe what I was hearing. Gazing out into the lot, I realized I was watching a group of lions stalking their prey. A sight of sheer perverted carnivores foaming at the mouth. My blood boiled at the thought.

"Dude, are you serious?" I snapped. *"Get the fuck away from me before I put your face through this asphalt."*

He casually laughed and told me he had to ask.

"Have a nice day," he added, with an extra touch of femininity, smiling as his tinted window rolled back up past his beady little eyes.

By the time the salesman showed up twenty minutes later, wondering why I was parked at a gas station a mile down the road, I had already polished off a full bottle of Merlot and was testing my eardrum capabilities listening to some early Iron Maiden, trying my hardest to put the experience behind me. I thought about telling him what happened, but couldn't, for fear that he too was partaking in this disgusting activity. The buzz that I gained from the bottle only momentarily lifted my spirits, and by lunchtime, I was so drunk that I could barely say Cabernet Sauvignon without slurring.

I somehow managed to get through the day, not selling a single bottle, and spent the rest of the night in the hotel bar playing Chinese checkers with an old man in a cowboy hat.

I had to move on despite this uncomfortable stain on my memory. But the amount of people that seemed to be getting in the way was growing rapidly in every direction. In addition to the endless mess of cars cramming every inch of highway, this time of year also turned out to be some kind of convention season—meaning the traffic problem had now moved *indoors* as well. The lobby of every hotel in the morning began to look like the entrance to a sold-out, general admission concert hall before they let the doors open. Shoulder-to-shoulder madness of the corporate variety. This unfortunately had the lines to get to the breakfast buffet typically backed up all the way into the registration area and out the side door exit. Due to a mixture of bad timing and lack of motivation to go elsewhere, I was continually forced to settle for the less desirable "iced tea and a package of crackers and cheese" meal out of the vending machine.

And it was because of these crowds that I had also begun to wait outside in the parking lot for the salesmen I was meeting. The scene in the lobby was too much to deal with, as it was clear that there were a horde of other people just like me, waiting to meet some stranger for work. My attempts early on to find a seat on one of the chairs and couches near the air-conditioned entrance ways were akin to being in a lineup down at the police station. The wandering eyes of anxious salesmen looked me up and down, curious if I could be the person they were supposed to meet at nine o'clock in the south side of the lobby. I tried desperately to avoid eye contact. I knew I could get away with a quick glance, but any hesitant stare or, god forbid, a double take, and I'd have a suit and tie at my feet in seconds.

Inexperience in these types of situations confirmed this. One guy even came up to me a second time, wanting to know if I was positive that I wasn't somebody named Dick Wilson.

The migration of salesmen and winery reps in these parts spilled heavily out among the streets and into the wine shops as well. Each place I went was three or four deep with other salesmen waiting to taste their wines with the manager. They were everywhere, glancing at their watches impatiently, lurking around the wine racks, and looking for their products like a pigeon bobs its head looking for food. Most of the time it didn't make sense to leave and come back; I'd merely wind up in another line someplace else, so I just had to be patient and wait it out.

The better of the lot made the most of this occupational imprisonment, whether it meant inspecting each bottle to make sure they weren't dusty (a customer might think it had been there for a while and no one was buying it) or seeing that they were displayed properly (labels facing straight and in the best available space, hopefully eye level). After checking voice messages and calling on a plethora of various accounts, there was always the possibility of a few friendly minutes of chitchat among the other salesmen: who's buying out whom, rumors on any new accounts, were things slowing down or picking up—that type of thing.

Maybe it had something to do with always having to follow a mob of other people, but I couldn't get anything done in these conditions. Before I even introduced myself, the managers were rubbing their foreheads and pleading with me to go away. "Please, no … Not another round of this. I have no room. Where would I even put it?" Through it all I had to put on the act and try to get them to see the light that was Bunglewood Vineyards. The dedication to selecting from only the finest regions, the various methods of refinement, the textures and nuances of a wine that tasted like it was worth twice the price. Rarely, if ever, did this even remotely spark any interest. At one place, in fact, the manager actually fell asleep during my routine. At first I thought he was just momentarily resting his head on his arms, but after five minutes or so it was apparent that this meeting was over.

"I think he fell asleep. Should we wake him?"

"Oh, forget it. Let's just go," the salesman I was working with said in disgust. "How the hell you got some of these guys to buy this shit in the first place is beyond me." He stomped out the door and immediately got on his phone, leaving me to gather and re-cork my bottles in embarrassment, as a few of the delivery boys peeking out of the back storage room tried valiantly to hold back laughter.

Now, I could go on forever citing shameful excuse after shameful excuse, but the root of this summer's steady decline into the red had to do with something much more plain and simple: blunt disinterest. There were days when I didn't even take the bottles out of my bag, never mind open and pour them.

On average, I would estimate that a half-dozen account managers per day told me that my wine wasn't worth the time to even *look* at. Right. I mean, it was nice that they were honest and all, but gimme a break. I wasn't claiming it was the greatest beverage known to man here; I was just trying to do my job. To make matters worse, the salesmen I'd been working with offered no help in combating this problem. Most were so unmotivated themselves in showing any interest in my small brand that I often got the feeling they were just going through the motions to satisfy their own job obligations. Their efforts basically amounted to being chauffeurs to and from each account. Once we got inside the place, they'd just stand toward the back fiddling with their various handheld computerized gadgets, not saying a word, and in many cases *pretending* to look busy. I know this to be true, because on several of these occasions I happened to catch some of these guys playing video games on the damn things. I never said anything about it, partly because I didn't care, but mainly because I'd probably be doing the same thing if I could.

Other times I'd simply gotten stuck with the bottom rung of the sales force—those rare individuals who possessed no social skills, no business etiquette, and no work ethic, yet were somehow able to hang on to their jobs long enough to get to spend a profoundly useless day with me. Take this one guy Herb, for example. Chubby with a shaved head and a black goatee, Herb had nothing to offer in terms of sales production, and repeatedly complained that it "was just too hot to do anything in this heat." He also had this annoying habit of talking over a question he just asked you.

"What kind of watch is that?"

"I think it's a—"

"Mine's from Italy. Got it last summer from a friend who lives in Naples. Have you been?"

"Actually I've never—"

"I go every summer. You really can't beat the food. Even the paninis in the airport are better than anything you can find here. You married?"

"No. My last girlfriend and I—"

"Yeah, me neither. Here's a picture of the chick I'm dating, though. Isn't she hot? Fucking model, bro."

In the car his voice grew even louder, due to the German techno music he had on at full blast. I had to close my eyes at one point because the bass nearly shook my contacts out.

"*Isn't this the shit?*"

"I'm not—"

"Oh, oh. This is my favorite part! *Listen!*"

"Yeah, well—"

"Don't tell me you listen to that geezer rock and roll nonsense?"

"I listen to a lot of—"

"Fuck that shit. No, Chet, *look at me.* Fuck that shit."

At lunch he had with him a bag of what must have been seventy-five vitamins. Although his rotund appearance looked to be anything but fit, he spoke volumes about maintaining his health. Flax seed oil for healthy cell membranes, ginger root to help lower cholesterol, Ginkgo biloba to increase blood flow, and so on. He followed this by ordering a bacon cheese steak with a side of gravy fries. When his food came, he politely asked for me to not talk to him so he could properly digest it in a timely procedure.

"It's a method I learned from my dietary specialist. You'd be surprised how many people cannot chew correctly."

Up to that point I hadn't been able to put forth much into the conversation anyway, so I sat back and let him eat. I spent most of lunch staring around the room at the various tables full of businessmen, all having separate barbaric conversations on their cell phones. Besides an elderly lady seated at the table next to us, no one else seemed to mind. I watched her as she gently placed her fork down and slowly turned to look at the guy behind her practically yelling into his phone.

"YEAH, THE HARRIS DEAL LOOKS GOOD. I'LL LET YOU KNOW THE SECOND IT HAPPENS."

She appeared altogether puzzled, pained, and frustrated. "I can't hear myself think ..." she mumbled.

"THOSE ASSHOLES DON'T KNOW A GOOD TIME FROM A HOLE IN THE GROUND! HAHAHAHA! HEY, LISTEN, LET'S MEET FOR LUNCH NEXT WEEK. YEAH. I'M WITH DENNIS RIGHT NOW. YEAH. HE'S A GREAT GUY. I'LL TELL HIM YOU SAID SO."

Her face cringed. I swear you could just see the years drip out of her by the second. What a depressing social scene, I thought. A perfect time capsule to show how ridiculous we looked at the turn of the century.

"That chicken you're eating isn't free range you know," Herb blurted toward the end of the meal.

"What?"

"Your chicken wasn't raised in a natural method that helps rid it of disease. God knows what they did to that poor thing."

"Dude, I thought we weren't talking. Wait a second ... *What about that bacon on your—*"

"Let it go, Chet. Let it go."

"Let what go?"

"This inner tension you're displaying. It's not good to get angry while your body is trying to digest. Of all things, especially that filthy bird on your plate."

After lunch, Herb announced he was feeling a bit tired and needed to "recharge." While he was taking a nap in the car for a half-hour, I was getting lectured by a French chef on how each of my wines failed on several levels to do justice to his culinary creations.

"This Cabernet is too weak, too feeble in structure to possibly work with anything like my Steak Au Poivre. A dish like this needs something that can stand up to it, not cower and run away—which is what this wine does. We do not serve hot dogs here, or were you not aware of that? And where is this Bunglewood winery anyway? Never heard of it. If I don't know it, how do I know my customers know it?"

As much as I would have liked to argue, what can I say, the guy was completely right. We only hit two other places: a small, Turkish restaurant that didn't have a liquor license, and an Italian bistro run by two gay brothers. When I walked back outside after the latter, Herb was gone. I immediately called him on his cell phone. He told me he was down the street getting his oil changed.

"Did Antonio buy anything?" he asked.

"No."

"I didn't think so. He hates California wine."

And so that was my day with Herb.

15. The Downfall of Outdoor Entertainment in America

"You think I still got one of those rotator dial phones, don't ya?" I didn't have to dig deep to realize that Gus wasn't a fanatic of modern electronics (or culture for that matter), but every once in a while it just came up, usually due to the incessant ringing of my cell phone.

"I'm not saying that, I—"

"Ahh, I'm just joking with ya. You know, I never had any problem with technology. I'm serious, Chet. I don't have a cell phone because I don't need one. You know? If I did, for work or whatever, I probably would. It's the trends that I never understood."

"Trends?"

"Yeah, like I remember when all the kids had spiked hair or some of those black fellows with the big afros. Now I had no problem with the actual look. It's the 'lemmings of the sea' thing I didn't like."

"What do you mean, 'lemmings of the sea' thing?"

"You know, the rodents."

"Yeah, I know what they are, Gus. But what's your point?"

He cracked open a fresh beer out of a small cooler to his right and handed me one.

"Well, I may not be the most original person in the world, but I'm me. I listen to Waylon Jennings, I like chocolate ice cream with blueberries, I keep my hair short, work in construction, you know ... whatever."

"Okay."

"So, why would I want to change all that to be like someone else? You know what I mean?"

"I understand what you're getting at, but what's wrong with changing with the current styles? Can't you continue to evolve with the times and all that?"

Wiping his forehead on his sleeve and picking up his cigarette that sat on the edge of the steps, he looked out into the street, seemingly in deep thought.

"Yeah ... I guess you have a point there," he said. I took a sip off my · beer and didn't say anything else.

"I tell you what, though," Gus said, breaking the silence a few moments later, "I got a feeling a lot of folks out there are doing things just because everyone else is. And I'm not just talking about haircuts or whatever."

"I don't doubt that at all."

"Well ... maybe that's what I meant to say, then."

"The death of originality?"

"No. I think we still got plenty of that."

"What then?"

Gus paused and took a drag off his smoke.

"The rise of persuasion," he said, "and the return of standardized living."

By mid-July there was no sign of improvement in sight. These exhausting days spent bogged down in traffic and working the streets were at least offset by a handful of various events, the first being the annual East End tasting in Westhampton Beach. The well-publicized affair was one of the most ritzy around, but as far as those of us who had to work it were concerned, it was also one of the most annoying. A collection of pure American high life. Pretentious young girls born into unconditional wealth teasing us with skimpy summer dresses and newly-developed curves, while Daddy walked around with his slicked back hair, deep orange tan, and shimmering gold watch, waiting for someone to notice his girl-friend's new tits. The shit gets old real quick.

The tasting was being held at a first-class tennis and racquet club overlooking the beach. Besides attracting a strong percentage of the rich socialite crowd that was gearing up for the second half of the summer, retailers and restaurateurs from the area would be there as well, looking for any late replacements to their summer inventory and all-important wine lists. Some other brand's failure was your only hope at this point. In the way that a baseball manager had to pull a certain player out of the starting lineup for not performing well, so it went with the wines. Either you had the chance to come in as a pinch-hitter and save the day, or you were simply left waiting on the bench until fall.

Apart from the business prospects, it was a beautiful early after-noon, and with the unobstructed sun beaming down hard it gave a soft, bright glow to the old white building. Before heading inside I took a stroll down to the beach and sat for a few minutes in the sand. A gentle breeze came through, rippling the water and ringing a chain on a nearby flagpole. Looking out into the distance, there wasn't another soul on the beach. Only a small gathering of seagulls and an endless row of monstrous houses. I found it a bit odd. For such a nice day, I would have figured to see somebody, a few tod-dlers with their mom, maybe, or an old couple walking along the water's edge. My guess was the UV index was too high, or there was some rumored high-bacteria scare. Possibly even a high-profile court case on television. I don't know … it seemed people would do anything these days to discourage a good time.

I walked back up to the building. Entering through an ornate glass doorway, the first person I saw was Tommy, whom I hadn't seen since the big New York tasting. He was sitting with a couple of club workers, all dressed head to toe in white, and playing cards. Looking up from his chair, he smiled and motioned for me to hold on a second. Calling on the last round of betting, he won the pot, holding two pair, Kings and Aces. "Nice playing with you boys, but it's time to earn my real paycheck," he said, standing up and slapping my hand.

We exchanged a few "how ya doin's" and went to the head table to get our name tags and table assignments. Although he was nicely dressed in a blue seersucker jacket and tan slacks, Tommy's face looked like he'd just left a week long bachelor party. Besides the pale complexion and heavy bags under his eyes, he was also rambling on and on about some television set the distributor owed him. Apparently he'd won it as part of an incentive plan last year, and his old company had yet to deliver it. As he was delving into the details, the two ladies at the desk were just staring at him, arms folded, while a line of impatient salesmen steadily built up behind us.

After a few minutes of this, one of the ladies finally interrupted him.

"Excuse me, sir. Can I help you? There are other people waiting."

Tommy turned in mid-sentence and excitedly yelled, "Tommy Jackson! Oregon! Parker Estates!" As if this outburst had never happened, he turned back to me and continued on about the television.

Somehow we ended up being next to each other in the far corner, underneath a banner that read "American Wineries." As we made our way up a flight of stairs to the main room, I looked back at the table of workers still playing cards.

"How long have you been here?" I asked.

"Since last night. I met one of those guys here last year. It wound up that we both went to the same college and all that. He has a place right on the water with his girlfriend, so I crashed there."

"How much did you win?"

"A few bucks. Enough to compensate for this." Reaching into his coat pocket, he pulled out a small baggy and flung it at me. It miraculously happened to land directly into my empty wine glass. I inspected it discreetly.

"Is this cocaine?"

"Nothing but the good stuff out here," Tommy grinned.

When we got to our tables, he popped open one of his sample bottles and poured himself a full glass. Things were about to get interesting.

Now, I'd done about 95 percent of these tastings drunk and about half of them stoned, but this was the first I'd done on the white. It was quite easy, actually. Underneath the long tablecloths, Tommy cut up a half dozen lines at a time on top of an empty box. Whenever there was a break in the action, or we simply felt the need for refueling, we'd just duck under the table like we were grabbing a bottle of wine. By the end of the first hour my brain was working at enormous speeds, but my hands were shaking. Under these conditions I could spit out information about the wine in striking accuracy and pace, but my pouring was substandard; many times I missed the consumer's entire glass.

The attention to detail must have been impressive though, considering that even the snobs weren't getting angry at my sloppiness of hand. Because of my intensely high spirits I was also able to somehow tolerate anything these swanky posers threw at me. The conceited attitudes of the restaurateur who had everything but found it necessary to demoralize my product just for the sake of conversation. No problem. The drunken heiress laughing that I'd never been to some private club in Prague before. No problem. The golden boy from UCLA who made a loud comment about my stained slacks to his yachting buddies. No problem. The only thing that was somewhat difficult to endure was the plentiful sight of female skin, mainly in the breast area. As hard as I tried, I just couldn't seem to look any of these women in the eye. It was like a magnet: my eyes just kept sinking downward. Well, either I was too fucked up, or they enjoyed the attention, because I didn't hear one complaint.

The day progressed more or less in this manner. Somewhere in the middle of all of this, I even came face-to-face with the vice president of our distributor. He had been waiting by the side of the table giving me strange looks while I took care of a few consumers. At this point the nonstop mental tempo of my presentation had me looking like I had just finished a marathon. I was sweating bullets, my hair was going in ten different directions, my jacket was off, and my sleeves were rolled up past my elbow. But I felt fantastic.

"Those were some amazing numbers from you guys this spring," he said, extending his hand. "Congratulations on the turnaround."

I shook his hand and smiled nervously, trying to gather my thoughts.

"I haven't seen the reports yet, but how do things look so far this summer?"

"Not good." I blurted out. "Well, I don't know, it's still too early to tell. I guess we'll see what happens. Things will pick up. I'm not worried. It's summer, you know, people aren't drinking much red. It's too hot for big wines. Have you been out here much? It's absolutely beautiful. Yeah, I've definitely got a good feeling about the rest of the summer. I haven't actually seen the numbers. Have you? No, you just said you haven't. Yeah, I'm not worried. It's gonna be fine. We just have to stay focused, that's all. So, uh, yeah, things look great."

Eek.

Just then some lady's bag swung around and accidentally knocked over a row of empty bottles I'd left on the edge of the table. They shattered on impact, sending shards of glass scurrying across the floor.

"Why didn't you take those away?" she screamed, trying to push the blame on me. "Look how unorganized and filthy your whole table is! You city people have no concept of decency!"

"*City* people?" I asked. "What are you talking about?"

She looked disgusted. Putting her hands on her hips and rolling her eyes, she huffed, "What, do you think that dumb accent of yours is from Ohio?"

"I'm from New Jersey."

A gasp came from the crowd as they all turned to look. The VP smiled and excused himself over to the next table. "Mr. Jackson! *How are ya, bud?*"

As the tasting drew to a close, Tommy wanted to continue partying, but I could hardly put one foot in front of the other. The never-ending glasses of wine that I'd poured myself throughout the day had started to kick in. The only logical thing for me to do was to go down to the beach and chill out for a while.

Tommy told me to give him a call later on, that there might be some people hanging out at his buddies' house or something. I told him I would, but at that moment, we both knew I was done.

Stumbling my way onto the beach, there was only one person in sight: an old lady with big wraparound sunglasses on, sitting motionless in a folding chair. My heart was pumping wildly, but the rest of my physical makeup was fading by the second. Before I lost total control of all bodily functions, I was able to shed most of my clothes and crumple up into a ball in the sand. Which is where I lay, staring like a beached whale into the ocean as the sun began to slowly disappear behind me.

After having slept practically naked in my car, in the parking lot of a grocery store (the cops once again kicked me off the beach), I managed to make it up into one of the luxury boxes at Richmond County Bank Ballpark, home of the minor league Staten Island Yankees, the following evening. As part of a promotion, the boss had set up a "night out" for a collection of our top buyers in the borough a few weeks back. Out of the twenty invited, a total of four had shown up.

The stadium was located right on the water with an impressive view of the Manhattan skyline across the New York Harbor. The box itself came equipped with everything one would need for a night of baseball: leather couches, a fully-stocked bar, a big-screen television, and a full spread of finger food. Shrimp cocktails, chicken wings, mini club sandwiches, hotdogs, hamburgers, chips, dip … the whole nine yards.

Our invitation encouraged the buyers to bring their families, so while they were silently moping on the couch, a half-dozen little kids were tearing the place apart, looking for something to do. Of course, there was an actual real live baseball game being played, but the kids showed minimal interest. Within minutes they were asking the hostess if the television was setup for a video game system. Their request was met with some initial trepidation, but by the second inning a Playstation was brought in by one of the security guards, who hooked it up on the agreement that he got first dibs on playing. The only complaint came from one of the fathers, who wanted to watch some reality show at eight, citing that he hadn't missed an episode in three years. He was outvoted three to one, and immediately called his wife in disgust to ask her to record it.

This rare gathering of store owners outside a business setting was a bit awkward at first. I'm not quite sure they remembered how to act like normal human beings and have simple friendly conversation. It was a bizarre environment to say the least; sort of like a bunch of shy, new kids standing around on their first day of grade school. My attempt to talk sports with them, hoping it would trigger a common spark, died almost instantly. To be fair, one of the guys did get halfway through a story about Willie Mays, but somewhere along the line, he lost focus and faded off into a quiet mumble. The others looked at him in nervous fear that they were next, so I quickly tried to shift gears and point out a few attractive ladies in the crowd. Based on their uncertain reactions, they weren't really following along with that either.

After a few minutes of minor success talking about where they'd all grown up, the room once again became a scene of blank emotion, pocketed hands, and unspoken tension.

"You fellas see that new Spielberg movie?"

A few head shakes.

"The war scenes are supposed to be incredible. Do you watch many action movies?"

A random blink, maybe a shoulder shrug.

"How about porno?"

Nothing.

Another twenty minutes passed before anyone said a single word. The situation was worse than I thought. This effort to try and speak like other humans simply wasn't panning out. It was torture. I literally couldn't come up with anything else to say.

I imagined they might be a bit more receptive, having distanced themselves from a work-like atmosphere, but the neutral setting, in effect, had no bearing on them. It appeared as though business *was* the only language these guys spoke. Their silence at least hinted that they wanted to break free of this, but their mental conditioning against it had already spread too far. And it was only at this point that I realized that their ability to leave work behind—even at the most American of entertainment pastimes, a baseball game—was beyond repair.

Deep down I had a feeling this might happen, but for some asinine reason I thought I might be able to help liberate these poor bastards. Sadly, it was not to be. Through their shifty eyes and suppressed expressions it was as if they were each praying for the other to bring up something work-related. Fortunately for them, that moment came sometime around the third inning, when one of the guys happened to pick up a beverage menu and made a brief comment about how poor the selection was. I couldn't be sure if this was planned, but the other three sensed the opportunity and immediately latched on with quick remarks. Within seconds they were busting through inventory shortages, distribution comparisons, and corporate buyouts. This left me in a position to be dumped by the wayside. No longer one of them, there came a point in the conversation where I was eventually tuned out, under suspicion that whatever they were talking about could be decoded by an outsider such as myself.

I spent the remainder of the game alone in an outdoor seating area that was connected to the box, slugging complimentary beer and wine among the rest of the fans at the half-filled stadium. The only other times I went inside were to grab another drink or pile some more wings on my plate, and even then the room would immediately grow quiet. Except, that is, for the sounds of dragon slaying and explosions coming from the video screen.

16. The Right Person for the Job

A depressing note to report came later that July. Citing that my expenses had actually overcome my monthly salary, the vineyard temporarily suspended my hotel privileges in lieu of the money owed. How it was possible that I actually owed them money was, without question, one of the strangest feelings I'd ever experienced on the job. Certainly, new heights in poor workmanship were being hit almost daily at this point, but this was one for the record books.

In a hungover state of denial, I spent a good two or three hours trying to figure it all out, backtracking over clumps of receipts and bills, and what I came up with was more or less what they claimed. Through a clogged mind of deflating self-confidence, I had indeed doubled over my monthly expenditure limit. The fact that I didn't see this coming was more a crime than anything, because in actuality, it had nothing to do with false calculations. I had merely stopped keeping track. It was foolish, I know. But at the time I was at the mercy of an exhausting work schedule that had taken full advantage of my brain, leaving no room for such menial tasks as bookkeeping, eating three square meals a day, or even showering on a daily basis. I just winged it, hoping everything would work out in the end. Well, it didn't ... So yeah, bad decision. Serving as a sad footnote to this whole situation were my latest sales numbers. Down 180 percent. It marked the first time since February that I was officially in the decline.

Shit. I didn't know what kept me from being fired, but I was beginning to think that this was some kind of sick experiment.

Whatever their reasoning may be behind such a slow execution, there was no sense worrying about it at this point. "Maybe the extra time on the road will do you some good," they told me, and maybe they were right. Unfortunately the five-hour drive out to Montauk that first day made me late for my first two appointments, and I had to go beg like a crack whore to get them to reschedule.

To further weaken morale, I got a rather distressing call from our distributor's office later that same afternoon. In short, I was informed that they had caught some suspicious activity going on in several different retail stores in Brooklyn. Apparently these guys were having such a hard time selling the product, they were doing whatever they could to get them out of the store—without losing money. This included switching the Bunglewood bottles into another brand's case box that had just been delivered, carefully resealing them, and quickly calling the distributor for a pick-up, claiming they were given the wrong item. The delivery guys never even thought to open the boxes, and promptly took away the hidden Bunglewood wines with them. Unbelievable.

The heat at this point also had me contemplating selling a bunch of stuff (guitar, some old Dead tapes, a signed photo of Sparky Lyle) in order to have an air-conditioning unit installed into my Jeep. I just couldn't take it anymore. On one particular occasion, half of the sample bottles I had stashed in the back seat had completely boiled over by the time I got to my first appointment. The Jeep must have acted like an oven, pushing the wine over the cork and collecting the liquid into a pile of gooey muck at the bottom of the case.

The drive only took me three and a half hours on that morning, but the humidity made it feel like weeks. It had to be damn near a hundred. You could literally hear the asphalt sizzle. I was constantly praying for any type of five-second stretch to get some breeze, but it was an absolute standstill the last two hours. The Verrazano Bridge was backed up all the way through Staten Island, and by the time I got out of the car I was soaked to the bone. It felt like I was draped in a wet tissue.

"Goddamn. You all right?" the salesman said upon meeting me outside a place called Liquor World. He was leaning on his back bumper, with a jaw-dropped look somewhere between horrified and disgusted.

I nodded slightly, slowly hobbled past him, and climbed into his car. I put the AC on full blast and placed my head directly on the vent.

"Give me a minute please … I think my brain is melting."

The seething temperature was a cherry on top of another long, unsuccessful day. I tried to break out my old lying routine, but these guys weren't buying it. They looked at me like I was speaking another language, which in most cases I probably was. I couldn't tell who spoke English anymore. Being ignored was universal. The only consolation came from the salesman I was working with, who was so wrapped up in telling me about the "old days" that he hardly had time to complain about my lack of production.

His name was Charlie Nunziato, and if there was one thing about Charlie that seemed immediately apparent, it was that the man shunned technology. With a toothpick forever dangling from his plump, mustachioed face, he went through near heart attack build up discussing his hatred for all things new and electronic. "So I tells the boss. If you's want me to have a cell phone, fuckin' buy me one!" he'd shout in a thick Brooklyn accent. "You'd think that after forty years in the business, I could get along without all these fuckin' gadgets beepin' and buzzin' every two fuckin' seconds." Every person that either cut him off on the highway, made him wait at a coffee shop, or charged him a penny over what it cost last week, set off a fury of ranting and raving about how things were going downhill in this country. He was a master of complaining. A true artist. His methods of tension and release as they partook to the one-sided conversation was something that I had only witnessed in some forms of jazz music.

The distributor must have had this guy down to a tee, because they gave him all the old school saloons and Italian restaurants in Brooklyn and Queens. Nearly every account was run by an old friend of his, as were most of the patrons that frequented them. Waddling his round body into the dimly lit rooms, he patted them all on the back and ordered a whiskey on the rocks, which was a necessity at every stop. In between this and topics such as "Jew broads," "Japs," and "Guess who died the other day," they would reminisce about simpler times: when you could get a gallon of gas for a nickel, and things like booze, cigarettes, and casual sex were all respected acts of the American culture. As for me, I just sat back, nodded my head, and on occasion added a small one word note of assurance that I too, was completely in agreement. I had no idea what half the shit he was talking about, and in no way did I feel like arguing. Let him have his Jew broads in peace.

One thing that I did learn from working with a guy like Charlie Nunziato was that it didn't really matter if you were a good salesman or not, just as long as you were in the right environment. If you substituted a gay Frenchman with all the business credentials in the world into his route or vice versa, the results would be disastrous. It'd be like planting a palm tree in Antarctica.

This idea was actually rather common in the wine and liquor business, and I saw several other examples of it, especially when it came to certain women. In case you hadn't guessed by now, this line of work was still by majority, male. I assumed this was due only to man's historically dominant consumption of alcohol (as well as with a certain machismo that went along with it), because under no circumstances was a single facet of this job any more difficult for a female. As a matter of fact, I'd been just as impressed, if not more so, with the days I'd spent with the growing number of women in the field. In general I found them to be better prepared, more courteous, and oftentimes much more optimistic. Yet in spite of this, it was quite clear that some of these ladies were benefiting in their assigned territories for other reasons. One such example came a few days after I worked with Charlie. Although my time working with this particular woman turned out to be awfully successful, a situation like this was a prime example of achieving high sales numbers *despite* a lack of actual business skills.

To put it simply, this young lady I worked with up in Ithaca talked a big game, but didn't know shit. And this is coming from someone who also didn't know shit, but knew enough shit when he had to. So let's get right down to it. My day with a Ms. Eva Laperierre began outside of her ivy-covered chateau in the cushy suburb of Cayuga Heights. Straightaway, everything about this woman seemed to exude upper class perfection. In fact, the first words out of her mouth were to apologize for her *three-year-old* BMW, which she pointed out "would have to do" until the new model arrived direct from Germany later this summer.

Dressed in a stylish, form-fitting women's black pant suit, she left just enough of the right buttons open to completely scramble any sort of game plan I might have wanted to convey. No doubt, Eva was extremely attractive. With long, wavy black hair; a fit, trim body; and the tanned face of a Brazilian swimsuit model; she definitely wouldn't have trouble finding work in the fashion world. Adding to this already dominating physical presence came a confidence and swagger that were absolutely staggering. Her aura alone seemed to render me insignificant. It was as if she might have been created in a lab.

As we made our way around the upstate area she spoke endlessly (in a pseudo-British accent) about how much respect she got and how much business she did, all backed up with a plethora of statistical examples and rags-to-riches stories. For the first hour or so, I just assumed she was every bit of the educated sales machine she claimed to be. But by the second or third stop, I caught on to something, and it quickly became clear how she worked her way into all this success.

In essence, her strict, no-nonsense way of talking to me in the car vanished the second we got inside an account. From that point on it was all pouty lips, hugs, and seductive teasing. She couldn't pronounce the name of the vineyard right, and I had to correct her at least ten times on the right prices and vintages. When it came time to actually taste the wines, her comments were often limited to descriptions like "yummy" and "super." To no surprise, this didn't seem to have any negative effect on the buyer. And why should it? There wasn't one place on her route that was run by a woman. Nope. Not even an asexual wine snob. All horny dudes, and all of them completely under her alluring spell, listening intently as she sidetracked into stories about her first time at a nude beach in Mallorca, or the time she dressed up as a leopard for Halloween, solely with body paint. Amazing. By the time the door closed on the way out, she was already back into business mode, ripping the poor guy she'd just seduced into buying ten cases of garbage wine.

Now, I could have cared less whether women used this to an advantage. To be honest, I was all for it if they had it—again, it was all relative to their environment—I just didn't want to hear that they were doing all this business because of any other reason. Seriously, what old slob or single young man wouldn't have loved seeing her on a daily basis instead of, say, some fat, balding guy named Ned who sweated too much and smelled like cabbage?

Sometime around her telling me that she was tired of her new clothes and that she wanted her boyfriend to move them into a bigger house by the lake, the boss called. I could barely hear him, he was screaming so loud.

"Who told you, you could just change your position?"

I assumed he finally saw a copy of my business card. I tried to blame it on the printmaker.

"I was only given a set number of titles … It seemed to me to be the most adequate. Is this a problem?"

"Is this *a problem*? You promoted yourself to Eastern Division Director of Sales!"

I played it cool and tried to make it seem like I didn't understand what he was getting at. After several minutes of this he finally calmed down.

"I'm sending you new ones; throw those out immediately. And I want a full report of the past week by Monday morning."

"Gotcha."

"How did the Staten Island thing go?"

"Fantastic."

"And the Westhampton Tasting?"

"Great people. We showed well."

"Mmm. All right. I guess that's it. Oh, who are you working with today?"

"Eva Laperierre"

"*Oh really*, I hear she's great. A friend of mine tells me she's one of the top salespeople in the state. Yeah, Eva Laperierre ... Huh ... How about that? Maybe I should take a trip out there sometime to work with her ... Late September or something. Can you ask her if she has any open days then? *Wait.* Don't do that. That's a little too forward, don't you think? Maybe I should call her myself or speak to her manager. Well ... uh ... all righty then. Hey, ah ... this is kind of funny, but just between you and me ... is she married yet, do you know? Hahahaha. I'm joking, of course ... But no, really, *is there a ring?*"

Ten forty-five the next morning. I woke up in an unfamiliar bed, sweating underneath a thick pink and orange comforter with flowers on it. My head was pounding and my mouth was dry. The room I was in had two twin-sized mattresses and was covered in Ithaca College garb. How I got wherever I was at that moment remained unclear.

There were no signs of anyone sleeping in the other bed, or anywhere else for that matter, as I peered out the bedroom door and into the living room, wearing nothing but a pair of New York Jets boxers. A TV set was on mute and CDs were strewn across the floor. Beer and tequila bottles covered an entire coffee table.

I hurriedly put on my clothes and tried to make sense of this. After bidding good-bye to the Miss America of sales, I had gone downtown to the Commons for a few drinks; I remember that much, but my recollection of any particular bars or girls was terribly cloudy. As I fumbled around getting my shoes on, I examined a portion of a wall covered in pictures. It was of the same two girls, neither of them looking at all familiar. Even more distressing was that they were polar opposites: one was rather slim and pretty with a huge rack, while the other was an absolute hog. Had I gotten lucky with a cute college chick on summer break, or had the beer goggles fatefully been strapped on in a fit of brief, drunken lust?

I didn't have time to think it over, and quickly got out of there. It was almost eleven o'clock and I had to be back down in Long Island, some 270 miles away, for another tasting at five.

As I searched the streets for my car, I pretended for confidence's sake that it was the cute blonde with the perky rack.

Well, I doubt blacking out in the middle of the workweek was beneficial in any way, but it did keep things interesting. At least for the time being. Still, there was no way to deny that the job at this point had taken on a different feel. Although I was still functioning on some sort of work mode, there was a sense of blind insensitivity that had crept into the equation. How long I could possibly continue to hold on without either a major breakdown or being fired was not even a concern anymore. It was like running a race with no finish line. I just kept going.

And yet, besides the paycheck and free booze, it all felt so meaningless. While my role as the observer documenting what lay deep within the structure of this job had no doubt revealed a lot, very little of it could convince me that I stood to gain anything here. I mean, my father and grandfather were both landscapers. At least they had something to show for themselves at the end of the day. A stone wall, a tree-lined park, whatever. In sales you got nothing but a list of numbers and a renewed hatred for human interaction. Which, for many, was perfectly fine. The paycheck was the only thing that really mattered, anyway. Whatever you had to do to get it was just accepted as part of life. In more ways than one, the idea these days that money will compensate (and validate) for a miserable existence appeared to be very real.

Going in and out of similar thoughts, I eventually found my car (it was parked outside a taco joint a few blocks away) and continued on the road through a collection of highways, bridges, and tolls en route to the tasting. All in all, the five-hour drive went smoothly, and I made it to the old store down near Massapequa, on the south-central part of the Island, in time. The manager was a quiet, timid fellow who doubled as the cashier and clerk, and wore blue-jean overalls on top of a plaid shirt and bow tie. He sat behind the register on a wooden stool the entire night, smiling and listening to some strange acid jazz that came out of two tiny speakers that had been attached to the wall with duct tape. Framed pictures of various jazz musicians and Las Vegas covered the remaining space from top to bottom. He told me Vegas was his favorite city in the world, and that it was one of the last places in the country where someone could really "stretch out and live." Interestingly enough, he also told me that he'd never been there.

"Someday," he said with a smile.

17. Shunned by the French, Shackled by the Elderly

"*Did the Yanks win? My antenna got ripped off over the weekend. They were up 2-1 when I lost reception.*" It was about eleven thirty at night, and I was just getting home from the tasting on the Island.

"*They lost,*" Gus said. "*Mussina fell apart in the eighth.*"

"*Shit. Red Sox win?*"

"*Yep.*"

"*Dammit.*"

I typically didn't see him up this late, only when the Yankees were playing out west. For a second I thought about having a smoke with him, but decided against it.

"*Well, I'm beat. See ya tomorrow, Gus.*"

"*See ya tomorrow.*"

As I was about to step through my front door, I paused for a moment, and turned back around.

"*Hey, Gus?*"

"*Yeah?*"

"*Does your job mean anything to you?*"

"*Yeah. It means I have to get up tomorrow morning.*"

"*Mmm, I see. Well ... Good night.*"

He tipped the bill of his dirty trucker's cap, and that was that. Sometimes his wisdom was a little tough to figure out.

Sitting down on my couch, I took off my shoes and slumped over on my side, clicking around the channels on the TV until I got to Sports-

Center. *I was drifting off to sleep rather quickly, but somewhere in between a report on a steroid hearing and a rape charge, I remembered it was garbage night. Damn, the couch felt good though. Creaking my body up, I grabbed the garbage bin out of the kitchen, scraped off the remaining food encrusted on the dishes piled up in my sink into the bag, and walked back outside.*

To my surprise, Gus was still out there.

"Almost forgot to put the trash out," I said, walking past him, and out to the curb. As I came back, he was sitting hunched over, looking off to the side, with his head propped up by his arm.

"What are you doin' up so late?" I asked.

Gus sat up straight and crossed his arms. "Just thinkin'," he said, with a slight frown. "My son was over last night."

"Oh yeah? What's new with him?"

He looked down for a second, then off to the side again. I got the immediate feeling he didn't want to talk about it. Picking up a small stone off the stoop, he glanced at it for a second, twisting it around in his hand, before chucking it into the street.

"Well, he's doing fine. You know, making a living and all that. I, uh … well … I just don't understand him sometimes, that's all."

I felt a bit awkward seeing him like this, not his usual confident self. "How so?" I asked cautiously.

"His attitude of late scares me a bit. I don't really get it, I guess." He paused for a second, as if he was struggling to find the right words. "Well … see, take last night for instance. His mother asks him if he'd like Chicken Cacciatore—his favorite—for dinner, and he just starts going into this long story about how he had the best Italian food at some fancy five-star place in Chicago last week. Mary just smiled, but I felt a little bad for her, you know? She lives to make her son a nice meal. So, anyway, a little bit later, I ask him if he caught the game the other night—Andy's two-hitter against Seattle—and he goes off into a whole string of stories about how many athletes and celebrities he's met in the city. Out in the bars and clubs or whatever. Ah … I don't know. It just goes on and on."

"I don't get it."

"Well, sometimes a simple question deserves a simple answer."

"Maybe he's just trying to impress you."

"There's a fine line between pride and vanity, Chet. And you don't just unknowingly accept the latter. That's a self-prescribed disease if you ask me. Sucks the soul right out of you."

I didn't say anything else as Gus continued to just look out into the street.

"What did you ask me before?" he said, a few moments later. "Does my job mean something to me?"

"Yeah."

"Well, I'll tell you what it means. It means I'm no better or worse than anyone else. I got a job, you got a job, so be it. Why this country glorifies one more than the other is beyond me."

"Do you think the money has an effect on your son, then?"

"Could be. Sure. But there's nothing wrong with making good money. Shoot, don't let anyone ever tell you different. Money solves a lot of problems, Chet. But I do think it also manipulates your natural intentions in life. Apparently it gets my son to forget how proud his mother is of her cooking. And celebrities and all that. Jesus. You know, when I was twelve I would've done just about anything to meet Mickey Mantle. But I was a kid, you know? If you're thirty-five and still acting like that, it just seems kinda sad to me. I mean, if you want to be a star, fine, you know ... be your own star. Practice singing or playing basketball. Whatever. But for Christ's sake, don't waste your time pretending to be one just because you can afford to rub shoulders with some B-list actor."

Gus stood up and arched his back, twisting to both sides. I followed him up.

"Ah, I don't know why I'm even talking about this. Sometimes I don't even make any sense to myself," he said, with his hands on his hips. "Just end up sounding like a cranky old man."

"No, I understand. Don't worry about it."

"Yeah? Well, all right. But just keep this between me and you. I don't need everyone in town mistaking me as the one chasing the Hollywood lifestyle," he said, laughing a bit to himself.

I smiled and walked back inside. Turning off the TV and getting ready for bed, I remember thinking that even Gus was aware—if not vulnerable—to the pressures of the outside world to be "somebody." In some way, I suppose, it made me feel good that I wasn't the only one. But like everything else going on in my life at the time, feeling "good" was only a temporary solution.

I was ten minutes late to meet a salesman named Francois the following week in the city, and he made such a scene that I nearly called it a day right there. Looking back, I probably should have. The fact of the matter was that I was actually a half-hour *early*, so I went around the corner to a music shop to listen to some new releases, and must have lost track of time. The second I arrived to meet him at some small café in midtown, he immediately shot up from his chair and began screaming at me in French from across the room. With his arms flailing in every direction, he looked like a monkey undergoing a seizure. In the midst of this bizarre fit of rage, he accidentally banged the table he was seated at and knocked over his little cup of vanilla chai tea, sending it shattering on the ground. It did nothing to disrupt his tirade, and he continued on for several minutes, dishing out a series of unrecognizable verbal attacks and random finger points.

The whole time this was happening I was standing there motionless, staring blankly at him. Mentally though, I was on the verge of laughter. In part because of this amusing tantrum that had gotten the entire café's attention, but mainly for these shiny black girlie shoes that he was wearing. They looked like big, pointy-toed ballroom slippers that would appear just as comfortable on a Barbie doll.

After he calmed down, and in broken English said he had to redo our whole schedule for the day due to my lack of punctuality, we hopped into his silver BMW and sped up Broadway. It's interesting to note that even though Francois was incessantly concerned about the time, he refused to take public transportation, and we spent about a half-hour outside each account, circling the block looking for parking spaces. When I questioned him on this later in the day, he snapped, "I didn't pay for this car to let it sit in my garage, just so I can take the subway with all the bums and whores."

Once we got inside, he offered me no help outside of a tired introduction, "Bonjour, Henri. This is Chet … He has some *California* wines," and spent most of the time laughing, presumably at me, with his countless French cronies in the far corners of each place, where they sat cross-legged and sipped tea.

Frankly, I don't even know why I was scheduled with this guy. He worked in the restaurant division of the distributor, a small sub-department that covered mainly four-star European bistros in the city—not necessarily the kind of places you'd find cheap American wine. The only thing I could think of was that our distributor had seen the decrease of my sales lately and decided to throw me a bone. Francois, on the other hand, probably saw it more as a slap in the face and was no doubt already tossing leads around to his connections, looking into a job elsewhere.

As we worked over both sides of Upper Manhattan, the clock—not Francois—seemed to be my worst enemy. The day was an absolute endurance test. One of those where you just had to suck it up and try to get through it. Everyplace we went I got nothing but bitching and moaning from the managers, telling me the same stories about how much work they had to do, how they didn't have any room for any new wines, how their back hurts, and why the prices coming from California were so high. Forget about giving me their attention; they barely had the common courtesy to look me in the eye for a single second. Francois' demoralizing attitude toward me was nothing compared to this. I could ignore him, but if I had any intentions of selling some wine, I had to try and at least give these guys the basic outline of the product. The results were excruciating, and anyone who had ever been in this type of situation would have agreed. Having to muster up the determination to humiliate yourself in front of someone who was angered by your presence and didn't even want to look at you was something that never came easy.

When put into such a miserable experience, it could be hard to concentrate on *anything*, and I had to catch myself from continually glancing down at my watch for fear that time was indeed rolling back. After one manager took a full bottle of my Merlot and threw it in the garbage to prove his point, I even resorted to the last line of mental dignity: the thought of "finding a happy place."

All the while, Francois seemed amused at my inability to sell anything, leaving each place with an assured grin that I had no idea what I was doing. "You are not having a very good day," he'd laugh. "You should tell your company to think about putting bottle caps on those wines."

Bottle caps. A totally degrading wine term far below screw-caps and plastic tops. The Bunglewood wines were not only unworthy of him, but in his view, unworthy of the tree used to produce the cork.

Dismissive remarks like this were the only time that he acknowledged my actual existence in private. His monotonously fluid phone conversations began and ended the instant we got out of the restaurants, give or take the few seconds it took him to light up another cigarette. The only thing that kept me going this whole time was the thought of crushing his skull in with a few steady blows to the face. The image of him squealing like a baby through a displaced nose and a shattered upper row of teeth calmed my nerves and made me feel good inside.

I guess you could say I'd found my happy place.

With the fantasy of unrelenting violence towards this man—as well as his snobby account managers—firmly in place, I managed to get through the day in one piece. In fact, by the end of it, Francois seemed in worse shape than I was. Constantly pounding the wheel, tapping at the clock in disgust, and mumbling about how much *other* work he had to do, his impatience and festering anger were indeed coming to a head. Although I felt completely drained and a bit antsy myself, I was in stable condition, and continued to merely pray for either a loose brick or a crowbar from the hands of a half-dozen Puerto Rican gangsters to come crashing through the driver side window.

"Sorry we could not sell any of your *California* wine," he said, pulling up to the Port Authority Bus Terminal, adding an air of pure arrogance to the word "California." "Maybe next time."

I grabbed my bag out of his trunk (he wouldn't let me keep it in the back seat), promptly gave him the finger, and spit in the general direction of his precious car. Probably not the best way to gain support for the product, but sometimes you had to find ways to keep your head up.

I heard him yell back something in French, but I couldn't speak French so, well, I guess that's all I have to say about that.

My frustration with salesmen continued to be especially hard to shake this particular week. So bad in fact that at three o'clock that Friday, I faked having food poisoning and went as far as sticking my finger down my throat in order to puke on a stack of rum cases inside a wine shop on Avenue B.

Ernest Poloski was his name, and he had to be the oldest guy in the business. If I would guess, I'd put him at close to ninety years old. A short, bald fellow with ruddy features, he walked with a severe limp, and was horribly hunched over on top of it. If that wasn't enough, he also had the worst memory and sales pitch to boot. A classic '50s dialogue spoken through the frail, cracking voice of an aging grandfather. Think an *older* Jack Lemmon in *Glengarry Glen Ross*.

I met Ernest at a small coffee shop in the Upper East Side, around the corner from where he lived. The first thing he told me was that his dog had given him a bad case of diarrhea. I didn't know what to make of this, much less what to tell him in response.

"Well then. Ah ... You gonna be able to work today or ..."

"Oh, you betcha. I'm ready to sell Rumblewood all—"

"*Bungle*wood."

"Yes, sir. Bunglewood. Oh, you betcha."

Hobbling down Second Avenue at our snail-like pace, we made it to the first stop at eleven and were promptly thrown out.

"I told you not to bring in any winery reps without calling first!" the manager screamed the second we got in.

"Oh. I didn't call? Well, let me at least introduce you to this fine young man—"

"Good-bye, Ernest!" the man screamed, looking down at his desk.

"Heh heh. This will only take a minute. Like I was saying—"

"*Good-bye, Ernest!*"

"Yes, of course. Well, I'll call you later in the week, then."

The man didn't respond, and we were soon back out on the street. Ernest was squinting in confusion, with his hands on his hips, looking in both directions.

"Is everything okay?"

He didn't say anything.

"*Ernest.* Is everything okay?"

Putting his hand on his chin he mentioned that he thought the next account was right across the street, but all that was there was a pizza place and a shoe store. It was around this time that he also began calling me "Ron" for some reason.

Our experiences at the next few places were equally disheartening. One had an electrical door lock which left Ernest banging on it and cupping his hands around the front window, shouting, "Vinny! Let me in! I want you to meet somebody!" The guys inside ignored him like he was just another bum on the street asking for spare change. The other place was boarded up with a "For Sale" sign on it. "What do ya know about that? This was a nice store, I wonder what happened?" he said, staring at it for several minutes. "There used to be this big barrel out front, and they had one of those old-fashioned ice boxes ..."

At lunch he ordered a bacon, egg and pepper sandwich, and must have had six cups of black coffee. Every now and then he would look up at me, smile, and ask if the food was all right, while he continually rummaged through a pile of notes that he had stashed in an old brown leather satchel. When I asked him politely about his heap of papers, he complained that he didn't like those new electronic devices and said he was forced to even get a cell phone by the company. "There's just no privacy anymore," he sighed. Indeed. His phone rang at an abnormally loud level. Ernest just shook his head looking at the thing. "Isn't that awful? I don't even know how to adjust it."

We took the subway downtown after lunch and had no luck. The "little Italian place with the best homemade meat sauce" wouldn't see us because Ernest got the date wrong and was supposed to have been there the day before. "We waited two fucking hours for you," the manager snarled, leaving Ernest scratching his head and going through one of his notebooks.

"I have it down here as the fifth. Well, what is today ... hmm, yes. I guess you're right. Heh heh. Well now, let me at least introduce you to—"

"Good-bye, Ernest!"

The next three places were all in the East Village, and all of them refused to speak to us. We were told that the managers were either not there or that they were too busy. Ernest simply smiled and walked out, sometimes just introducing me to one or two of the Hispanic delivery boys.

At around three o'clock, I made the decision to put this day to rest. With my stomach still feeling as round as a beach ball from the massive chicken parmesan sandwich I had devoured at lunch, I proceeded to force myself to vomit in the back corner of Bee Liquors while Ernest was trying to explain a wrong order he had placed last week. It was my only way out. I just couldn't bear telling this man the truth: that I could no longer endure his confusion and the anger it brought out in these people as a result.

I felt bad for the old guy, taking abuse from everyone. And although I dreaded the idea of someday ending up like him, I have to say he was still the most honest person in the business that I'd ever met. So, in a sense, I liked to think my premeditated vomiting was an act of respect for an old timer, whose mind could no longer keep up with his heart.

Well, maybe not. But it sounds better that way.

18. Manhattan Meltdown

O ver time I had developed a sort of love-hate feeling in regards to summertime in the city. On one hand, I certainly admired its plentiful attractions of all things immediately accessible to those who could actually afford them. The alluring aromas of every type of food imaginable blowing out of the swaying front doors of each air-conditioned restaurant; the never-ending rows of bars and outdoor cafés filled with carefree, sun-soaked day drinkers; and, of course, the abundance of hip, beautiful women in their short skirts and summer dresses. It was enough to make a single, barely-making-rent man in his late twenties dream of better days ahead.

On the other hand, the scorching August heat meant that the city's most unattractive sights and smells were also amplified. The concrete that you saw frying an egg on the evening news also fried dog shit, week-old garbage, cigar butts, and those strange lime green puddles that seemed to pop up everywhere. In certain parts of the city, the stench was unavoidable, namely down in some of the more ancient subway platforms, where the heat was so suffocating that the walls literally dripped with sweat and grime. The trapped smell of urine didn't help, either. It seeped into your pores and burned your eyelids. Well, not really, but the mind can play tricks on you in such wretched conditions. All it took was a simple delay on the line to signal an inner panic that could result in a steady increase of body temperature and overall paranoia—whether you were trained in the ways of achieving inner peace or not.

And while the influx of tourists became rather annoying and in the way, it was everyone's favorite, the bums, who turned the city especially foul this time of year. Back in town at full force, the summer signaled the end of their excursions elsewhere, leaving them full of hope for the upcoming begging season. Although I got bad looks from an increasingly staunch opposition, at the end of the day I usually gave away an unfinished sample bottle and a few smokes to some of the regulars. So what. Nine times out of ten, these people would rather have that than a cup of tap water and a half-eaten bag of potato chips.

"Goddamn, you look like shit," Mike said. "What the hell happened to you?" I was downtown in SoHo at my old high school buddy's restaurant/lounge/bar, looking for a place to cool down and clear my head. I'd just spent the last hour in a bulletproof store in the Bronx waiting for a manager to show up, just to find out he'd quit two days earlier. Prior to that I'd accidentally knocked over a case stack of wine—breaking seven bottles at $12 a pop—and somehow got my bag stuck in a subway turnstile, quickly sending a line of impatient rush-hour travelers into a unified rage. I needed to see a recognizable face. Ironically enough, it was mine which was hardly that.

When I arrived, the cute hostess at the front didn't distinguish me from our previous meeting and, once again, gave me a considerable dose of attitude when I asked to speak to Mike. This time I don't blame her. Over the past month, not only had I shed my standard business attire, but I'd also grown a substantial beard and gained about fifteen pounds due to a strict diet of garlic buttered noodles. They were all I could afford. In addition to suspending my hotel expenses, the vineyard had also limited my restaurant expenses to compensate solely for entertaining important guests, claiming that it had always been company policy for all area representatives to pay for their own private meals on the road. Seeing as how I basically lived off my expenses, the decision had forced me to retreat back to alternative methods of finding ways to eat, hence the all-carb college diet that I had bought in bulk.

The first few days of this started off fine. By keeping the garlic-to-butter ratio at an even balance, I was able to enjoy a rather hearty meal, considering the fact that it barely cost me a penny. As the days went on, though, my taste buds began to whine for something different. I remember that first night of panic, scouring my cupboards in desperate hope of coming across anything else to work with. The results were disappointing. Mostly what I found was some sort of basic food additive: sugar, pepper, an unopened bag of flour, Old Bay crab seasoning, etc. The fridge was more of the same: some mustard; a bag of lemons; a half-used, year-old jar of salsa; and a few plastic containers of food that were tucked away toward the back and in some strange sort of cocoon phase. No liquids whatsoever. I hadn't bought a non-alcoholic beverage in probably three years and lived on one of those filtered water containers. It was the first thing I got when I moved out of my parent's house. Seven years later, the apartment only had a CD rack and a tin Anchor Steam beer sign as further additions.

To go along with the added girth, my once short and neat hair style had also been replaced with a more, let's say, shaggy appearance. I thought I looked rather bohemian-hip, but Mike had other thoughts.

"Dude, you look like a prep school hippie."

"This jacket is vintage. You don't like it?"

"It's hideous," he said, inspecting it closer. "You smell like the bottom of a hash pipe."

Not necessarily comforting, but in actuality he was correct. I did smell like a hash pipe, because that's what I'd been smoking in the alleyway before I got there. I scored it from one of my cousin's boyfriends at a wedding over the weekend, somewhere in between the bouquet toss and the cutting of the cake. My parents, whom I hadn't spoken to in months, were up for the occasion as well. My mother had a truly obnoxious tan and kept telling everyone how warm it was down in Florida during the winter (as if they hadn't already figured out that Florida is like a thousand miles south of New Jersey), while my father sat quietly next to her in a really loud Hawaiian floral print shirt. Our only conversations were about a sailboat he was thinking of buying and some random comments on the previous night's Yankee game.

Anyway, for the next half-hour or so, Mike and I sat at the back table of his place talking about what I'd been up to the last few months. Over several glasses of Bunglewood wine, I explained to him the sad state of my life in regard to its all-encompassing attachment to this job. The business lifestyle, I told him, was becoming too much. I was tired of not having some time of my own.

He was not impressed. "Listen, man, I get salesmen in here all the time trying to sell me shit ... and they've been doing it for *thirty years*. So don't tell me you're burned out."

"Is it possible to just be burned out on the idea?" I asked.

"What idea are you talking about?"

"The one that says I'm wasting my life doing something I hate just because it's a 'good job.' I mean, I'm still fairly young. And single. Aren't I supposed to be enjoying life?"

"Look. Life isn't always ... enjoyable, I guess."

"Well, that sure seems like a wrong way to look at it."

Mike leaned back and ran his fingers through his hair, glancing around the room.

"Jesus Christ, man. What do you want to do then?"

"I don't know. I think that's the problem."

"*What* don't you know?"

"What I want to do. I don't really *like* to do anything. At least nothing that I can get paid for."

He sighed and looked blankly at me for a second.

"What about snowboarding, you know, professionally?" he said. "You were pretty damn good back in the day. Do you still board?"

"*Snowboarding?* Bro, I'm twenty-eight and I live in New Jersey."

"Right. Well, what about sportscasting or, uh … or *music*. I mean, you still like music, don't you?"

"Yeah."

"So there. Why don't you get into audio production or something like that? Go back to school and—"

"School? No. That's out."

Silence.

"Dude, I can't help you."

Following a long night of drinking at his restaurant/bar/lounge, I nearly fell apart for good the next day. Twice. It was straight downhill from morning to night.

My first four stops could hardly even qualify as account visits because all four managers refused to speak to me. Apparently making an appointment carried no weight among the core group of Korean-run stores. This resulted in my introduction, product summary, follow-up questioning, and farewells to be conducted entirely under the lifeless, dead stare of silence. Not a word.

The fifth stop on my list was a tiny shop in TriBeCa. It appeared to be another stoic battle between good and evil. This particular guy was an absolute master of the death stare. It was as if he could possibly be sleeping with his eyes open. Very Zen.

I was wrapping up my visit, thanking him for the time, and had begun to roll my wine bag toward the front door when I heard him clear his throat. I turned and he said, "Do you have T-shirt?"

It took me a moment to come to grips with the thought of actually carrying out a two-way conversation.

"T-shirts? Well, I think I could probably get a hold of some from the—"

"Good. Send some T-shirt."

I was a bit confused.

"Uh … I'm not sure what wine it is you wanted. Would you like to—"

"Just send T-shirt," he moaned.

"I'm sorry. I don't understand. Usually we give merchandise to stores who actually—"

"Don't want wine! Just send T-shirt!" he shouted.

I came within a split second of snapping. This asshole just wanted me to send him some free fucking T-shirts? For not even taking in some of the wine? It was a genuine slap to the face, and had it not been for the cloudiness of the booze still lingering in my system I probably would have strangled him with that cheap eyeglass chain dangling around his neck.

All I got out was a meager "Go fuck yourself," to which he just laughed and muttered something in Korean.

Later that evening I was not so restrained. After grabbing a quick bite to eat at Gray's Papaya, I scooted over to Sixth Avenue where I was scheduled to work a small in-store wine tasting. The lady that ran the place turned out to be pretty cool, and we got to talking about things like new music and old dive bars. She lived upstairs and managed the shop with her husband, who owned several others in Jersey as well. Considering my recent history, I was having a decent time selling some stuff ... when the night took a sudden— and violent—turn for the worse.

It was around eight thirty that a certain couple walked in and started browsing around the store. I could hear them giggling and cracking jokes to each other as they walked down the aisles, trying to decide what they wanted. Exchanging a quick smile with the manager, it was obvious to both of us that they had a few drinks in them already.

Somewhere along the line the two separated, and the woman, a cute mid-thirties blonde in a cutoff jean skirt, noticed me alongside the register. I asked her if she'd like to taste some Chardonnay, and she smiled and said, "Yes." We talked for a minute or so about the wine, and she seemed to like it. Calling her boyfriend over, she handed him a cup and asked him what he thought. The guy—an ex-linebacker type with a shiny bald head and rough features—

took a sip and immediately acted like he was going to gag before spitting it out into the garbage bin to my left.

"Honey," she said, "it wasn't *that* bad, I actually—"

"Ugh!" he shouted. "That's the worst fucking wine I've ever tasted! What was that?"

"It's a Chardonnay," I said. He continued to groan and hold his tongue out.

"It tastes like dog piss, bro."

I was not amused.

"Well, I'm not forcing you to drink it, *bro*."

They were just about to walk away when I said this. I knew right away it was a mistake. The man slowly turned back toward me, his eyes widening.

"What did you say?"

I tried to be rational about it—and again, explain that it was his decision—but for some reason this enraged him, and he lunged across the table and grabbed me by the shirt.

"Don't you ever talk back to me, you skinny little piece of shit!" he screamed. "I'll end your life right here! You got that!"

Letting go, his steroid-induced veins were having a spasm all over his body. I didn't know what to do and remained motionless, staring at him in disbelief.

As he turned back and put his arm around his girlfriend, something began to boil inside of me. Months of putting up with verbal degradation had finally reached total capacity. And unlike the other instances, my mind couldn't handle it with mere words. So while the manager stood paralyzed behind the register, looking on in confusion, I took a full cup of Merlot and threw it on him. He came back at me quick, but I came quicker and popped him hard right between the eyes with my fist. Stunned, he briefly staggered toward me before collapsing awkwardly in front of the register.

I grabbed one of the empty bottles as he struggled to get back on his feet, blood gushing from his nose. Both of the women were now screaming as I came around the edge of the table. My adrenalin was ready to finish him off on any sudden movement in my direction. The man looked at me with anger through his hands, but didn't say anything else, as he continued trying to cover up the blood that was now spreading rapidly over his white Bruce Springsteen tour shirt.

He took a few cautious steps back, while his girlfriend nervously attended to him. They then turned and quickly shuffled out the door.

Although I was scheduled to pour wine until ten, this, for all intents and purposes, brought the tasting to an end.

When the boss called at ten in the morning (seven Pacific) the next day, I knew it couldn't be good. My fears rang true when I was told that my numbers had fallen off by 60 percent from last months and a whopping 285 percent from May's, putting me in second-to-last place on the company standings. Only Jerry from the Southeast trailed me, and he died of a heart attack back in the spring.

My year-to-year numbers were something entirely different.

"Being you didn't sell much last August, your numbers didn't vary much over the year. Which doesn't necessarily make it any better or worse. You still can't sell shit."

It was the "shit" that hurt. Blunt, honest, yet strikingly out of his peaceful Californian nature; it gave me a sense of complete failure. They had lost all patience with me, and I was now a marked man. All that remained was the inevitable termination speech.

But again, it never came. What I got instead could be best described as a loose threat. Some shit about how "my youthful spirit hadn't turned out as they'd hoped" and how I was "gonna have to make some serious adjustments, and quick" or, you, know, they were gonna make them for me. Of course, merely *saying* this was ridiculous. Why not just fire me while you're at it? What were they waiting for?

I didn't have much of an opportunity to dwell on this, because at the time of the call I was already working with a salesman named

Bob down in Little Italy. Trying to brush off the near hatchet job, I felt as though I was in some sort of slow-motion phase most of the day. The majority of impatient, crass remarks and actions of the restaurant managers seemed to roll right over me, without the blink of an eye. My mind, like my bandaged right fist, simply went numb.

I could easily point to a number of reasons for this—lack of motivation and excessive intake of alcohol for starters—but in truth, it was Bob who unknowingly became a help throughout the day. He seemed to be going through a lot of troubles on his own, which in a way, deflected away the thoughts of mine.

I found this sort of role reversal to be quite therapeutic. As for Bob, I wasn't sure. His manner was so depressing to begin with that I was convinced the man was on the brink of disaster. At only thirty-two years of age, he had black rings under his eyes and wrinkles on his forehead—which, mixed with a receding hairline, made him look old enough to be my father. With his shirt sleeves rolled up and his tie yanked off, he spoke of his problems at great length through a series of deflating sighs and drifting thoughts. It was like a roll call of unwanted responsibility: the hours he put into the job; his payments on everything from a car, a house, and his Italian leather briefcase; all the way down to his girlfriend. "I don't even know if I *like* her anymore, never mind love her," he mumbled over a third cup of coffee. "Nevertheless, I'm somehow three months into paying off an engagement ring ..."

In spite of all this, I liked Bob. It took a while to warm up to his defeated outlook on life, but as we continued to trudge across the streets of lower Manhattan, I got to understand him more and more. In some way it actually reminded me how detached I'd been from other people's lives, including most of friends and family, by being on the sales road. Time certainly flew by when you were trying to earn a living. One that you might have never envisioned, but rather one you'd been brought up to believe as a reality nonetheless. When life began to feel this way, decisions began to be made out of fear. Fear of not living up to expectations, fear of what others will say, and fear of the consequences should you fail.

Every once in a while we'd check into an air-conditioned bar or coffee shop to avoid the sticky August heat, and it was here that Bob spoke of such thoughts. I didn't so much offer any help to his problems, and I wasn't sure he even wanted my opinion. Maybe it was just nice to have someone simply listen once in a while. I remember at one point, he did mention that he was sorry for dumping all this on me. "I guess I just have to suck it up … This is what you're supposed to do with life anyway, right? Wife, kids, house, car …" he said, trailing off, as he looked out into the bustling city streets.

I thought about what he said for a minute.

"You can do anything you want," I told him. "You only live once."

He didn't say anything in return. But for a brief moment, as he continued to look outside, a smile came across his face for the first time all day.

This period of tranquil reflection was short-lived. The following morning I stood in the entranceway of a diner on Thirty-Fourth Street for an hour, waiting for a salesman named Marco. We were scheduled to meet here at nine thirty, but by a quarter after ten, I hadn't seen or heard from him. Looking up his number in the distributor's contact sheet, I decided to give him a call to make sure I was at the right location or whatever.

Turns out the guy stood me up. When I finally got a hold of him, he mentioned that he wasn't going to be able to make it today. *Wasn't going to be able to make it?* I quickly became incensed that he didn't have the decency and respect to even let me know this. He fired back a snide remark about me being late and unproductive with other salesmen in his territory, and just like that it escalated into the magnitude of a grade-school playground argument.

I think I called him a pussy and threatened to snap his legs off at the next meeting.

19. Drunk by Noon and Fading

*W*e were sharing a few beers and breaking down the remainder of the Yankees schedule one evening that summer, when a string of three or four trucks came down our street, honking as they passed our complex.

"Throw me a beer, Gus!" one guy shouted.

"Feel like clocking back in?" said another.

Gus just smiled and waved them off, as the sight of the big machines and the roaring sound of their engines eventually faded off in the distance.

"How many guys you got working over there, Gus?"

"Well, we got our core group of fellas, you know, and a few managers, on-site and off. And there's always someone new or some part-time help here and there … Shoot, I have no idea. Never really counted, I guess."

"How's the overall vibe? I mean, you know, uh, like how—"

"I know what 'vibe' means, you asshole. How old do you think I am?"

"Sorry, man," I laughed.

"I don't know. We get along … Some more than others. What kind of question is that?"

"I was just wondering, that's all. I used to hate working in the same place every day, dealing with the same shit over and over. God, we used to get on each others nerves. Now it's the total opposite. I'm constantly on the road, working in different places with different people."

I paused for a moment, as another truck came rumbling by. "I think I'm actually starting to miss having some familiar faces around."

"Well, I'm sure both situations have their pros and cons. As far as getting along with everyone, I can't control what people say and think. I can only control what I say and think. And even that is a problem sometimes."

"Ever get into a fight over something?"

"Over what?"

"I don't know, anything."

"With words, no. At least not since I was kid. But if someone starts pushing me, I push back."

"No one's ever pushed you over the edge with words?"

Gus didn't say anything right away, but then after momentarily scratching the back of his neck, he asked, "Who's the greatest center in Knicks history?"

"What?"

"Who is the greatest center in Knicks history?"

"That's easy. Patrick Ewing," I said.

"Well, see, I disagree with you. I'd go with Willis Reed. He got us two championships, didn't he? What did Patrick get us? None."

"Yeah, but Patrick led the team in scoring like every year he played."

"Okay. Now I can either choose to argue with you and get angry— or get us angry at each other—or I can just say my part and leave it at that. I don't need your approval on everything I happen to believe is right, Chet. Life doesn't have to be a competition."

"Yeah, I hear what you're saying, Gus. But, you know, what if someone started saying something nasty about your mother ... or your wife?"

"Well, then that person would have to die."

"I thought you just said words don't affect you?"

Gus finished off his beer and belched.

"You sure got an awful lot of questions, Chet."

My hand was still swollen from the punch a few days later as I struggled to pour lefty at an ocean front wine tasting down the Jersey Shore. Unable to properly grip the bottle with my right, it gave the impression that I was not only an amateur, but also perhaps, physically disabled.

Minor embarrassment notwithstanding, I was relieved to be out of the city on what turned out to be a beautiful summer day. The tasting itself was actually a last-minute change in my schedule. And a good one at that. Especially when you consider that I was originally assigned to do a wine event at a Polish National home in Brooklyn. I didn't have the experience to confirm it, but I assumed a few hundred unwashed senior citizens boogying to the likes of Len Schwartz and "Big" Ollie Stanski would have been every bit as exciting as it sounded. Luckily for me, our brand's New Jersey rep, Jane, called the night before asking for help. I agreed, and we spent most of the morning in a nearby office superstore making copies of tasting notes and looking at several volumes of her baby pictures.

While most of my days came and went looking into the eyes of the bored and the unsatisfied, a day with Jane was the exact opposite. She actually loved her job to the point of constant giddiness whenever it was mentioned.

"I couldn't wait to get back to work after having the baby. Aren't you excited about the upcoming fall sales drives? Have you tasted the new Chardonnay? It's absolutely fabulous!"

Comments like this were tossed around randomly throughout the morning and early afternoon. I was unsure of whether they were parts of actual questions or merely spur-of-the-moment observations. Most of the time I just smiled and nodded my head.

There was no way to deal with Jane's attitude, other than to just accept it. And had it been all sunshine and giggles, it would have been totally bearable as well. But in many ways, preparing to take on a tasting with her was like preparing to host dinner for the Queen of England. At times it bordered on the pinnacle of anal-retentive behavior.

"All of the bottles need to be spaced exactly two inches apart and in rows of four, with each opened bottle adorned with a silver pouring spout ... If so much as a single drop or smudge graces the label, discard that bottle immediately and substitute it with a clean one ... From the front edge of the table to the first bottle of each row is precisely fourteen inches, and facing each row should be a small container holding fifty laminated information cards on each wine ... The ice bin, which we'll use to chill our white wines, needs to be kept at forty-seven degrees at all times. To help ensure this, I've brought in a thermometer that will beep anytime it moves more than two degrees either way ... And don't bother with regular ice; I've made my own, shaped into the form of grape clusters."

She even brought her own napkins, which took me nearly an hour to fold in the correct manner so that they formed a flower bed along the outer edges of the table.

Following the construction of a fifteen-foot interactive map of the Sonoma Valley, Jane announced that it was time for us to get "in sync." Rummaging through a cardboard box, she pulled out a pair of large floppy hats and placed one on my head and one on hers.

"What's this?"

"That, Chet, is a straw farmer's hat with a Bunglewood Vineyards logo on it, and this is your personalized name tag. It has a button on the back that turns on the flashing lights."

She also handed me a note card that was titled "Keys to Success for Today's Event."

I was inspecting this a few minutes later, when I noticed her looking over at me with a big, shit-eating grin.

"I made those last night. Pretty awesome, huh?"

I didn't say anything and continued to skim over several of the topics such as "Leaving a Sincere Expression" and "Tapping into the Consumer's Heart."

"Chet, we're gonna meet a lot of great people today. Heck, the way I see it, it's like gaining hundreds of new friends!"

Well, maybe it was because I was standing with the most hyper-active, jolly rep in the room, or maybe it was because my motivation to try was simply waning, but my efforts on this day turned out to be borderline acceptable, at best. Not even the perfect setting imaginable could sustain any of the initial positive emotion I had. That motor in my brain which had been able to click on and off just as recently as the tasting in downtown Manhattan had finally run out of batteries. My fake smiles barely made the impression that I was delighted to be there, and my informative speeches about the wines were limited to a few drab, basic statements. "This is our Cabernet Sauvignon. It costs like ten bucks." The words just weren't there anymore. In their place was a mounting feeling of depressed uncertainty that had previously been forbidden to enter my thought process due to a hectic, brainwashed schedule.

So why was I still here? What was I waiting for? Looking for? *Hoping* for? As I reflected back upon the past year, my mind went completely blank. No answers, no reassuring visions, not even a single, solid idea of any kind. For a brief moment I panicked, feeling altogether worthless and lost, as if my entire reason for being had been erased.

But as quickly as I had sunk into despair, something began to dawn on me from underneath the darkness. By merely thinking of nothing, maybe I'd found the answer after all.

And then it hit me.

There was no pot of gold to be found here, no winning lottery ticket to be held. I had merely succumbed to the normality of life: getting up, going to work, getting paid, going to bed ... and doing the whole thing over the next day.

My standing as an average guy living in an average town and making an average salary had been verified after years of bumming around trying to subconsciously avoid it. It was nothing shocking or revolutionary—billions of people wallowed in mediocrity the better part of their adult lives—but I think when it finally hit me, and I was able to accept it, there was a tiny sense of defeat. Perhaps growing up in a country like America, where the lifestyles of the rich and famous were bombarded upon anyone within striking distance of a TV, radio, or newsstand, made the reality of the situation sink in just a little bit deeper.

Or maybe it was just me. Not every story had a fairy tale ending.

Regardless of whether or not I was supposed to feel good about being another rat in the rat race, I knew that I no longer wanted this job, and had to control myself on several occasions from falling deeper into these thoughts. As much as I tried, it didn't always work. Oftentimes I either missed an entire series of questions from the consumers or, even worse, just plainly ignored them.

She never said anything specifically, but I could tell Jane was clearly embarrassed by my performance. Her bright and cheery attitude had been cut down to a forced, tight-lipped smile sometime around the end of the first hour, and by the halfway point she was more or less pushing me out of the way, trying to handle all the consumers on her own.

Finally, with about thirty minutes left before the tasting was slated to finish, she simply told me I could go.

"Look, why don't you get a head start home. I can finish up from here," was all she said, but I knew what it meant.

Although I felt as if I'd been reduced to a child after that comment, I was more than happy to get out of there. It was almost five o'clock, and there were swarms of people awkwardly carrying beach chairs, umbrellas, and coolers throughout the parking lot. If I had any intention of beating the traffic, I would have to leave soon.

But at that moment, something in my head was telling me that going back home was a bad decision. So I didn't. Instead I drove a few miles down the road and found some shitty motel on Ocean Avenue. The place reeked of chlorine and had a television set that could have easily predated the property. No matter. I was acting on a strong hunch, and intended to follow it out for the sake of my own mental stability.

My workday the next morning was supposed to include a run through Queens, but that too was decided to be a bad decision. It would've been a cold-call run, so what the hell. I didn't have to make up some excuse for cancelling any appointments, and because the boss didn't have it on record, I couldn't get in trouble for not showing up. Besides, most of the stores I was planning to go see were left-for-dead shit-holes that had multiple reasons for not buying my product anyway. For one, they were so undersized that they had no room to buy anything. Secondly, they did such small business that they had no *money* to buy anything. Come to think of it, even talking about the wine was useless because all they ever wanted were plastic jugs of vodka, cheap cognac, and the kind of wine that came in a box. That it was from Italy or France or even Delaware made no difference, as long as it was inexpensive and in liquid form.

Be that as it may, I always ended up trying to state my case for the Bunglewood wine. Somehow they always claimed they had it already.

"No. Already have. Already have."

"You have this wine?"

"Yes. Already have. Already have."

"Where? *Here?*"

"Already have. Already have. Yes."

"I don't see it. Can you show me?"

"Already have. Thank you."

This could go on for ten minutes at a time. It was like a bizarre Abbott and Costello "Who's on First?" routine featuring an Indian shop clerk and a derelict salesman. I think they used it as some sort of confusing defense against me.

Along with the enduring sound of a nearby jackhammer (I'm fairly certain every square inch of Queens is under eternal remodeling) there would also be constant interruptions from construction workers and neighborhood crackheads coming in to buy nips of vodka. I assumed this was a recurring theme throughout the day, as on the odd chance that I would be in these stores for more than a few agonizing moments, the same guys would often return for multiple rounds, saying things like "Yeah, gimme one more of those little fellas. Heh heh. Long day."

Now, that was *supposed* to have been my day. But like I said, it wasn't. No, instead I was situated on the outside deck of Martell's Tiki Bar, overlooking the beach and five drinks deep by noon. Rum and cokes, and damn good ones. With no appointments to make, no meetings to prepare for, and no salesmen in sight, all my troubles were mere reflections at the moment, and it felt rather liberating to be removed from the midweek business world mayhem. This was a time to relax and take in the sights of youthful female flesh that came, like the waves, in sets. Indeed, there were few things in life like a dripping wet, fit body ordering a Pina Colada next to you in such a setting. For nothing more than a brief moment, it made you feel like everything in the world was good and running according to plan.

Other than a few immigrant workers helping to sweep up whatever remained from the night before, the bar was nearly empty when I arrived. At ten thirty, most of the vacation crowd was still staking out their territory down on the beach, underneath the beginnings of another picturesque summer day. Slowly but surely, though, more people began to pour in, and by the middle of the afternoon it became a raucous mixture of business suits and bathing suits, all finishing up their day at the same spot.

If one thing *was* lacking, it was a breeze. So every once in a while I'd leave my seat at the bar and take a dip in the ocean, floating low among the waves, the bottom of my eyes on up the only visible portion of my body. Although the shoreline was filled with people, I felt completely isolated, in a world all my own. The frenetic energy that had been stuck inside my brain for the past year had finally been allowed to settle. Sort of like one of those water-filled snow globes after it had been shaken and set down for a few minutes. I could actually feel the stress and unhappiness leave my body.

Sure enough, I became rather drunk. Pushing my credit card and tolerance level to the limit never felt so good. The buzz was going so well, in fact, that I made the decision to skip lunch so as not to ruin it with a full stomach. This put me in quite the jovial mood, and by the time I would normally have been stuck in rush hour traffic, I was left trying to control myself from heckling a cheesy Sublime cover band. Laughing at botched chords and booing a "Witchy Woman" tease in the middle of "Santeria" was not taken kindly by the lead singer, who at one point announced to the crowd, "This next song is dedicated to the drunk asshole sitting at the bar." My hysterical behavior would surely have reached another level had it not been for the kindness shown by an attractive young bartender. Without asking, she continually brought me pitchers of ice water, refilled my pretzel bowls, and kept my open seat away from others when I went down to the ocean. Compared to the other lunatics at the bar, who were pawing at her as if she were a newborn kitten, I must have seemed rather tame.

She had bleached blonde hair tied back in a bun, and wore a pair of low-cut board shorts with a white collared polo shirt. I couldn't quite pinpoint her accent, but it was definitely some place in the south.

"Alabama," she said with a smile when I asked her, following another round of cold beer. I apologized for posing a question that I was sure she got all the time, but she politely shook it off as no problem.

"So what made you come up to New Jersey?"

"I don't know," she laughed. "It's just one stop on the list, I guess."

"What do you mean, 'list?' What do you do?"

"Nothing, really," she said, shrugging her shoulders with a smirk. "That's sorta the plan."

"Well, you must do something. I mean, you're a bartender, right?"

She took my glass and poured me another.

"Today I am and tomorrow I may not be. I try not to think about it too much."

I looked back and smiled. Finally, someone who had it down right.

At four o'clock the next day, I was still in Point Pleasant. Rent money was now in jeopardy. The afternoon started out decent, but by two o'clock, some Mafioso type characters rolled in and cut short my quality time back at Martell's. Nothing ruins a scene quite like a group of bonehead Italian posers who would rather look at the definition in their biceps than the ladies. I spent the rest of the day in the motel watching *Beach MTV* like a pathetic loser and staring at my cell phone resting on the table next to me. The ringer had been off for the past forty-eight hours, and the red light message indicator was flashing and beeping to no end. An obscene amount of salesmen had left messages. So much so that my phone malfunctioned and started listing the numbers in what looked like hieroglyphics. The attachment to this thing was unbelievable. To the paranoid, it was almost like a homing device: *They can find me anywhere. I can't get away.*

I was about halfway up to Albany on I-87 a couple of days later when I realized that I wasn't even working in Albany that day. This was precisely what happened when the mind and body were not connected: when everything felt glazed over and fuzzy, I was still drunk from the night before, and the responsibility meter was teetering just above zero. So at one of those countless rest stops that dotted the thruway, I had to turn around and head back down in the opposite direction to the Island. Not before I ran inside to use the bathroom, which in turn led me to get one of those mutant foil-wrapped burgers under the heat lamp, a New York State traveling coffee mug, and a pair of cheap, yellow-tinged sunglasses. In all, this made me two hours late to meet the salesman I was working with, a mental miscue that did not go unnoticed.

"You know, you cost us two fucking hours of sales," the guy said to me, leaning up against his car when I pulled into the parking lot. Not even a handshake.

I said nothing and just stared at him. I don't know why, but I thought it might be interesting to see how long I could do this. Of course within about thirty seconds he began screaming at me to snap out of it. But I didn't budge. He tried for another minute or so, serving up an assortment of idle threats and unflattering comments, before he just went blank and said, "Fuck it."

He then hopped in his car and peeled out.

I stood there for a little while longer, not really thinking about anything. Just sort of standing there and listening to everything around me. After that I walked down the street to a diner and ordered a roast beef sub. Double mayo. With gravy fries and a beer.

A few hours later I was headed back up to Albany—this time for real, as part of a last-second emergency to help try and fix a problem with one of the biggest stores in the state. I don't remember why I even answered the phone in the first place, but before I knew it, Betty was informing me that the vineyard had received several threatening phone calls from the head buyer regarding his quantity discount. The word was that he flipped his shit upon finding out he was paying the same price for fifty-six cases as the guy down the street was paying for three. Not good. The boss thought going up there in person would show our glowing appreciation of his first-class business, as well as how serious we were taking this unfortunate matter.

The ride up was significant for two reasons: one, a Johnny Cash marathon on the radio; and two, a quick dissection of both my mental and physical breakdown. The scene inside the Jeep explained it all. The seats and floorboards were heavily littered with every kind of fast food and candy wrapper imaginable, with dozens of Styrofoam coffee cups, Gatorade bottles, rolling papers, and empty cigarette packs mixed in. Much of this material dated back to the pre-buttered noodle days, as evidenced by a collection of gas receipts and newspapers toward the middle that were marked April and May. Either type of diet (along with a sporadic showering schedule and no exercise) could probably explain the gut that hung over my seatbelt as well as the oily, pimply skin that appeared in the mirror.

Other notable highlights included a crack in my windshield that resembled a swastika and a heavy slathering of bird shit on my hood that had hardened to withstand the most torrential of downpours. Apart from cosmetic damage, though, the Jeep was in decent shape, considering I hadn't changed the oil since February and my tires were as bald as plastic inner tubes. Christ … even my local garage called to see if everything was okay.

As far as the mental side goes, I knew it was bad when some of the best conversations I'd had in recent memory were the ones I'd had with myself. Up until that point, I hadn't realized the seriousness at which this had been going on, but somewhere in the middle of an hour-long discussion concerning the influence of Pink Floyd on modern music, it became clear to me that I had a problem.

Looking back on these inner chats was rather discomforting. They often became so heavy that I unconsciously took the role of both sides and argued between them in complete solitude. Half the time, though, I believed that I *was* aware of this. And that was what bothered me the most: I had become my own best friend.

When I finally got up to the store, the man was nowhere to be seen. I was informed by one of his assistant managers that he "overreacts sometimes." When I told this woman that I had called earlier and driven up three hours just to see him, she casually brushed it off.

"I don't know what to tell you. All I know is that he left this afternoon to go fishing up on Lake Ontario.

"I'll let him know you stopped by, though," she added.

20. Quality Time with Unemployed Dominican Gamblers

*A*round the same time I confronted Mike about my problems, I began to speak more directly about them to Gus. His solution was much different.

"Let me show you something. Hang here for a second," he said one evening.

I watched as he walked inside to the back corner of the kitchen, where he put his arm around his wife, Mary, and began speaking to her as she was hand washing some dishes in the sink. Although I couldn't understand what they were saying, I'm fairly sure I overheard her laughing a bit.

"Come on in," he said, opening the screen door, a few moments later.

It was the first time I'd been in his apartment, and it was every bit as low-key as I'd imagined. I felt immediately transported back to my grandparent's home: quaint, and filled with vintage charm. The living room was decorated in matching antique furniture and some ornately framed photographs, with a few random pieces of moderately updated technology: a cordless phone, a fairly decent-sized TV, and what looked like a small cassette player. The place was nicely kept, with bits of detail on just about everything, from the laced drop covers on the couch to the matching cherrywood coasters on the living room table.

As we passed through the kitchen, Mary turned and smiled somewhat nervously, as if she was in on some kind of joke or something. I smiled back as Gus led me into their small bedroom. Turning around as we entered, Gus faced the near wall and smiled looking up at a picture hanging above the dresser. It was a rather large painting, about three feet by five feet, of a nude woman sitting on a window sill.

"Mary," he said.

She looked very young, maybe in her early twenties. Her face bore a very similar, albeit smoother, appearance, and her hair was light brown and wavy, moving down past her shoulders. She was exceptionally beautiful.

"Wow. When was this done?"

"A few weeks after we'd gotten married. We'd just come back from the Cape. One of my friends in the area was a painter."

"You let one of your friends paint your wife like this? That must have been tough."

"Actually, that was the fun part."

"What do you mean?"

"He only became a painter to romance women. Sort of like a musician or a movie star, I guess. And I gave him a woman that he could never have."

"That was pretty confident of you."

"When you know you have something great, you tend to hang on to it, Chet. And I wanted to hang on to that feeling forever."

"Did it work?"

He looked at me and then back at the painting.

"Every single morning I walk past that and smile."

Walking back out front—Mary turned once again, this time giving me a blushed look and a very childlike grin—I was a bit confused by the whole thing.

"Gus, uh … that was pretty cool and all, but what did you mean to say right there? You know, about my job situation?"

"It's very simple," he said. "Either it's a keeper or it ain't. You don't want a painting of a mistake hanging over your dresser your whole life, just because somebody else might like it."

The no-show in Albany only further cemented my fading inter-est in this job, and by late August all motivation for work had become solely built around the idea of doing as little as possible for as long as possible. I knew where this would lead me, and you know what, I didn't care. Being a rather healthy individual had allowed me to use the "sick card" on two separate occasions where I was assigned to work with salesmen, and my reliable Jeep had offered me the chance to use it as an excuse on why I couldn't make it up to Rochester for a meeting. The vineyard even offered to help pay for the "repairs." I assured them it wasn't a problem, that I could han-dle the cost, which in saying so probably extended my position even further. As for the mountain of people I had to call back, I answered about half of them, dishing out bogus inventory projections and obscure product details, while trying at all costs to avoid any sort of situation that could potentially rope me into more work. The sec-ond I sensed it coming, I quickly faked a bad reception or another incoming call. Overused and obvious, yes—but still effective.

So, the last week of the month was spent at the only semi-pro-ductive place I could think of: the track at Monmouth Park, trying to win enough money on the horses to compensate for a hotdog and a day's worth of cold beer. It was my only hope of maintaining some form of sanity. My cable television service had been cut weeks ago, and the food and beverage down at the beach were too damn expensive. And besides, sitting alone in my apartment and eating buttered garlic noodles without a buzz was no way to live outside the laws of business protocol. At least down at the track, a good run could get me a few weeks of fun out of it and possibly even a couple of extra bucks on the side.

The scene was not new to me. I used to come down here all the time with my friends in high school. The beer was cheap, and they never ID'ed us. It had been nine or ten years, though, and time away from any type of gambling brings rust and scattered, indeci-sive thinking. I needed to get back into the flow—and quick. Fortu-nately, by the end of the second day, I had fallen in with two old

Dominican guys named Lefty and Miguel. They didn't speak much, even to each other, but their vibe was good. More importantly, they were also excellent handicappers. *Regulars*. Under their tutelage they got me back into betting shape in no time, hitting daily doubles and trifecta boxes with confidence. Miguel put the bets in, Lefty collected the money, and I bought endless rounds of beers and drank heavily like no tomorrow.

I had reached the point of no return.

Epilogue

A Phoenix Rises from the Gooey Wine Muck

*T*his foray into an abyss of unprofessionalism lasted approximately two weeks, though in retrospect, it could be argued that it lasted my entire time on the job. I was fired on the fifth of September on accounts of bottoming sales, incomprehensible reports, and overall unacceptable behavior stemming from a multitude of missed dates and, on the days I did show up, disheveled appearances. I'm surprised it took them that long, although I didn't exactly answer my phone for the last week or two. The notice came the old-fashioned way, in a letter postmarked "urgent" in red ink. In my mind I could have just as easily quit and avoided the obvious stain on my resume, but instead chose to hang around long enough to see if I could collect another paycheck, which I did, allowing me to pay off rent and move into a cheaper apartment near the Delaware River. The place doesn't have air-conditioning and the bathtub looks like it was attacked with a pitchfork, but the tap water is drinkable.

Of course, this also meant I had to bid good-bye to Gus. I didn't realize the effect he had on me at the time, but once I began to reflect back on my decisions, where I was, and where I was going, all the conversations with the man came to light. His unexpected turn as my neighbor makes his role in all of this a strange one. Philosophical genius? Probably not. Even-tempered realist? More likely. Unbeknownst catalyst? Definitely. Whether or not I'll see much of him in the future, I can't say, but we did exchange numbers and a handshake before I left. Knowing Gus, I'll probably have to be the one to reach out, but at least, as he once put it, "I know where he's at, and he knows where I'm at."

And so, my story ends here. My apologies to the readers who anticipated a life-changing conclusion wherein a juvenile, semi-alcoholic slacker is somehow reborn into a snappy, clean-cut businessman, but hey, it doesn't always work out that way. The point of all this was to observe what went on *within*, and to see if I could transform myself into the job, or if the job could transform me. While a fourteen-month stint in the wine industry may not grant the clearest view of the business world, it did afford me the opportunity to see everything that I needed to. I couldn't play it straight, I couldn't play it dirty, and after all was said and done, I knew I didn't care to either way. Yeah, my parents were upset, and most of my friends thought I'd made a bad decision, but what can I say? This kind of life is not for everyone. *Although* I do recommend giving it a try. Seeing how terribly addicted some people can be to their jobs will give you a whole new perspective on what it means to be alive. Now, I don't want to imply that being dedicated is a bad thing—hard work is hard work—but the American dream has never been about what you *do* for a living, but rather, the ability to *do* what fulfills your own definition of happiness. As far as I'm concerned, you can either stand looking over the edge, following the person in front of you and clinging tightly to the guardrail your entire life, or you can take the leap and see what happens.

But with that, unfortunately, comes the consequences of being part of the minority. Yes, it requires a bit more courage to follow your own path these days, so if this is what you desire, I wish you well. As for myself, I'm just satisfied spending these last few weeks of warm weather doing odd jobs around town, picking up whatever comes by, while enjoying my spare time down by the river's edge, practicing my guitar and sipping on vodka lemonades. I've even tossed around the idea of enrolling in a few writing courses over at the local community college. Creative Nonfiction and Journalism

101. Not sure where I'm headed with any of this, but one thing's for certain: I'm gonna live my own life while I try and figure it out.

And maybe it was all for the best. Maybe tomorrow I'll get a dog, or maybe I'll just pack up and move to Colorado. It's still a free country ... on the surface at least. And that's all I ever really wanted to be. *Free.*

978-0-595-44118-1
0-595-44118-1

Printed in the United States
108622LV00002B/61/A